"It's hard to find anyone who is willing to indulge my fantasies. They are somewhat ... extreme."

"Really?" Leaning forward, the woman crushed her cigarette in a tin ashtray. She smelled of sandalwood and cloves and Caitlin could see the outline of her erect nipples through her sheer, intricately beaded flapper dress. There was a glint of silver in the dark pink flesh. "Do tell."

Another test, another level. Caitlin's mind and heart were racing. She was unused to flirting with women in any context, and it seemed an entirely more dangerous, more delicate operation. With men, all she really had to do was cross her legs and make them to do all the work. This was a whole new ballgame. She took a deep breath and a calculated risk.

"I like ... " She fished in her purse and extracted the stiletto. Reaching forward, she slid one hand behind the woman's neck and drew the point of the knife along the curve of her jaw, br~~inging it to rest in the soft place~~ just under her chin. "Blades."

— from *Control Freak*

D1636842

Control Freak

Control Freak

Christa Faust

BABBAGE PRESS • NORTHRIDGE, CA

This book is a work of fiction. Names, characters, places, references and incidents are the product of the author's imagination or are used fictitiously, and any resemblance to actual persons (living or dead), events, or locales is entirely coincidental.

ISBN 1-930235-14-3

First Babbage Press edition: September, 2002

Babbage Press
8740 Penfield Avenue
Northridge, CA 91324

www.babbagepress.com

Printed in the United States of America

For my father, who loves me anyway

Thanks again to everyone I thanked the first time around plus new and improved thanks to Lydia and Art, to Ramsey Campbell, for getting it, to everyone who e-mailed wanting to know where they could get a copy of this damn book (you asked for it!) and to Butch, who knows all my secrets.

August, 2002. Los Angeles.

It's been nearly 10 years since I first put pen to paper with the idea that eventually grew up to become *Control Freak.* That seems impossible and yet my life couldn't be more different now than it was then. For one thing, I no longer live in New York City, the city that raised me, the city which is as much a part of the vital meat of this book as Los Angeles is in the work of Raymond Chandler and New Orleans is in the work of Poppy Z. Brite. Not to mention the fact that when I first started dipping my toes into this project that might be a book, I could not even imagine what it would be like to have someone pay money for something I wrote. Now, on the other side of a mountain of calendar pages, I have chance to jump in the literary way-back machine and remember the gestation and birth of the paper creature you even now hold in your hot little hands.

This book went through a lot of changes in it's awkward teen phase. There was even one draft that had actual, supernatural elements. I crossed out and crumpled up and rewrote and banged my head against the keys and then once I finally had a draft I could live with I got to experience the fun of being rejected by editor after editor. Too graphic they said, too perverse. Of course it seemed funny to me because I had deliberately softened things, writing what I was foolishly hoping could be a mainstream novel. But after all, when you are dealing with kinky sexuality, you can't just cut to the blowing curtains and every one will automatically know what's happening. Most of what's going on is totally foreign to nearly everyone and I didn't want to write something so exclusive that I'd wind up preaching to the converted and leaving everyone else in the dark. In a way I think it's a lot like writing a Michael Crichton novel. Writing about stuff that maybe a handful of people fully understand but presenting it in a way that makes it accessible and real to people who've never worked in a deep sea habitat or studied medieval Europe or tied someone up and flogged them.

In my case I think most of the problem I was having with people that were upset or offended by *Control Freak* was that I had made all these creepy, unnatural sex things a little too real. I didn't want to write about a wild edgy person who was into kinky sex. That would be too easy to dismiss as science fiction. I wanted to write about someone "ordinary", someone "just like you" who finds these curious, unconventional desires inside herself and makes peace with them. There, enlies the real problem. It's ok for villains to be into evil perverted sex. We can relish their naughty misadventures while clucking our tongues and disapproving and then cheering when they get their comeuppance at the end. It's even ok to have a "normal" person get sucked into naughty debauchery, like in a *Chick* comic or a high school anti-drug reel, as long as they suffer a righteous *Reefer Madness* crash and burn, leaving everyone with the simple kindergarten moral that anything but married hetero love will destroy you. The reader can enjoy the nasty stuff and come away feeling morally superior. What horror critic David J Skal refers to as the "Tsk Tsk Yum Yum" Syndrome. Americans love to watch bad guys do bad things. To relish the bizarre native rituals of alien tribes. To watch *COPS* and "reality" programs and these "Real Sex" shows they have now about every conceivable kink, but it's all just cheap vicarious thrills that the norms in Nebraska can disapprove of every week. Everyone loves to go to the freakshow and *ooh* and *aah* as long as there is a clear line between the audience and the freaks.

I was trying to blur that line. To let the reader see things through the eyes of a person discovering her kinky sexuality, to feel what she feels and maybe even see a little bit of themselves in her without the safe, reassuring punishment and return to normality at the end. This was a tough sell, not only because it was morally unconventional but because the protagonist was a strong, dominant female, a sexual aggressor who acted rather than being acted upon. This character was not a victim of desires that would eventually destroy her. She was not the poor helpless heroine tied up in the trunk of a runaway car. She was behind the wheel, making her own choices and taking responsibility for her own actions, right or wrong or somewhere in-between. This was more than a lot of (mostly male) editors and agents were ready for.

In the end it was an "erotica" publisher who decided to give *Control Freak* a go. Considering that I had toned the manuscript down in hopes of mainstream publication, it's kind of ironic that Masquerade Books, who's various fiction lines included everything from romantic, girly erotica to balls-out pornography, was the only one who would take a chance on it. At the time it seemed like a good choice. My book was on newsstands, in Tower Records, everywhere. Of course I had no idea that once the first print run sold out that would be the end of that. There would be no second printing. They were far more interested in cranking out the next one and the one after that, sending them on down the conveyer belt like auto parts or fast food burgers. Obviously this concept didn't do so well since I haven't seen a new Masquerade book in ages. Meanwhile I get e-mails all the time asking where people can get a copy of *Control Freak*. I myself own only one dog-eared copy of the Masquerade edition. Hence, this book. Now, finally, I'll have an answer to all those pesky emails.

Before I let you get on with it, here are a few things to keep in mind when reading this book:

This book was mostly written between 1993 and 1995. The internet was in its infancy. You could still smoke in restaurants. All the window dressing of pop culture and fashion was in and of that decade. So much has changed since then but I do sincerely hope that this book will stand the test of time. That it can be set in that past decade in the way anything period is set within the time of its conception without seeming dated. The flaw that renders many books and movies of the past dated and silly is a overreaching need to be "hip" and "with it". To exploit whatever's trendy at that very second be it 1930, 1966 or 1995. Stories that transcend their decade are not about how cool the characters (and by extension the writers) are for being into the latest hot trend, whatever it may be. They are about the story itself and the characters that inhabit it. I hope that the emotions and struggles of the characters in *Control Freak* will still have relevance in 20 or 50 or 100 years and that the decade in which the events take place will be nothing more than the stage on which the events play out, the set dressing that allows Constant Reader to travel through time and experience what the world was like in that moment through the eyes of someone not too different from themselves. I have no idea if it will or not. I've had to read through the damn thing so many times I can't even tell if it's any good anymore. I guess that's up to you.

So read on, Constant Reader. I want to tell you a story. It's about a woman in New York City in 1995. It goes a little something like this ...

Part One

ESCAPE

i.

Fourteenth Street, as far west as you can go without swimming. Hot heart of the meatpacking district. Slick cobblestone streets and acrid steam. Dead things, bought and sold.

Cruising carloads of suburban frat-boys prowled in slow, drunken circles, trawling for hookers with dirty fingernails and wild, crack-bright eyes. Rag mummies with bare black feet rooted through red plastic bins stamped INEDIBLE — slaughterhouse leavings, scraps too foul for glue. The air was thick with the smell of death and desperation, of cold meat and loveless hearts. Blood ran in the gutter, studded with broken needles.

Two girls held hands as they walked along the foul, oily sidewalk, not slow like spring lovers, but with barely contained urgency. They were clean and fearful and utterly out of place, like a pair of hand-fed finches broken loose from their fancy cage and lost in the sprawl and tangle of this urban landscape. Above their heads, bright red and yellow signs cheerfully advertised whole rabbits and fresh baby lambs.

"Where are we going?" Jez asked, a thin thread of anxiety woven through her tiny voice.

"Away," Eva answered, nervously running her free hand over the prickly blonde stubble on her scalp as she glanced back over her shoulder. Jez's pulse fluttered in Eva's palm, a seductive rhythm against her skin. Her fingerbones felt so fragile.

"He'll find us," Jez whispered, grey eyes downcast, fixed on the toes of her cheap new sneakers as she walked.

"No." Eva stopped and took hold of Jez's bony shoulders, trying to look stern but afraid the girl might be right. Paranoia plucked at her nerves like an insistent harpist, forcing her to constantly scan the empty length of the street. Was there someone in the shadows of that doorway? Why was that car driving so slowly as it passed? She found she did not entirely trust herself anymore. The future was a vast ocean before them, teeming with possibilities and Eva felt lost, terrified. There were too many choices, any one of which could be disastrously wrong. She found herself missing the ritual predictability of captivity and was immediately ashamed. She could not allow herself to look back, to miss him. Full of conflicting urges and painful need, she cradled the tender curve of Jez's skull in her hand. They were nearly free, now.

Eva trapped the girl's face between her hands. Desire and fear flowed together in her belly, forming hot tentacles that flexed and coiled between her legs.

"We're safe out here," Eva told her, fingers up under Jez's shirt, caressing her belly, toying with the strip of unyielding leather that showed above the lowslung waistband of her brand new jeans. Jez's chastity belt, the last reminder of their old lives, of him. Horrified, Eva knew in that moment that she still longed for him, for his knowing hands and demanding mouth. He always knew just how to touch her, how to coax and tease her, to take her to the razor edge of her own endurance and over, into the demonic ecstasies that lay beyond. He had taught her things, opened doors. And now she was running away and taking Jez with her and there could be no going back.

"We're already gone," she said, forcing herself to breathe deeply, to think only of the future. "Just one last thing."

She pushed the girl into the shadowy mouth of an alley and kissed her, her mouth sore and bruised, voracious, starving. Her heart was slamming against the cage of her ribs. A slow burn simmered between her legs, making the friction from the seam of her jeans seem unendurable. She felt like she was falling, dying, being born.

She pushed Jez away and held her back against the wall. Reaching into her waistband, Eva pulled out a knife and flicked it open. She unbuttoned Jez's jeans with one hand, pushing them down to her knees and exposing the complex buckles and straps of the hateful chastity belt.

"What are you going to do?" Jez's eyes were round and fearful, shiny as drops of quicksilver.

"I'm taking this off." Eva held the knife up in front of Jez's face and ran a thumb over the wide silver lock.

"Eva, someone's coming." Jez was pale, shaking.

"Shhh." Eva caressed Jez's cheek with the flat blade of the knife. "There's no one."

"I'm serious." Jez squirmed. "Maybe we should go back."

"Jez," Eva said. "There's no time. Don't make this any harder than it has to be."

"Someone's here," Jez said. "I hear them."

"Shut up!" Eva slapped her face, not very hard, but Jez's eyes still glistened with a sheen of tears.

A strange flush of power pulsed under Eva's hot skin and she found that she wanted to push the girl to her knees here in the alley, to press that tear-stained face into her crotch and *make* her apologize. This sudden desire to take control was what had given her the strength to leave, but she found she still feared its intensity, its unpredictable demands. And she knew this was no time for play, especially if someone really was coming. So she drank in a deep breath to steady her hand and whispered, "Hold still."

She bent down and held the knife up to the thinnest of the leather straps. Jez squeezed her eyes shut as if it was her own skin about to be cut. Rats went about their business in the overflowing dumpsters, indifferent to the noisy drama unfolding in the alley's mouth. The moon above was a razor crescent in the captive sky. In the distance, the city muttered to itself in it's own language.

Part Two

INFILTRATION

2.

Caitlin and Mike, making love in a pool of afternoon sunshine. The slanting yellow light that bathed their sweat-slick flesh gave the clandestine feel of a secret affair. The sun loved Caitlin's hair almost as much as Mike did, playing deep in its Irish whiskey gold and honey amber. Conventional couples made tired love in the dusky blue evening, but Mike loved Caitlin in the afternoon.

He had endured much good-natured ribbing from his partner to steal this time with this woman. She made him greedy, and his life had become an unbearable desert punctuated by lush oasises like this.

Her body was racehorse lean and finely sculpted, her buttermilk skin dusted with pale freckles. Vargas-girl legs a mile long and mischievous heat in her glass-green eyes. Her breasts were small but she had nipples like thumb-tips, excruciatingly sexy beneath the thin t-shirts she always wore. She was the tallest woman he had ever met, six-two in flat shoes. When they kissed, their faces were exactly level. Although she was not model-pretty, the angles of her face were strong and compelling, her wide mouth curiously sexy.

Her true beauty was a by-product of form and grace, her every movement like unconscious ballet. Unlike many tall women who stoop and curl into themselves in an unconscious attempt to apologize for their height, Caitlin was never awkward with her body. She danced through the world without fear, without compromise.

When they had first met, she stalked up to his desk like a bad girl from a hard-boiled thriller and whispered in a husky, raw-silk voice straight out of the forties.

"I'm a desperate woman, detective. I have nowhere else to turn. You're my only hope."

He just sat there with his mouth open while she tossed her hair and laughed, thrusting out her hand and introducing herself. She was a writer, a piece of information she dispensed with a twist of wry sarcasm. She had spoken to his partner, weaseled her way up through the precinct hierarchy. Would he mind if she asked him some questions? How could he refuse?

Now, every time she turned her hot green gaze on him, he felt awkward and out of control, like an overeager child. When he met a woman who used the same shampoo, the smell would keep him uselessly hard for hours. He was utterly in love, and utterly unprepared for the consequences of that love.

She held his wrists up over his head, the powerful thrust of her hips controlling him completely, as she always did. He could do nothing but surrender to her, as he always did. His orgasm was frighteningly intense, swallowing everything.

Pressing her face into his neck, the length of her body shuddered, the damp curtain of her hair spilling across his vision. He wrapped his arms around her, unsure of where his flesh ended and hers began. He took a deep breath and held it, knowing that if he let it out, it would form the words she had made him promise never to speak.

"Don't fall in love with me," she had told him in the warm euphoria that followed the first time. "I'm not saying that to be coy, or trying to play hard to get. I'll be your friend and your fuck-buddy for as long as you like, but that's as far as I can go, OK?"

At the time, it had seemed refreshingly honest, exactly the kind of thing that he needed after the murky, guilt-shrouded labyrinth of his failed marriage. But now, the restriction was agony, a thick, impenetrable barrier between his mouth and his feelings. Even when it was good with Maura, it was never as good as just walking next to this woman.

"Caitlin," he said, pushing a heavy handful of tangles back away from her face. Her eyes had gone a smoky evergreen. He stroked her cheek.

He had no idea what he was going to say, but it hardly mattered. Just saying her name was another way to say 'I love you'. She turned her mouth to his fingers.

"What is it?" she asked.

The silence between them was a primordial soup of subtle emotion. He was afraid to breathe. Her eyes were like sunlight filtered though fathoms of green ocean, and he swore that there was something there, some silent answer to his silent declaration.

The shrill, electronic cicada call of his beeper broke the fragile surface tension of the moment and the half-glimpsed emotion was gone, leaving Mike alone with his unmentionable love. He closed his eyes, hiding under Caitlin's hair and cursing silently. He pressed his lips to her temple.

"I don't have to answer it," he said.

Caitlin laughed, low and rich but with the unmistakable cadence of someone letting out a long-held breath. She slipped off and he made a wordless sound of protest, clutching at her hips. Dancing out of his embrace, she extracted the offending machine from the tangled heap of their clothing. Her golden brows knitted.

"It's probably Eric," she said, tossing him the beeper.

He glanced at the display and groaned. He could feel the euphoria burning off in a hot wash of stomach acid. It could only be bad news. He peeled the damp and wrinkled condom from his limp dick and tossed it into the trash.

Caitlin sat cross-legged on the floor, pulling fuck-knots from her waist-length hair while she watched Mike on the phone, nodding, frowning. When he hung up, his expression was dark and serious.

She came forward and put her arms around him, her body warm and quiet, understanding. He let her hold him for a silent minute, drawing strength from her familiar scent. A sad echo of the earlier intensity rippled through him and was gone. He kissed her mouth and drew gently away.

"Eric just caught a case down 14TH," he said, running his fingers through his sweat damp hair. "Some kind of sexual mutilation or something. I gotta go."

Caitlin's eyes glittered.

"Call me later," she said, meaning that she wanted all the details. He shook his head.

"Sometimes I think you only fuck me for material."

He kissed her forehead, his mouth lingering, his hand cupping the back of her neck. He waited for her to protest, to say *of course not* but she said nothing. He sighed.

"I'll tell you all about it tonight, OK?"

She smiled.

———

Caitlin watched him dress, feeling less vulnerable with each layer of clothing that separated them. He was preoccupied as he buckled his shoulder holster, ran his fingers through his hair. His goodbye kiss was quick and he was gone.

Alone, she sat down naked at her desk and woke up her laptop. While the machine hummed and clicked, she piled her matted hair on top of her head and secured it with a pencil.

"Good afternoon, Lady Morrigan," the computer said, its voice deep and courtly. "How can I be of service?"

"Draw me a bath, Jeeves," she told it, her voice sharp with forced hilarity. She dug through a pile of CDs, selecting one by feel and slipping it into the boom box on the desk. "Use the gardenia oil and have a cold supper laid out, I'm famished."

The computer sat in the helpful silence of a foreign vender who speaks no English. The greeting program was the extent of its vocalization.

Caitlin rocked back on her chair and pressed her fingers to her lips. She closed her eyes and breathed in the lingering smell of Mike's body. It was his unapologetically masculine scent that had first caught her attention as they traded flirtatious banter in the drab antfarm of the 10TH Precinct. He was much older than she was, 41 to her 23, and nothing like the pale, contemptuous computer geeks that she normally paired with. He was vital and unselfconscious, an Alpha-wolf who inspired little dog rage in all her friends, bitter nerds with deep racial memories of high school abuse.

For a long time, she was able to convince herself that her affair with Mike really was nothing but a phase in her relentless hunt for material to fill the hardboiled crime novels that paid the bills. But today, in the moment before the pager went off, Caitlin's heart had stopped in her chest, and she was sure that he was going to tell her that he loved her.

During her introspection, the screen had flipped over to screensaver, a strange pattern of flying worms and clocks. She shuddered and called up her personal journal.

> Cliché #1: We are so much alike under all our surface differences. Both logical. Both detached. Don't trust easy. Don't give easy. We have the same dark sense of humor, the same cynicism. We piss each other off and we make each other think. I've never been with a man like him before.

> Cliché #2: Great sex. Everyone likes to think they are the best ever, but this man is light years ahead. He not only knows where it is, he knows what to do with it. He does everything I want like it's an honor without the eager-to-please desperation of most men. I tell him to get down there and lick my pussy and he gets this look, almost worshipful. He's so respectful. Chivalrous, even. And I love to watch his face when he loses control, when all the toughness peels back and there's nothing but raw vulnerability and need. I know I could have anything I wanted from him. He makes me feel like a Goddess.

> Cliché #3: Last and worst. When I'm with him, it's like everything else just goes away. The world shrinks down to the size of our skins. He makes me feel like anything is possible.

> Be logical, Caitlin, Are you falling for this guy? Because if you are, you'd better take it out in the back yard and shoot it before it gets any worse. There are scientific theories based on less evidence than you have to prove that love = pain. Besides, where's it gonna go? Can you really picture yourself a cop's wife?

Caitlin passed a hand over her eyes. Billie Holliday wailed in the background, her acrobatic voice raising and falling all sweet milk and razors.

Closing her file with vicous keystrokes, she pulled in a deep breath and dialed up TruthNet.

The BBS greeted her with cheery familiarity. She downloaded her E-mail and thought about leaving a note for Wilson Bergin, TruthNet SysOp and her best and oldest friend. The structure of the BBS was very similar to a magician's cabinet, full of secret compartments and trick doors. Invisible commands and hidden menus nestled one within another like Ukrainian dolls. Caitlin knew maybe one tenth of the whole maze and had little desire to know more. She cruised the latest postings, the latest banter, only half-curious. A handful of virtual-acquaintances violently debated some topic too convoluted and obscure even for her, but Wilson's disembodied opinion was conspicuously absent. She decided to pay him a physical visit.

"Wilson," she typed. "F2F @ 19:00"

It was always smart to warn Wilson of face to face interaction well ahead of time, and even though she was one of the few people on earth who could get away with showing up in the flesh unannounced, she usually tried to avoid startling him.

She logged off and shut down, pulling on an old pair of jeans and a man's white, v-neck undershirt and stuffing her feet into her boots as she hopped towards the door. Grabbing her leather jacket off the back of a chair and groping for her keys, she danced out into the hallway, motorcycle helmet banging against her denim hip.

3.

The uniforms already had the alley cordoned off when Mike arrived. Juana Carrera and Ray Nolan were flanking the victim like dogs guarding a fresh kill while Eric knelt at Carrera's feet on one of the few bloodless patches of cobblestone.

He was a thickly built Italian with a wide, smirking face that always seemed to be hiding some secret joke. His suit was pearly grey over a dark shirt and his tie was narrow black silk. His wiry black hair was carefully gelled, drug lord stylish. It was a look that came from working five years in Vice.

"Juanacita," Eric said expansively, spreading his arms wide as if proposing marriage. "You know I can't live without you."

"Detective Antonucci," she said, her lips turned up in one corner, the barest hint of a smile. "Will you please try to conduct yourself with some measure of professionalism."

"Do you see how she does that," Eric asked Mike as he ducked under the yellow tape. "Women. You give 'em your heart and they spit it back in your face."

This ritual was old and familiar, Eric throwing himself at Carrera's feet and Carrera cutting him down. If she ever accepted his advances, he'd probably die of shock.

"Tell me," Mike asked, stretching a pair of white latex gloves over his scarred hands.

"Just what ya see." Eric stood up, brushing off his knees. "White female, late teens. No ID. Extensive genital mutilation."

Mike squatted down beside the sprawled body, frowning at the deep, football shaped stab wounds and arching bite-marks beneath the girl's uptilted chin. Blood was everywhere, long, clotted splashes and coagulated rivers between the uneven cobblestones. Nothing unusual. But the mess between her legs ...

"Who found her?" Mike asked.

"A transvestite prostitute," Carrera told him.

"Wonderful," he said, eyes rolling skyward. "Anybody else see anything?"

"Nope," Eric said. "Nobody saw dick."

"How 'bout the trannie?"

"Davis is leaning on her, but she's swearing up and down that she don't know nothing."

"Figures," Mike said. "I got a bad feeling about this one."

"You and me both." Eric shook his head. "I need a fucking vacation."

A round of agreeable noises and sympathetic nods.

"I'm telling you, this one's gonna be a bitch," Nolan said, wrinkling his lips in disgust, not at the state of the sleepy-eyed corpse, but at the hopelessness of the case. "I can smell it. Media'll be all over it, you can be sure of that. My condolences, Antonucci."

"Fuck your condolences," Eric smiled. "You can give me condolences on your fucking knees after I put this bitch down. I'll be shaking hands with the mayor and you'll be suckin' my dick."

"Well, Detective" Carrera said, her pretty Latina features smoothly deadpan. "I suppose everyone needs a dream."

Mike shook his head and bent to examine the dead girl more carefully. She must have been girlishly pretty, beautiful even, before the bland anonymity of death washed away all traces of personality. Long pale eyelashes, freckled pug nose. Lush whore's mouth and blonde stubble on her head. There was a silver ring in her septum and an intricate tattoo on her right biceps, a capital A composed of twisted organic shapes that seemed to writhe like tortured flesh. Her jeans were around her knees.

Whoever had done this must have taken their time, lovingly carving what was once a vagina into a twisted sculpture of mutilated tissue. The clitoris had been trifurcated, peeled back like reluctant petals. The inner labia was segmented into thin strips that had been braided to form four separate coils. Long fillets of meat from the inner walls of the vagina had been almost entirely removed, pulled inside out and attached only by the thinnest of veins.

"Shit like this takes dedication, that's for sure." Eric said, squatting down beside his partner.

Mike nodded. He fished in the pocket of the jeans, pulling out a single crumpled ten dollar bill and a price tag for the jeans themselves.

"Must work fast." Eric smirked. "Must've had the new Ronco Pocket Slicer-Dicer. It mutilates, it amputates ... "

The detectives snickered. The victim stared sightlessly at the blank white sky.

Mike handed Eric the tag. "Check this out. These clothes are brand new."

The detectives heard Sergeant DeSalvo before they saw him, his anything but dulcet tones echoing down the alley, turning the heads of jaded rats watching from a respectful distance.

"Jesus fucking Christ I need this like I need a fucking hole in my head."

He appeared from around the corner with the air of a high school principal ready to break up some unruly students.

"Alright, who caught this fucking mess?" He glared at his underlings, scowling dramatically.

"I did, sir." Eric took a step forward.

"You did?" His scowl deepened. "I thought you was getting sandwiches."

"I was in the neighborhood." Eric shrugged. "Just call me Mister Lucky."

"Well, *Detective* Lucky, you caught yourself a fucking media shitstorm. We just ID'd this little honey. One of the uniforms recognized the tattoo from an old missing person report. Her mom's Ruth Eiseman, that loudmouth Self-Help cunt who writes all that crap about men who blow dogs and the women that love them. You clear this one and they'll be lined up to suck your dick. If not, you better be ready to suck mine. Because I tell ya ... "

Like Eric's wooing of Juana Carrera, this little macho vignette was so predictable, Mike barely heard it. DeSalvo was just passing down the shit he had doubtlessly received from Lieutenant Leary. Wrathful gravity in the good old Homicide foodchain. 'Twas ever thus.

The coroner's dark van pulled up to the mouth of the alley and disgorged a pack of industrious techs like some intellectual swat team.

A neat black woman knelt beside the body, fingers gentle in their impossible search for life.

"Dead," she announced.

Eric snickered.

"Gee," he said. "Do you think?"

The woman smiled.

"She's all yours," she said to the waiting techs.

Flashes popped and sent red and yellow ghosts chasing across Mike's vision. He shook his head to clear them, wishing childishly that he were still in Caitlin's bed, breathing the lingering aroma of their exertion.

He found somewhere else to look while the techs rolled the corpse. He's been staring at dead bodies for ten years and although they seldom bothered him while they were lying still, there was something about the way the techs tossed them around like sides of beef that dug underneath his objectivity. He made himself focus on the crime scene itself, scouring the cobblestones for something overlooked.

The quiet alley told him the story of a struggle, of blood flowing as if running away, pointing back to the place where the knife had first met flesh. Of a girl's life spilling out and her vacated shell being dragged out of sight and subjected to lunatic revision.

The depth of sickness that would lead someone to mutilate a fellow human with such relish and creativity was pretty rare. Killing was easy, and with the wide array of firearms available to the vengeful, it became almost like a video game. Mike saw the aftermath of this bang-you're-dead mentality every day. But this was so unspeakably intimate. Mike had seen a lot of sex-related crimes in his career, but there was something about this guy that made his skin crawl. Mike was glad he had forgone lunch in favor of Caitlin.

"Jesus." This from Nolan, cupping a protective hand over his genitals and watching as they loaded the girl into the van, as if her mutilation was somehow catching.

DeSalvo was in the mouth of the alley, verbally abusing the knot of reporters clustered on the other side of the tape.

Eric sucked air between his teeth and fished in his pockets for a cigarette.

"I don't know, man," Nolan said.

"Fuck what you don't know," Eric answered, lighting up.

"Well." Nolan smirked. "I know one thing for sure."

"Oh yeah, what's that?"

Nolan leaned in and snatched Eric's cigarettes, shaking one out and clamping it between his teeth.

"Better you than me."

4.

Caitlin straddled her classic Harley Sportster, coming down with her full weight on the starter. The bike coughed, spluttered and then caught, and she took off down 25TH Street, heading for the West Side Highway.

The motorcycle was one of her few luxuries, purchased with money from a small inheritance, and she felt cool as nobody's business with her heavy leather gloves and steel toed boots. She was not normally prone to such frivolity, but in the strange summer of her grandmother's death, the Harley had seemed like the ultimate symbol of freedom and escape. Escape from the icy hell of the silent dinner table, from the frozen wasteland of her father's eyes. From the empty place where her sullen, raccoon-eyed sister Megan used to sit before she carved up her delicate forearms and bled to death behind a locked bathroom door.

Her Grandma Talbot, her mother's mother, had wanted nothing to do with her only daughter since she ran off with a poor Irish fiddler fresh off the boat from embattled Belfast. But nonetheless, she made sure that Caitlin and Megan went to private school and had brand new dresses at Christmastime. Caitlin was seven when an unmentionable cancer had chewed up her mother's insides, a wild and voracious sister, devouring and out of control. Grandma Talbot refused to give a dime to help with the escalating hospital bills and when the malignant child had finally claimed her daughter's life, she tried to get custody of her granddaughters.

Their father had fought with unflinching ferocity to keep his girls and eventually, Martha Talbot backed down, contenting herself with subtle control from a distance. Caitlin's clearest memories of her grandmother were of a tall and softly menacing presence with an intricate crown of platinum hair and a lingering scent of lavender-water and medicine. She was always there for graduations and other school functions. She would sit in the back row at Megan's recitals while Caitlin sat like a good girl itching in her opaque tights and watching the nine year old prodigy play her violin like she was trying to start a fire. Megan drove her teachers crazy, playing with the fiddle low on her arm and always refusing to stick with the sheet music. She played with apocalyptic abandon, astonishing the sweating crowd of relatives with the amount of passion coming from her small frame. Caitlin's father would stand, applauding wildly with fierce pride nearly bursting through the seams of his best suit. Megan's recitals were the only thing that could still make him happy in the bleak years that followed her mother's death, and it wasn't long before Megan spat her talent back in his face, throwing down the violin and picking up the electric guitar. Caitlin tried every day to make up for her sister's rebellion by bringing home glowing report cards and big red As on all her essays and stories, but he would never look at her the way he had looked at Megan on the rickety elementary school stage. This knowledge was heavy on her ten year old heart even then, in those black moments in the stuffy auditorium when she would turn away from Megan with tears blurring her vision. There, in the back row would be Grandma Talbot, stiff and dangerous like some rococo weapon from another age.

Grandma Talbot would not go to her daughter's funeral. Or her granddaughter's. The only funeral Caitlin saw her at was her own. She would never forget the fancy maroon funeral parlor packed with relatives she'd never met, all full of saccharine sympathy for the wild Irish seed with her too-short dress and cheap shoes who had the audacity to inherit everything.

Her life had been punctuated by funerals. First her mother's, Megan's hand small and sweaty in hers as they knelt at the rail, leaning in to kiss the corpse's cool, powdery cheek and her father beside them, tough, Irishman's tears nothing but a liquid brightness in his anguished blue eyes. He played his fiddle for the last time at the funeral of his only love, an aching lament that flowed like the tears he could not shed. Years later, as the twin devils of hard liquor and hopelessness slowly ate her father alive, Caitlin would remember that song and her heart would break in a thousand places. Her stepmother, Irene, was as good to him as she could be, but she was not his Rose, and their marriage was as cold and empty as a church, nothing but dark Catholic gravity keeping them locked in their loveless orbit.

Then there was the quiet shame of Megan's funeral, the sealed casket and Caitlin alone with nothing but the bitter company of secrets and the black hope that maybe now that her sister was gone, there might be some love left over for her.

Caitlin could not make herself believe that Megan was really inside the glossy blond-wood casket (paid for by Grandma Talbot, of course.) Megan who had everything and wanted nothing. Megan who was small and dark, like their mother, while Caitlin was so tall and fair, mirror image of the hated grandmother in her proud youth. Megan who was loved too much, while Caitlin was forgotten.

Her father was drunk and silent. Irene was silent too, her worn face hard with righteous disapproval. In some deep part of her, Caitlin knew that Megan Rose McCullough had been dead for years, that she was already dead when their father broke Irene's nose for suggesting in a fit of bitter rage that her husband preferred his own daughter to his lawful wife. Caitlin had heard her sister's dying screams in the hot darkness of their shared bedroom and had done nothing to save her. The cold, bitter girl with her vicious music and her porcupine haircuts was a walking corpse, a pale skeleton with smeary black eyeliner and chipped black nailpolish. She changed her name constantly, but she was calling herself Rose the day she died.

Grandma Talbot died two months after Megan. The stiff Protestant pomposity of her grandmother's funeral was like another planet. Gleaming strands of pearls and expensive navy blue suits. The whispering of pursed orange lips and creamy aroma of rare flowers. The music was syrupy and impotent. It was the first day of her adult life.

That inheritence had paid for her college and her computer. The first year in her apartment and her beautiful motorcycle. She had tried to give half to her father but he had glared at her and spat on the scarred wood floor, told her to keep her goddamn charity. She fled, never looking back.

Now, a year after her graduation, the money was just starting to run low. She was frugal by nature, and combined with her income from the cheap novels, she expected it to last through till Christmas. Soon, she was going to have to start thinking of earning a real living.

As she laid a pair of singles in the toll collector's outstretched hand, she found herself thinking again of Wilson. It had been weeks since she had seen him in the flesh and his mother's massive house had been more like home than the tiny apartment where she grew up. A place to hide when the bleak chill of the dinner table became more than she could bear. It would be good to see him, and he would doubtlessly be able to add some flesh to the teasingly ephemeral bones of Mike's mysterious *sexual mutilation.*

5.

Mike and Eric sat in their unmarked Plymouth Fury outside the lush Scarsdale home of Ruth and Jacob Eiseman. It was the largest house on its block, dark green shutters and a well swept path flanked by neat, geometrically perfect rows of pink and white impatiens. The lawn was vibrant, recently mowed and there was a gold Lexus and a clean white Range Rover in the driveway. Potted ivy and soft copper wind chimes hung beside the door.

"God, I hate this part," Eric said, toying unconsciously with the wedding band on his thick finger.

Mike nodded.

"I'd rather tongue kiss a fucking floater than tell a woman her little girl is dead."

"I know," Mike said, pocketing the car keys and extracting himself from behind the wheel. He straightened his tie and headed up the neat brick path.

"It just gets to me sometimes, I don't know." Eric ran fingers through his crisp hair, a few steps behind.

Mike did not need to respond. Eric always did the talking, but when it came to dealing with the family of the deceased, especially wives and mothers, he inexplicably clammed up. On the rare occasions when he was able to open his mouth, it almost always spewed something utterly inappropriate. It had been standard operating procedure in their partnership for Mike to handle the family, but even after ten years, Eric still felt it necessary to explain each time.

"Shit, I fucking hate this part," Eric muttered as Mike pressed his palm against the doorbell.

A soft flurry of footsteps on carpet and then silence as they were sized up through an eye level peep hole.

Mike held up his shield.

"Police," he said. "We'd like a word with you."

The door opened on an aggressively thin woman with carefully styled ash-blond hair and casually tasteful, mail-order clothes. She eyed them warily. She smelled like skin cream and pencil shavings.

"Detective Kiernan." Mike said. He gestured over his shoulder. "My partner Detective Antonucci."

Eric ducked his head and muttered a greeting.

The woman was obviously not interested in social niceties.

"Is it Eva?" she asked. "Did you find her?"

"Could we come in for a moment?" Mike kept his voice soft and non-threatening, as if he were coaxing a suicide off their ledge.

She took in a single quick breath and closed her eyes.

"She's dead, isn't she?"

Mike nodded.

"I'm afraid so, ma'am."

Behind him, Mike could feel Eric tensing up, ready for the hysterics.

There were none. The woman nodded silently and motioned for them to come inside.

The living room was very modern, mushroom walls and terracotta throw pillows on the pebbly beige couch. Like the woman, everything was subdued and tasteful, catalogue-like. A long mantelpiece of pale marble held framed photographs of the dead girl and several academic awards. The flawlessly neat, *Better Homes and Gardens* feel of the room made Mike feel grungy and unclean. The rich sweat he had worked up with Caitlin had long soured on his body and the fact that he had spent the last few hours in a bloody alley with a dead girl had left a clinging psychic sediment that made him feel unfit to stand in this woman's spotless living room.

A man appeared in the curved doorway at the far end of the room, squinting at them with the unmistakable expression of someone who normally wears glasses, but isn't. He was sandy haired and intellectually pale with a boyish face that bore no small resemblance to the deceased.

"What is it, Ruth?"

The woman did not turn towards her husband.

"These men are detectives," she said in a strange flat voice. "Eva is dead."

The man staggered as if he had been hit.

"Oh my God." He clutched at a thin backed wooden chair and pulled it around to sit. His face was grey with shock and his hands clutched at each other like drowning lovers.

"How did it happen?" Ruth asked, her eyes dark and narrow, almost as if they might try to pull one over on her.

Mike wiped his mouth, struggling to put the facts into as delicate terms as possible.

"Well," he said, finally. "It seems to be ... sex related."

"Sex related?" Ruth scowled. "What do you mean, sex related? She was raped?"

"Not exactly." Mike turned to Eric, who was absorbed in studying the wide leaves of a small potted tree.

"Well what exactly *do* you mean then?"

The man was cradling his head in his hands, calling on God in a soft monotonous voice.

"She was ... mutilated. Sexually mutilated."

"Mutilated," the woman echoed. Her lipsticked mouth was a tight slash, eyes like nail-heads.

Vast silence in the tasteful room and blood was pounding in Mike's temples, making him sweat under his new jacket.

With a long, slow breath, he dug out his "let-this-terrible-tragedy-not-go-unavenged" speech. Most of the time, it had distraught mothers kissing his feet and offering up the most intimate details of their wayward child's history. This time, it only made the woman slightly less antagonistic.

"I suppose we'll need to ... identify her."

This from the man, speaking into his own lap.

"Yes," Mike said. "We'd like one of you to come down to the Medical Examiner so we can get a positive identification. Then we'll need to ask a few questions."

"Fine," the woman said. "I'll go."

"Oh God," the man said softly. "Oh God."

6.

Caitlin tapped on the leaded glass set deep in the thick door of the Bergin residence, an indecently large, castle-like structure on Fieldston Road, in Riverdale. Mrs. Bergin herself answered the door with a cellular phone tucked in between her shoulder and her ear. She was a small woman with a serious face and expensive shoes. Her mysterious executive position at IBM took her all over the world so Caitlin was always surprised to see her. Her chestnut hair was perfect.

"How ya doing, Mrs. B?" Caitlin stage whispered, swinging her helmet by the chin strap.

The older woman spared a brief smile, then waved Caitlin in, her mind already returned to ruthlessly running the world. She did not have an off switch.

Wilson was in the dojo, or the wide, empty room that bore that name, practicing Kendo with a Louisville Slugger. Not that he didn't have a real *katana* and *wakisashi*, along with a massive two handed Scottish Claymore, an authentic Confederate sword and scores of other swords and knives that Caitlin couldn't name. It was just his own strange fetish, an idea he'd gotten from some cyberpunk potboiler. He found it obscurely amusing to use this quaint piece of Americana for a Japanese martial art. It was also much heavier than the traditional wooden swords used in Kendo and no doubt it was a subtle form of male display behavior, though he would never admit it.

"Respectful salutations, Will-San," she said, bowing from the waist.

Wilson rolled his eyes and groaned appreciatively over her pun. He was naked except for a pair of boxer shorts printed with ones and zeros and his body was sinewy as an animal used to running from predators.

He had an intense and not altogether pleasant face with dark eyebrows that met in the middle and sharp blue eyes that missed nothing. His mousy-brown hair was pulled back in a oily braid and there was a rash of pimples on his wide, pale forehead.

"Lady Morrigan," he said, returning her bow. "Surely you have come for reasons other than wordplay." He swung the bat inches from her nose. "Something has you quite pixilated. Perhaps the squealing down at the 10TH Precinct has your erstwhile paramour up in arms. A girl with her sexual organs creatively mutilated. Rather brutal, I understand."

"Christ, Wilson, you ruin all my best surprises."

Caitlin fell to her knees and began to mime *seppuku*. Wilson shook his head.

"Do not kneel before me, wench, lest you plan to take full advantage of that position."

Caitlin laughed.

"Are you flirting with me?"

He blushed. In the whole fifteen years she'd known him, he had made a direct sexual comment maybe three times. He was prone to intensely chivalrous, platonic affairs with totally inaccessible women who would never love him back, but Caitlin couldn't say with any conviction that he had ever actually been laid. She knew better than to ask.

"I meant no offense, lady," Wilson said, blush darkening.

"I'm over it," Caitlin said, leaning in and kissing his hot pink cheek. She loved Wilson when he was flustered. She mimed his long, sweeping Kendo moves with an empty hand and found herself wondering if she could ever sleep with him, if he would want her if she offered. Wilson viewed all women as aliens, some hostile, some benign, some goddess-like. Caitlin, over the years, had been accepted into a fourth category. An honorary boy. He sometimes joked with her in the same way a secure hetero-boy makes mock-flirtatious remarks to a gay friend, but there was a very clear line she knew better than to cross.

As she moved across the empty floor, she realized that she had not been with another man since she met Mike. The word "monogamy" filled her with nameless terror, but she found that she had little interest in other men, and that fact was just another bad omen in a long line of ominous developments.

"Wilson," she said as he moved to parry her invisible blade with the bat. "I think Mike is falling in love with me."

"They frequently do, you know," he answered, executing a series of ritualized thrusts, stopping the bat as if it could really be blocked by her imaginary *katana*. The long muscles in his forearms rippled.

"But he's such a sweet guy," she said, parrying. "I don't want to hurt him."

"Look," he countered. "You are, as usual, allowing yourself to become far too neurotic about this. You told him at the outset that he was not to fall in love with you, Am I right?"

"Well yeah, but ... "

"*And* you assured him that you were quite serious, and he understood and accepted your terms?"

"Of course."

"Then just *feed*," Without warning, he broke form and slipped under her block to lay the bat against her ribcage, stopping it enough that the impact was only mildly painful. He bowed. "Just take what you need, like you always do. Stop driving yourself crazy over animal rights."

"Ow!" She blinked, rubbing her side. She could still feel that strange, pregnant silence before the beeper. Shuddering, she changed the subject.

"If I had a real sword you wouldn't have thumped me like that."

"If I had a real sword, you would be in two halves right now." He grinned, as if this concept pleased him. "And besides, you couldn't have blocked the blow from that position with air or steel. Your reflexes are still quite substandard."

"They work when I need 'em," Caitlin sang, pirouetting like a ballerina across the wooden floor.

"You are undisciplined," he told her. "Your approach to the martial arts is like your approach to sex. Hapkido last week, kendo this week. Next week, who knows?"

Caitlin shrugged.

"Maybe I'm still searching for my true calling."

This was truer than she wanted to admit. All her life, she'd felt unglamourously different. Megan had her rebellion spelled out for her by her musical idols, a melange of painted leather and safety-pins and butchered hair bleached and dyed, bleached and dyed. But Caitlin never had a style, a direction. She was just a long, lanky girl in men's jeans and men's boots, too tall for the fashionable little scraps of bright cloth that passed for dresses in trendy boutiques. Other women disliked her, threatened by her quiet ease with a body that defied the standards of femininity. Many thought she was a transsexual. Others saw her as a freak who was not properly humbled by her inappropriate anatomy. Men were simultaneously captivated and intimidated, wanting her and fearing her and always wondering what it might be like with her. To them, she was a desirable freak, but still a freak.

Caitlin bit her lip to clear her head of this reflection. She took Wilson's callused hand and dragged him out into the long hallway.

"You gonna turn me on to the mutilation scoop or what?"

"But of course," he said, his mouth stretched smug in the corners the way it always was when he had something she wanted. He stepped aside at the door of his room, motioning for her to enter first.

This room had hardly changed in the 15 years since she first walked in the door. There was a constant subtle updating of technology, but the narrow child's bed and scruffy blue carpet, the battered wooden desk barely containing the overflow of machine guts and paper, the boyclutter of socks and throwing stars and old copies of *2600* and *Wired*, these things were the only stability in the treacherous sea of her childhood and adolescence. In the corner, a hulking Digital PDP11-34 that they had stolen from their school storeroom. Wilson had strained his back trying to get the refrigerator-sized dinosaur onto the cart he had built to hold it and transport it silently past the snoozing security guard. He spent the next month in bed for that stunt. It was their first illegal act, and in a fit of victorious glee, they named it Robbie after the robot in *Forbidden Planet*. Wilson's subsequent discovery that it was virtually useless without a second component as large and unwieldy as the first never dampened his affection for the thing. It was never missed.

And in this room, leaning up against that bulky machine, Caitlin had lost her virginity with a forgettable friend of Wilson's. He had been so eager that she found herself making him jump through hoops just for fun, demanding that he perform all sorts of unreasonable tasks in order to earn the privilege of taking her cherry. When ever she entered the familiar chaos of Wilson's room, she found herself recalling the image of this hungry boy kneeling before her with his desperate cock straining towards her like a leashed dog while she forced him to describe, for the third or fourth time, how beautiful her pussy was. That memory never failed to make her smile.

The only area in the Wilson's room that was vaguely ordered was the small cluster of hardware that ran TruthNet. The modest BBS prided itself as being an unregulated farmers market of information, rumors, urban legends and all manner of former secrets. It was, as many boards are, a labor of love. She knew that Wilson liked to think of himself as the Robin Hood of the information age. When he was feeling particularly pompous, which was almost always, he described himself as the new Martin Luther, wresting power away from the access-privileged priests and distributing their secrets to the common people. Not that the common people would know what to do with electronic keys to the phone company's lingerie drawer, but it was a fine sentiment, nonetheless.

In truth, he was lying to himself and they both knew it. Knowledge as power and competitive one-upmanship was the skeleton of their relationship. The pretentious fulminations of the Hacker's Ethic meant nothing next to the amphetamine rush of secrets, of slipping in and helping yourself to hidden information.

Wilson gathered up the pieces of an eviscerated cellular phone from a chair next to his and balanced them precariously on the top of an awkward pyramid of books. Caitlin sat.

"As of my last visit to PigNet," Wilson said, his fingers flying on the keyboard. "They were still compiling the forensic information. But they are certainly moving with almost supernatural speed, considering the nature of bureaucracy. They are quite excited."

The singing tones of dialing and then a burring ring. The NYPD information network's unsuspecting computer picked up, asking for a clearance code. He checked a list of names and codes taped to the wall and chose one of a few highlighted in acid green. The information spread open before them like a well-tipped whore.

"Female, blond and blue, 5'7", 113 lbs.," Wilson chanted as the information scrolled past on the screen. "Cause of death, blood loss due to extreme laceration of the throat and genital area."

Wilson licked his lips and Caitlin rolled her eyes.

"The victim had rings in both nipples and a ring in her septum. It is likely that a ring was also present in the hood of the clitoris, before the wounds were inflicted. There were bite-marks as well as stab wounds on the victim's throat, some fresh, and some healed and not all from the same set of teeth. Also noteworthy, an old burn in the shape of a letter A on the left buttock. All the major alterations are post mortem. The victim was not tied during the attack, but appears to have been restrained repeatedly to the point of scarring over a period of months prior to her death. She also appears to have extensive scarring on the back, thighs and buttocks, some as recent as two or three days old. These marks indicate the use of various devices associated with sado-masochism."

Wilson arched one half of his thick, connected eyebrows.

"That's new," he said. "And, wait ... "

He leaned forward as if to make himself more streamlined, fingers clacking away on the keyboard.

"The victim has been identified as Eva Eiseman, 19, of Scarsdale, NY ... Eva Eiseman. Caitlin, do you know who that is?"

Caitlin shook her head and he laid a hand on her shoulder.

"Apocrypha," he told her as if he were presenting her with a diamond ring.

"Apocrypha?" Caitlin said. "The self-proclaimed Queen of Cyberspace? Holy fuck!"

Wilson nodded sagely.

"Isn't she the one who hacked that crawling news thing on the Sony building in Times Square?"

"That's right. She made it repeat 'Absinthe, my blood for you' for 3 minutes and 47 seconds during rush hour. It was a stunt to impress the reclusive but very powerful owner an SM club in the meat packing district. Not far from where she was found with her vagina turned into modern art. I suppose it worked."

"S&M club?" Caitlin frowned, thoughtful.

"SM, not S&M. there is no *and* in Sadomachochism. It's not Sado-*and*-masochism, hence no *and* in SM. Anyway the House of Absinthe is not just any SM club, my dear, it's *the* SM club."

"Is it that place that runs an ad in the back of *The Voice*, you know, 'Indulge Your Darkest Fantasies!' What's that place called ... ?" Caitlin turned her eyes up to the ceiling. "The Crypt?" She did not mention the little shiver that had traveled up through her body as she ran a nail over the letters of that ad, the little drawing of a naked woman in chains. How she had wondered what it might be like to go there.

"Oh, please." Wilson smirked. "The Crypt is like Disneyland compared to Absinthe's place."

"Well shit, Wilson," Caitlin said, grinning. "Since when did you become an expert on sadomasochism?"

"You forget," he said. "I'm an expert on everything."

Caitlin laughed and Wilson shrugged as if he were above it all but she could see the bright spark of humor in his eyes.

"I wonder if the cops have picked up on the Apocrypha angle yet," Caitlin mused, rubbing her hand over the back of her neck.

"We are talking about the New York City Police Department." Wilson snorted derisively. "Hardly Mensa candidates."

Caitlin wrinkled her lips but said nothing.

"Eva Eiseman is the daughter of a prominent self-help author. It was her mother's clout that got her out of various scrapes involving electronic indiscretion back before the training wheels came off. No doubt it is her influence that is inspiring the 10TH Precinct to such fervent investigation. If they don't have it yet, they will soon."

Caitlin closed her eyes, the vague glimmerings of an idea coagulating in the back of her mind. Gather the facts. Talk to people. Get the jump on everyone and be the first to come out with a true-crime account of the *most gruesome murder since Jack the Ripper ...*

She shook her head. Like they say, *It's so crazy it just might work.* Lurid description and sleazy, eyecatching phrases were her specialty. So was speed, slamming out sixty thousand words in two sleepless weeks. No reason to confine herself to made-up murder for six grand a pop, when she could exploit the madness of the real world and walk away with a bestseller.

"It's getting hot in here," Wilson said mildly, gesturing towards the screen. "Time to go."

A few quick commands and he was out, leaning back in his chair and lacing his fingers behind his head.

"Well?" Caitlin asked.

Wilson waved a disk under her nose and she threw her arms around him kissing him wetly.

"Please," he said, squirming out of her embrace. "Try to control your gratitude."

"Are you gonna post the Apocrypha info?" she asked, sliding the disk into the pocket of her jacket as if it were solid gold.

"Of course," Wilson answered. "Why do you ask?"

"I just thought ... " She trailed off. "I don't know."

"No, please," Wilson said. "By all means, share with the rest of the class."

"Well," she said. "Maybe we should sit on it for a while."

"Excuse me?"

"I mean, maybe hang on to the info until I get this piece a little tighter. I just don't want everyone and his grandmother making off with my story."

"*Your* story?" Caitlin could see he was gathering steam for another lecture. "When exactly did information obtained by me become your intellectual property? You should know better than to claim ownership of information."

"Don't patronize me, Wilson." Caitlin could feel anger rising in her spine, drawing her up tall. She was about to let him have it with both barrels of unbridled Irish wrath when he tipped back in his chair again and gestured at the monitor.

"Well, I guess that renders our argument somewhat pointless."

The message screaming across the screen was:

"THE QUEEN IS DEAD, LONG LIVE THE QUEEN!"

7.

The board was alive with rumor and speculation. Phone lines teemed with electronic opinions, arguments and outrageous lies. Hackers spoke reverently of the deceased's exploits and boasted of their own. The forensic reports were cooed over and lovingly dissected. Theories were put forth and shot down.

In a private chat room set up just for the occasion, hacker royalty from around the world held an on-line wake for the deceased. Extra lines had been pirated and hardly anyone was stepped on. Occasionally someone would get nasty and X's would start appearing in their words with increasing frequency until they had the sense to shut up. Names both famous and obscure crawled out of the electronic woodwork to put their two cents in. Mostly it was very civilized.

>Sometimes death makes perfect sense and
>sometimes none at all. Apocrypha was
>arrogant and flashy, but she was a good
>cowboy, for a girl that is. Nobody deserves to
>die like that.

>There is no death here. Only in the flesh world.
>The Queen lives on here, with us.

>I'm telling ya man, we can't let this sex pervert
>get away with shit like this. they can't do this
>to one of ours, its like The Ethic here man, ya
>know? now who's with me on taking out this
>bletcherous fucker? we'll trash his credit rating
>for the next 10,000 yrs ...

>hello?

And on and on like that. An impassioned debate on the possible existence of monsters raged between those who found the idea intriguing and those for whom such a fleshy, old-world concept was beneath contemplation.

>'Any sufficiently advanced technology is
>indistinguishable from magic.' - Arthur C.
>Clarke.

>'Any sufficiently brilliant hack is
>indistinguishable from magic' - Untergang

>This guy is no more supernatural that you and
>me. It only seems magic to you children
>because you don't understand how he did it.
>You're nothing more than a bunch of primitives
>clinging together and shuddering during an
>eclipse. He's not a monster, just a smart
>motherfucker who hasn't been caught yet.

There was a brief scuffle over who would answer back, but a new voice spoke up and silenced them all. It was the voice of the reclusive Lucio, a well known New Orleanian hacker who had gone underground to shake a feeding frenzy of federal interest several years ago.

>The world is much bigger than you think.

Then, like a binary manifestation of the Blessed Virgin, he was gone, leaving nothing but awed speculation in his wake.

On and on and on.

For all their opinions and moralistic tirades, no one really seemed to understand that Eva Eiseman, only child of Ruth and Jacob, was dead. Not just game over, deposit 25 cents to continue. Dead, lying in a grungy alley with piles of leaky trash bags and rats and roaches just helping themselves.

One of the few who seemed to regard the situation as anything more than a grand whodunit was a kid calling himself Elric. He claimed to be a friend of Apocrypha, though rumor had it that he was really an ex-lover. It took an hour of careful wheedling for Caitlin to get him to agree to meet her.

8.

Caitlin sat in a swanky, upscale diner in Scarsdale, drinking bitter coffee and wondering if Elric was going to stand her up. Her brain had kicked into high gear and the story was growing and expanding at an astonishing rate. She was on the scent of something huge. She felt hyperaware, wildly alive, bursting with detail. Facts and images mated and recombined inside her head, assuming a loose, frighteningly massive shape. What to do with this thundercloud of information was almost beside the point. She would never admit it, but at the core of her desire to know was a dick-measuring competitiveness, a need to be the first one with the answer.

She pulled a pencil from her hair and opened her notebook. More than half of its pages were filled with her military-neat handwriting.

Waiting for Elric, she wrote.

> 20 minutes late, but I'm not surprised. Wouldn't tell me anything online. How can I make him trust me? The old world media still hasn't picked up on the Apocrypha connection, so, unlike the unfortunate Eisemans, he hasn't been approached by any other journalists. Gotta to play it cool. Sympathetic, but not condescending. Understanding. A shoulder to cry on. Do this right, Caitlin Anne. Don't fuck it up, now.

"Morrigan?"

A gawky, white haired boy with ugly sunglasses and a single, angry pimple on his chin stood across the table, his arms wrapped defensively around himself. His t-shirt had a pentagram twined with leaves that read "Witches Heal" and his left earlobe was pierced with a clunky sliver stud like the kind you get when you have your ear pierced at a mall. Her mind carefully filed each detail for future examination. His hair was, on second glance, not pure white but streaked with yellowed ivory, caught away from his face with a soft black hair tie. He looked curiously old.

"I'm Elric." He sat opposite her in the booth and removed his glasses, blinking in the afternoon light. His white-lashed eyes were as pink as a Draise-test bunny's. "You can see where I got the name."

Caitlin nodded. She had followed the adventures of the albino warrior when she was younger, but she had always preferred hard science fiction to fantasy. She refused to let herself be unsettled by his alien gaze.

"Do you want to order something before we start?" she asked, setting her pocket cassette recorder on the glossy table top.

He shook his head and lit a cigarette.

"Look," he said, words and smoke spilling out together in a warm rush. "Things aren't the way they used to be. I have a real girlfriend now. It's not like everyone says."

Caitlin nodded and took a sip of coffee, waiting for him to continue. Her sensors picked up on his discomfort and she could feel herself slipping into good listener mode.

He pulled a napkin from the dispenser and began carefully shredding it. When it became obvious that he was not going to elaborate, she spoke, pitching her voice low and respectful.

"Well then, why don't you go ahead and set the record straight?"

Elric looked sideways at her, taking a deep drag of his cigarette.

"She wasn't my girlfriend or anything. I know that's what people are saying, but it's not true."

"No?" Caitlin watched him over the rim of her cup. His face was tense, washed in complex emotion.

"It was ... " His raw pink eyes seemed to be studying the air between them as if there might be some answer in the slow ballet of dust in the weak sunshine. "Like a game, y'know. I was scared that people would find out what we were doing but Eva didn't care. She never cared what anyone said about her. But if anyone said anything fucked up to me, she would flip out. She fought this kid once who used to tease me, calling me Rat-eyes and Pinky."

His voice was unbearably bitter, recounting the childhood nicknames.

"This kid used to tease me every day, throw my library books in the mud, steal my lunch, that kind of thing. When Eva told him to leave me alone, he pushed her into the wall.

"He goes: 'What are you, trying to protect your little lesbian girlfriend?'" He made his voice low and nasty. "'Maybe I'll take your freak girlfriend home and see if she'll put out for me, too.'

"I never saw Eva so angry." He laughed, a sharp snarl. "She fought that kid. He didn't want to fight a girl, but she turned around and punched him right in the face. Then, every time the kid would hit her back, she would grind her hips and go; 'Oh yeah baby, hit me again, I love it.' She was all fucked up, spitting blood and blowing kisses. In the end, the kid just gave up, disgusted. I'll never forget that.

"That night, she stayed over at my house so her Mom wouldn't see her all bruised." Elric looked down, red blood coursing under his white skin. "She wanted to ... y'know, do it ... as soon as we got home from school. Her mouth was all cut up ...

"Afterwards, she told me that I should never let anyone tell me I was ugly. She said that I was beautiful and exotic, just like Elric. She was the one who gave me that name. I always hated the way I look, but she made me feel OK about it. Like I was something special, instead of just a freak."

He crushed the cigarette out in the glass ashtray bearing the restaurant's logo. He looked as if he was struggling with tears. He fumbled for his glasses and put them back on, sealing the rift in his armor.

"Did you know where Eva was going when she left home?" Caitlin asked.

"Of course. She wouldn't shut up about it." He lit another cigarette. His voice had taken on a knife-edged sarcasm. "Absinthe this and Absinthe that. She was crazy for this guy Absinthe who owns some club downtown and runs around pretending to be a vampire."

Caitlin nodded, waited for him to go on.

"She was obsessed, determined to win him over. You see, she was one of the few females to make a name for herself in that nasty boys-club of computer nerds and she was so cocky, wearing her sexuality on her sleeve. Anything you can do, I can do better and she meant it, pulling off outrageous pranks and skating away scott free while all they could do was stare at her ass as she went."

He paused, sucked smoke from the end of his cigarette.

"For her," he said. "Getting Absinthe was just another elaborate hack."

Caitlin wondered if this was true, or if this was just Elric's was of dismissing his rival. She decided not to ask.

"She would go for days with no sleep," Elric said, exhaling sharply. "Working on these crazy plans to make that guy notice her. She pirated the signal from his cellular phone and made it spout poetry every time he tried to make a call. She was totally in love."

"Were you jealous?" she asked.

"I wasn't her boyfriend," he said, mouth thin and twisted. "I mean, it's not like we were a couple or in love or anything. It's not up to me to tell her what to do with her life."

Yes, Caitlin noted silently.

"Did you know about Eva's taste for sadomasochism?" she asked, diverting his anger.

"Yeah, I guess," he said, eyes cutting away beneath the green glass of his cheap shades.

Caitlin waited while he smoked, unwilling to push him. The wheels of the tape recorder turned. Silverware clinked softly and low conversation drifted like the smoke from Elric's cigarette.

"One summer," he said finally, "Eva's parents sent her to this computer camp. She met an older guy there."

Another smoke filled pause. Caitlin wanted another cup of coffee, but she was unwilling to distract him. She waited.

"He taught Eva a new game. A game called "prisoner of war". One person was the prisoner and the other was the interrogator. Eva was always the prisoner." He shook his head. "She didn't tell me about it for a couple of years. When she finally did, she tried to get me to play it with her. I thought it was stupid, but she really wanted to, so I tried it.

"I never saw her get so ... excited. I wasn't all that into it, but it got her so hot, we must have done it for like nine hours that first time. I guess I sort of liked it, not so much because I liked the idea of it, but because she loved it so much and it made me feel good to make her feel good."

He laughed again.

"That sounds really sick, doesn't it, hurting someone because you want to make them feel good. I was really confused for long time after that. We sort of started drifting apart, and the next thing I know she's got that stupid ring in her nose and she's tattooed a big fucking letter A on her arm. And then she's dead."

A small drop of moisture slipped out from under the curve of his sunglasses and left a glistening track down his colorless cheek. He crushed out the cigarette.

"She's a Gemini," he said. "I mean ... she was." He paused for a moment, swallowing. His voice soft and unstable. "She had these two sides that were always at war. The intellectual side that rejected the flesh, and the carnal side that wallowed in it. She took everything she ever did as far as it could possibly go. She was looking for gods in the farthest reaches of experience. She found Absinthe."

"I think I want a cup of coffee," he said. He looked suddenly too young to want coffee, but he went ahead and ordered a cup for himself and another one for Caitlin. He took it black, like her.

They drank in silence for a while as Caitlin studied him.

"Do you think this Absinthe is the one who killed Eva?" she asked.

Elric shook his head.

"Does it really matter?"

He dug in the pocket of his army surplus pants and laid a much handled photograph on the table between them.

It showed two geeky looking third-graders posing with some kind of unfathomable machine built from tin cans and television parts. The tall boy was obviously Elric, his sunglasses far too big for his small face. The girl was sunburned and squinting, curly blond hair wild and badly cut. There was a dust of freckles across the bridge of her turned up nose and her wide goofy smile revealed torturous metal braces. She held what appeared to be the control box for the strange machine.

"That's Eva and me," Elric said. There were still tears on his face, but his voice was steady. "I don't think they're ever gonna catch the guy who killed her. They hardly ever do in real life."

Caitlin shrugged, unwilling to contradict or interrupt.

"Imogene, that's my girlfriend. She says that the law of karma is gonna turn around and bite that guy right on the ass. She says everything you put out comes back to you three times more. I would like to believe that there could be some kind of justice or revenge or something, but it hardly matters, since catching that guy isn't gonna bring Eva back."

Caitlin waited to see if he would continue.

"But wouldn't you like to see the guy put away?" she asked. "Before someone else gets killed?"

He shrugged. "It would be nice, I guess."

Caitlin was about to speak when he produced another photograph. It showed a chubby, sweet-faced girl in a midnight blue medieval gown. There were flowers in her glossy black hair and a silver pentagram hung against her ample cleavage.

"That's Imogene," he announced as if it was some sort of evidence.

"I met her three years ago, at the Renaissance Faire with Eva, but we've only really started seeing each other over the past few months. She and Eva were very close." He lit another cigarette, the last in the pack. "I think she would talk to you."

9.

Imogene lived in an enormous, Victorian house in Ossining whose bottom floor was an occult shop and a natural food restaurant. Caitlin parked her bike between a brightly painted Volkswagen bus and battered Honda hatchback covered with stickers that said things like "Love Our Mother", "Pagan Power", and "My Other Car Is A Broom".

The name of the occult shop was "She Provides" and its interior was dim and fragrant. Bundles of dried herbs tied with colored string hung from the ceiling along with hand dipped candles and refracting crystals. Incense burned on the glass counter, its fragrant smoke coiling sinuously towards the door. A smooth white cat with mismatched eyes nursed a litter of kittens in a wicker basket in one corner, and a hand-made broom of birch twigs and green ribbon lounged in another. Tentative harp music drifted with the smoke, trailing off as Caitlin entered.

"Morrigan," the young woman behind the counter said, fingers wandering over the strings of the small, intricately carved harp she held in her ample lap. "Great Raven. Celtic goddess of battle. A strong name for a strong woman."

Caitlin frowned, unsure what to make of this girl. She had gained weight since the photograph that Elric had shown her, and her eyes were clear, penetrating blue. The pagan decor and the silver pentagram around the young woman's neck rattled the ghost of Caitlin's Catholic childhood, but her grown up, journalistic objectivity kept the video camera in her mind running full speed.

"My real name is Caitlin," she said, extending her hand. The girl took it in both of hers and held it for a bit longer than what is normally considered socially acceptable. Her chubby fingers were heavy with silver and turquoise.

"My real name is Rhianna Imogene Morningsong, Daughter of Artemesia Starfire Morningsong, but you can call me Imogene."

Caitlin smiled.

"Well, Imogene, is there somewhere we can sit and talk for a few minutes."

"Of course," Imogene said, returning Caitlin's smile.

She motioned for Caitlin follow her and pushed aside a heavy purple curtain, leading the way down a long narrow hallway.

"Crow!" Imogene called, motioning Caitlin through a doorway into a small room with two soft chairs and a tiny table covered by a velvet cloth.

A small boy appeared in the doorway as Caitlin sat down. He was dressed in a loose tie-dyed t-shirt and rolled up jeans, and his ratty black hair and bright blue eyes mirrored Imogene's.

"Mind the store and call me if anyone comes in, OK?"

The boy nodded gravely.

"You're not going to let her do it, are you?" he asked, his dark eyebrows knitted.

"Do what, my Owlet?"

"Go down to the bad place that swallowed Eva."

Imogene looked at Caitlin, frowning.

"Well, she's a grown-up lady, and I'm sure she can make her own decisions." She hustled the little boy out into the hallway.

Caitlin sat, shifting uncomfortably on the mushy-soft chair. She set her recorder on the table and hoped that it this interview would provide something worthwhile.

Imogene returned and sat slowly in the chair opposite. Her careful posture as she lowered herself into the seat and the way she held one hand on the small of her back made Caitlin realize that she was not fatter, she was pregnant.

"Don't mind Crow," she said. "He hasn't learned to keep his vision to himself yet."

"Is he your son?" Caitlin asked.

"Yes," she answered. "He's an amazing spirit. Eva used to watch him for me, used to sit him on her lap while she worked on that computer.

'You see this, Crow?' she used to say, putting his little fingers on the keys. 'The whole world is in here'. He really misses her."

"Have you told him what happened," Caitlin asked.

"Are you kidding?" Imogene laughed. "He knew before I did."

She fidgeted with a large chunk of rose crystal, turning it over and over in her hand.

"The night it happened, I dreamed of this ... presence. This tortured, desperately lonely soul." She shivered and touched a violet pouch on a ribbon around her neck. "I woke up with tears on my face and Crow was standing beside the bed, his face white as death. He told me a bad monster had cut Eva up."

The crystal wove through her fingers like a magician's trick, walking from one hand to the other. Her black eyebrows were drawn together and her lower lip trembled.

Caitlin could hear a very mercenary, very professional voice inside her head. *Talk to the kid,* it said. Although she didn't give much credit to so-called "psychic powers" the Sunday supplement crowd loved that kind of shit. She weighed her options, and decided she would ask as soon as seemed right.

"Do you have any idea who killed Eva?"

Imogene frowned. "I've never felt anything like it."

"When you say 'it', are you referring to the presence you felt in your dream?"

"Yes."

"And you think this presence killed Eva?"

"I'm sure of it."

"You say it, rather than he or she. Why is that?"

"I don't know," she said. "It didn't even feel human." Imogene closed her eyes, grimacing as if she were straining to remember. "I know that sounds hokey as hell, but it's true. If it is human, it's become so horribly isolated, it sees itself as the only one of its kind. It can't relate at all to anyone, though it aches for love and human comfort. It sees itself as the only color in a black and white world."

The lines in her forehead smoothed but her eyes remained closed.

"It is so lost, so full of pain."

Her voice became a strange monotone, dull and without inflection.

"There is one other person. For the first time in its life, it is becoming attached to someone. Falling in love even, in a strange and obsessive way. It wants this person very badly but I'm not sure why. This person is in terrible danger. They need to get away, but it will never let them go until they have been completely destroyed. It controls them utterly. Be careful, Caitlin Morrigan. It is much stronger than you think and predator-smart. It will trick you. It will make you forget everything you believe. If anyone can save this person, it is you, but it will be the hardest thing you've ever done, and you will lose everything else."

Imogene shook her head and opened her eyes. There was a sheen of sweat on her round face.

Caitlin shifted uncomfortably in the calico mire of her chair. She wished she could come up with something witty to break the spooky mood, but she was just silent.

The boy poked his head in the doorway.

"Mama?"

He had two steaming mugs balanced carefully on a wooden tray.

"Gramma said bring you this tea."

He smiled shyly and Imogene motioned him forward. He came, walking slow to avoid sloshing, and set the tray on the table.

He looked up, anxious, into his mother's face.

"Are you and Niniane OK?" he asked, laying his hand on his mother's belly.

"Fine," Imogene said, passing a hand over her eyes. She lifted a cup and smiled into the steam.

"I'm going to have a little sister with white hair and pink eyes just like Elric's," Crow announced. "A brand new Eva."

Imogene laughed and ruffled his hair.

"Crow tells me that Eva will reincarnate in my daughter. I guess anything is possible."

Caitlin smiled and lifted her cup to her lips. It smelled sweetly herbal and tasted of rosehips and peppermint. She tried to make ordinary conversation, as if such a thing were possible.

"This tea is wonderful," she said.

"My Gramma makes it with herbs from the garden." Crow told her. "The tea for guests is much better than the icky stuff she makes me drink when I get sick."

"You're very smart," Caitlin said. "How old are you?"

"I'm four," he said.

Caitlin raised her eyebrows.

"Really, I thought you were at least eight."

"I'm articulate," he said, beaming.

"You certainly are."

"I'm only eighteen," Imogene said. "He couldn't be much older than he is."

"Is Elric Crow's father too?"

"No," she said. It was obvious that she was not going to elaborate.

Caitlin's tape ran out with a loud clunk.

"Well," she said. "I guess that's the end of the interview."

She stood up and pocketed the little machine.

"I really appreciate you speaking to me. This information will add an interesting dimension to the story."

Imogene stood and took her son's hand.

"Be careful, OK," she said.

"Listen," Caitlin said, weighing her words carefully. "I'd like to ask Crow a few questions about Eva. Off the record of course."

Imogene frowned.

"It's OK, Mama." Crow said. "I can handle it."

Imogene shook her head. "Such a little grown-up," she said, laughing. "Just five minutes. And don't let him fool you. He really is only four."

She picked up her mug and left, glancing nervously back over her shoulder. Crow made the OK sign with his small fingers.

Caitlin pulled the chair around and sat back down.

"Crow," she said. "Can you tell me what you remember about Eva?"

"I remember the computer. I remember jelly beans and the pool in the back yard. I remember the ring in the middle of her nose."

The boy stood remarkably still for a child, not fidgeting or squirming. His blue gaze was direct and unnerving.

"Elric sure misses her, doesn't he?" Caitlin asked.

"Sometimes he wishes he was dead, too. He thinks about Eva all the time and what they did together. It makes him embarrassed. He's afraid of not loving Mama as much."

Caitlin nodded, reminding herself that this was a four year old, no matter how astute. She took a deep breath in preparation for her last and most delicate question.

"Do you know who killed Eva?" she asked.

The boy's dark eyebrows knitted in unconscious imitation of his mother.

"A really bad monster."

Patience. Caitlin told herself.

"Can you tell me what the monster looks like."

"Just like a person on the outside, but really, really bad on the inside. Like the stuff under the sink that kills you if you drink it."

He took her hand in both of his, an odd, priestly gesture.

"Don't go down there where it lives. Stay with that policeman who loves you. If you go there, it will eat your life."

Imogene picked that moment to appear in the doorway.

"Is everything OK?" she asked.

Caitlin pulled her hand away from Crow and stood.

"Fine," she said.

This psychic thing was going way too far and it was making Caitlin's head hurt. She felt like she was watching a bad horror movie, spooked and irritated at herself for letting it get to her. She wanted desperately to go home to her own, normal apartment and do something mundane and grown-up, like pay the phone bill. Anything to wash the doomy, ouija board taste out of her mouth.

"Thank you both," she said. "I appreciate your ... candor."

Imogene showed her to the door, Crow trailing close behind.

"Wait," the boy called, just as Caitlin laid her palm against the door.

When she turned the boy shyly offered a small white bundle tied with red and black beads. Caitlin took it, examining it more closely. As she brought it near her face, she could smell bitter chlorophyll and the sharp tang of sage. There was an angular runic character stitched on one side with red thread.

"For protection," he said.

Caitlin gave a tired smile.

"Thank you," she said, pushing the door open. "Good-bye."

"Blessed be," Imogene said.

"Blessed be," Crow called from behind her skirt.

Caitlin waved, unhooking her helmet. The evening air tasted like cool wine after the rich, incense miasma of the store. She strapped the helmet on and pounded on the starter. As she peeled out into the street, she could still see the boy's pale face through the dark glass, small hand waving like a starfish in a vast night ocean.

10.

Mike and Eric flashed their shields to the bouncer at the bottom of cement stairs that led down into a dingy fetish club called The Crypt. The bouncer was huge but sweet-faced, like a friendly animal who might kill you accidentally while trying to hold you down and lick your face. He had a tiny gold stud in one nostril.

He exchanged a few words with the blonde behind a scarred Plexiglas window and then led the detectives through the empty club.

Mike lagged behind while Eric engaged the bouncer in animated conversation, lubricating the witness with idle chit chat, warming the guy up, as he always did, for the serious questions. They had this routine down to a science, Eric schmoozing up front while Mike lingered behind, observing, filing away every detail.

Mike bit his lip and made himself concentrate. His eyes struggled to capture and catalogue everything they passed. There was a thick, spermy basement smell to the clammy air. A square bar, sagging couches, a dark pinball machine. There was a net of chain, an eyelet studded cross, a steel frame with leather cuffs dangling empty over a padded, chest high bench with kneeling rails on each side like a malformed church pew. Drawings of men in engineer boots and undershirts with big, leaky dicks and stern women with impossible waists and spike heeled shoes. The place was dim and haunted with the clinging spectre of need.

The bouncer led them to a small flight of steps, through a locked door marked "private" and long storeroom, into a cramped office.

"So the next thing I know," the bouncer was saying. "These two bitches was goin' at it, and I don't mean fuckin', I mean pullin' hair and screamin' and rollin' around on the floor. The one chick took off her shoe and cracked that blonde bitch right in the mouth, BAP, just like that."

He motioned for them to take what seats they could find. Mike pulled up a battered folding chair and Eric sprawled back on a soft yellow couch.

"So needless to say," he continued, wide grin full of pantomime modesty. "This was a job for El Diablo. I broke them bitches up. I was like, "scuze me ladies,' coppin' a little tittie here and there while I dragged 'em apart. They both had them silicone jobbies, you know what I'm talkin' about."

"Yeah, I know how that is," Eric answered, stretching his legs out long in the cramped office. "Just like feeling the arm of this fucking sofa. Give me a good old-fashioned set of 100% natural baby suckers any day."

"Word, man, you got that right." Diablo reached out and slapped his massive palm against Eric's, laughing.

"So, listen," Eric said, leaning forward. "You wanna tell us what you remember about Eva?"

Diablo sobered up.

"That's a fuckin' shame what happened to that kid, I tell you. She used to come around Fridays, weekends too sometimes. Hang out the whole night usually, but I never seen her go home with no one. Always came alone, always left alone. This was a while back, though. She was a good kid, always sweet. I never really knew her like a friend, just like a girl you see a lot. Now I'll tell you I was buggin' out when I heard she was 17. Her ID was good, man. I mean, I seen a lot of fake IDs in my life, but I swear the kid had a perfect driver's license said she was 23. A fuckin' driver's license. You can't fake a fuckin' driver's license, right?"

Mike and Eric exchanged glances.

"You'd be surprised," Eric said.

Mike nodded and scribbled a note to himself.

"So do you think that Eva was straight or gay?" Eric asked. "Bisexual, maybe?"

"I always figured her for straight, even though I never really seen her with anyone. I hadn't seen her for like six or seven months and then when I seen her that last night she was with this other girl."

52

He bit his lip as if struggling to remember.

"This girl musta been like 14, so there was no way in hell I was gonna let her in. I just assumed it was a girl, but now that I think about it, maybe it was a boy. Y'know how sometimes it's hard to tell."

Eric leaned forward, thick eyebrows raised.

"What did this kid look like?"

"Well she had a shaved head and light eyes. Kinda strange lookin', like Chinese or somethin', but really pale. Small." Diablo indicated the girl's height in the air with one hand. "Like five feet, five one maybe."

"What was she wearing?" Mike asked.

"Jeans and a white t-shirt. Real loose, y'know how they wear it now."

"Did they look worn at all?"

Diablo frowned.

"What, her clothes?"

"Yeah, I mean were they dirty or clean or what?"

"They weren't dirty at all." Diablo looked up at the cracked ceiling, remembering. "They looked brand new."

Mike nodded, writing.

"What time did they show up?"

"Pretty early, ten, ten thirty maybe. I only talked to her for like five minutes. Said she was in trouble, that she needed ten bucks. She was always a good kid, so I gave it to her."

"Did she say anything about the trouble she was in?"

Diablo rubbed his big hands together, frowning.

"She didn't say she was in trouble, I asked her if she was in trouble and she goes, 'sort of' or somethin' like that. She said she wanted the money to get on the train or some shit."

"You don't think this other kid could have killed Eva, do you?"

Diablo made a soft spitting noise.

"Are you kiddin'?" He shook his head. "I coulda picked my fuckin' teeth with this kid. Y'know I wouldn't be surprised if that kid's body turns up floatin' in the river."

Mike nodded without looking up from his notes.

"Oh yeah, and one other thing." Diablo looked down. "I uh ... I gave her this knife."

Mike and Eric exchanged sharp glances. Diablo looked back up, studying their faces as if gauging how much trouble he was in.

"What kind of knife?" Eric asked.

"Just a cheap old thing, y'know. About this long with one of them leapin' tigers on the handle. I just thought she might need it if she was in trouble."

"Do you remember where you bought the knife?"

"In this martial arts store in Chinatown."

Diablo was giving Eric the address of the store but Mike could barely hear their voices. He was utterly absorbed in the assimilation of the new information, patiently fitting it together with the old, searching for the larger pattern. This guy seemed as close to honest as they come, and that was a stroke of pure luck. An honest witness was a rare and coveted thing and it could mean the difference between another point-less, unsolved sheaf of paperwork and a conviction. One thing that twenty years on the force had taught him was that for whatever reasons, everybody lies. They lie to make themselves look better. They lie to protect their lovers or their family or themselves. They lie, because everyone knows better than to tell the truth to a cop.

Out of the din of information, a memory of Maura's innocent brown eyes and wounded pout.

Of course I'm not seeing anyone else.

And when the truth finally came out, he had been utterly blindsided. He had gone against all his instincts and believed her because he loved her and there didn't seem to be any other choice. When it all went down in flames, his first emotion was shame, shame at being so thoroughly suckered.

Didja hear the one about the homicide detective who can look at a pool of blood and tell you the perp's shoe size but couldn't see that his own wife was playing hide the salami with another guy?

Mike shut his eyes. He was sure he had killed all those memories the day he signed the divorce papers, but once in a while one would sneak up on him. He crushed it down before it could multiply and forced himself to concentrate on the situation at hand instead of ancient history.

"I couldn't fuckin' believe it when I seen the papers, talkin' about what happened," Diablo said. "Shit like that shouldn't happen to a fuckin' dog, you know what I'm sayin'?"

Eric was standing, slapping Diablo's wide shoulder and thanking him for his time.

"If you remember anything else," Eric told him, pressing a card into the bouncer's hand. "Give us a call, OK?"

"Sure thing, man," Diablo said. "You got it. And anytime you guys want to come down and see the club when it's jumpin', it's on me. Anything to help you guys out. Personally, I hope you catch that mother-fucker."

He leaned close.

"Just so you know," he said. "Word's out in the scene, and there's a shitload of angry leatherwomen out there who would love to get a hold of that guy. You better make sure you get him first."

Eric and Mike both burst out laughing.

ii.

When Mike answered the door, he looked exhausted, his eyes bright from too much coffee and too little sleep. Caitlin slid her arms around him and held him as he leaned into her embrace, tense muscles relaxing gratefully against her.

"What are you doing here?" Mike asked, brushing his thumb over the contour of her jaw.

"Oh, well if you're busy ... " Caitlin turned away, grinning.

He caught her and drew her back into his arms.

"I'm always busy," he said, pressing his mouth to the curve of her throat.

"Well," she said, face turned up to the ceiling. "You don't have to neglect your duties on my behalf." She patted a bicycle messenger's satchel slung across her back, filled with faxes and printouts and scrawled notes. "This is business."

"Business?" Mike slid a hand up under her shirt, toying with her nipples. "Really?"

Across the hall, an old woman opened her door the length of the security chain and peered through the crack like a curious vole.

"Who's out there?" she asked, her voice thin and wraith-like.

Caitlin giggled and pulled away, composing an expression of mock innocence and turning towards the inquisitive voice.

"It's just me, Mrs. Costa," Mike called, sneaking his fingers back under Caitlin's shirt.

"Cut it out," she whispered, twisting away.

"Detective Kiernan. I thought it might be you." The old woman smiled vaguely in their direction. "I just like to be sure."

"Of course," Mike said. "You have a good night now."

"You too, Detective."

Mrs. Costa pulled her door closed, multiple locks clicking.

Caitlin threw a mock punch to Mike's head and he ducked, laughing.

"I can't believe you," Caitlin said, struggling to rein in her smile.

"We could be naked," Mike said. "She's blind, she wouldn't even notice."

Caitlin arched an eyebrow.

"Really?"

She smiled sideways at him and pulled her shirt up over her braless breasts.

"Jesus." He stepped in front her, hands spread open in a protective gesture. "Are you crazy?"

Caitlin laughed and sauntered through the open door, into the apartment.

Mike's apartment was spare and immaculate. After the divorce, Maura kept the house and all the furniture. All the little artifacts collected during seventeen years of marriage. Mike left them behind with no regrets. His new home was stripped down and functional, unpretentious. A tough-skinned couch. A small table where one person could eat a comfortable meal. Handmade bookshelves lined the walls, crammed full of science fiction paperbacks that he read like literary potato chips. When Caitlin first saw them, she had laughed with disbelief.

"What," he had said. "You think because I'm a cop, I'm too dumb to read science fiction?"

She had flashed him an embarrassed smirk.

"I don't know, I just thought you'd be reading cop thrillers or something."

He laughed.

"What, are you kidding? My life is a fucking cop thriller."

It was these books that she drifted towards, fingers brushing the battered spines of Heinlein and Asimov and Pohl and Niven. Her shirt was still pushed up over her breasts. She pretended not to notice.

Mike came up behind her and ran his hands over her naked belly. She smiled and pressed her body back against his.

"Do you have a copy of the Eiseman file here with you?" Caitlin asked.

His fingers stilled.

"Sure, why?"

She turned towards him.

"I have some information pertaining to the case. If you're interested."

He blinked and then glanced down at her exposed breasts.

"Uh ... right." He closed his eyes and pushed his fingers through his hair, mentally switching tracks. "Let's see what you got."

They sat together on the couch, limbs intertwined, paper strewn across their laps and spilling over onto the low table. Mike made another pot of Cafe Bustello and Caitlin told him about Absinthe between hot, brutal mouthfuls.

"Where did you get all this information? You've probably got more on this case than we do."

"I have my sources," she said, preening.

"Fucking nosy writers," Mike muttered.

"I heard that," she warned, raising her hand as if to strike him. He caught her hand and kissed it.

Still holding her hand in his, Mike studied each new piece of information with unhurried thoroughness.

"So you think this guy did it? This guy Absinthe?"

Caitlin shrugged, as if it was all the same to her.

"Could be."

She tapped a photo on the coffee table. Eva's biceps, close-up and subtly discolored. "That tattoo stands for Absinthe. She left home to be the man's slave. Even if he didn't do it, he must know more about it than we do."

Mike nodded, thoughtful.

Pride raced through Caitlin, chasing the caffeine in her veins and making her feel larger than life.

"Have you got a picture of this Absinthe character?" Mike asked, draining the last mouthful of his coffee.

"Of course." Caitlin dug around in her bag and pulled out a glossy magazine featuring a doe-eyed brunette with vast implants and no pubic hair being menaced by a regal blonde in skin tight leather. *Fetish Quarterly* was its title.

"What are you doing reading this kind of trash?" Mike took the magazine out of her hand and eyed the cover models. "Hey, not bad."

"Give me that!" Caitlin snatched it back and rolled her eyes. "God."

Mike chuckled and peered over her shoulder while she flipped pages.

"Wait wait wait," he said, trying to stop her from turning pages featuring naked women.

"Calm your penis," Caitlin said, swatting at his fingers as if they were flies. "I'm trying to be serious here."

"Oh yeah, she looks real serious," Mike said, pointing to a black-haired goddess who looked like an escapee from a Frazetta wet dream.

Caitlin made an exasperated sound and turned the page.

"There," she said.

Absinthe, seducing the camera. Dripping with dark sexuality. His eyes were curious and arresting, the color of bloody amber. His skin was alabaster, translucent almost, and Caitlin found herself imagining its texture under her fingers. Tender, it would be. Like a infant's. She looked away, ashamed suddenly of her inexplicable attraction.

"What, you like this guy?" Mike asked.

Caitlin shrugged.

"You do, don't you?"

"Well sure," she said, teasing, testing his reaction. "I wouldn't kick him out of bed."

"Yeah well he'd probably kick you out of bed, unless you grew a dick since I last saw you."

"Maybe," Caitlin said. She shivered.

"I don't see what the big deal is anyway." Mike said, glaring at Absinthe's two-dimensional beauty. "He just looks like another skinny fag to me. And a possible murderer, too."

Caitlin laughed and kissed Mike on the mouth.

"What?" he asked.

"You're jealous," she said.

"Get outta here."

"Jealous, jealous, jealous," Caitlin sang, waving the magazine under his nose. He smacked it away.

"Well, what if I am?" he asked.

Caitlin's belly fluttered. Insidious tenderness crept over her, blushing her cheeks and making her look away.

"Yeah, well how do you think I feel when you go drooling over all those girls with big old hooters?"

She crossed her arms over her A-cup breasts. Her heart was beating furiously.

"Aw, come on now." Mike pulled her close, gently uncrossing her arms. "You got no reason to be jealous of a buncha fat sluts in a dirty magazine. You know I think you're beautiful."

Caitlin looked up at him, his broken nose, his honest blue eyes, the strong angle of his chin.

"I think you're beautiful," she said.

"Yeah right." He smirked. "I been called a lot of things in my life, but beautiful ain't one of them."

"First time for everything," Caitlin said, her mouth inches from his.

He lingered for a moment, then closed the distance, parting her lips with his tongue. Paper tumbled to the floor and they followed, making hungry love amid forensic reports and starkly-lit victims staring at the camera with heavy-lidded eyes.

———————◆———————

In Mike's bed, when it was all over, Caitlin lay with her whole back fitted against his body. His arms encircled her, his breath warm on the back of her neck, his sticky, tired cock nestled between the cheeks of her ass. After the first time, on the floor, he had lifted her up like a rag doll and carried her to the bed where they indulged in long, slow passion, culminating in a single shared orgasm that broke down all the walls with its heartbreaking intensity.

Listening to the rhythm of his breath, she shut her eyes and luxuriated in the rich opiates pulsing through her system. She thought he was already asleep and she was drifting gently when he startled her by speaking low in her ear.

"Caitlin?"

"Yeah?"

"You know the way we were talking about the case before, talking about the scene and the forensics and all that?"

She made a soft noise of agreement, snuggling deeper into his embrace. His arm tightened around her.

"It's really weird for me to talk about that kinda shit with you. I mean not bad weird, just different."

"Why?" Caitlin asked.

"Well ..." He kissed her shoulder, resting his mouth against her skin for a long moment, thinking. "Talking with you is almost like talking with Juana Carrera or Trish Connelly or any of the other women on the job. Except I know what you look like naked."

He followed the curve of her thigh with his palm. Caitlin chuckled.

"You mean you all don't take showers together or whatever."

"Please," he said. "I don't think I'd want to see Trish Connelly in the shower. I'd be scarred for life."

They laughed together for a moment, and then let it trail off, lying still and silent, comfortable.

"Really, though," Mike said. "You're an amazing woman, really sharp, y'know. You have a way of seeing around the corners of things."

He paused and Caitlin held her tongue, waiting for him to go on.

"It's just so strange to be talking like that with you. Not just me talking and you putting up with it, but really discussing stuff."

Another pause, but Caitlin could sense more coming. She waited.

"Maura hated hearing about things. Back when we first met, she would at least listen and sort of nod her head, but it got to the point where she didn't even wanna hear it. Said it gave her nightmares. She was always having nightmares."

He turned over on his back and she rolled with him, cushioning her head on his arm, listening.

"Like this one time, I was down by the playground on 24TH. This was back when I first started working with Eric. We were jacking up this Jamaican dealer, he was a suspect in this shooting, y'know, and he's telling us he ain't got no *ganja*, he didn't shoot no one. So Eric's getting in his face and I'm checking to see where he tossed his stash. There's this paper bag under the bench and I kinda reach my foot under there and slide it out. Now I can tell by stepping on it that there's a gun in there, so I sorta kick it over to Eric and he puts his foot on it and feels the gun.

While he's cuffing this guy, I start kicking this bag over to the curb to have a look. When I get it there, I bend down and pull the gun out of the bag, big ass 9MM it was, and when I pick it up, I see that it's cocked and loaded. Here I am, kicking a loaded gun down the street. I'm lucky I didn't blow my own foot off, or God forbid, shoot somebody's grandma in the head. I mean, it was stupid but when it was over, it seemed pretty funny, me kicking that gun down the street like that. So I told Maura the story, thinking she would laugh. It was a pretty innocuous story, right? I mean, I was always real careful about telling her things. Like I didn't tell her about the time this fourteen year old kid put a bullet in the wall right between my legs. She was about an inch away from having a eunuch for a husband, but I don't tell her so she won't be scared. I respect her feelings, right? But I figured this was no big deal, just a funny thing that happened. Boy that was almost as stupid as kicking that gun."

Caitlin nodded in the dark, fingers tracing the shape of his ribs.

"She flipped out," Mike said. "I mean, she really lost it. She cried, told me how every time I'm late, she waits by the phone to hear that I'm dead in some crack house, and then I come home and joke about accidentally shooting myself. She told me never to tell her about things like that, that she didn't even want think about it. She wanted to just pretend that I was working some safe job in a nice boring office. Can you believe it? When we were first dating, she told me that she liked me being a cop. She said it made her feel safe."

Caitlin couldn't imagine how to respond to this sudden bitterness. She wanted to do something to negate this old hurt, but felt pitifully inadequate. Wishing for brilliant or insightful words, she held him silently.

He turned to her and framed her face with his hands. She could barely make out the lines of his cheekbones, the wet reflection of distant streetlights in his eyes.

"But you," he said. "You don't need me to make you feel safe. You're strong. You're not afraid to look at crime scene photos. You could break a man's arm if he tried to grab your ass or take your pocketbook. No one would try to tie you to the railroad tracks. It makes me wonder sometimes, what you're doing with a used up old wannabe hero like me."

Heat swirled and pulsed in the coils of Caitlin's guts. Her hands traced the geometry of his spine again and again, moving like separate creatures while torrents of conflicting emotion collided in her head.

"All my life," she said, staring into the dark beyond his shoulder. "I've been working to make myself strong, to be the best at everything. Testing myself, preparing for some imaginary just-in-case. I never trusted anyone else to protect me, so I had no choice but to do it myself."

It was his turn to be silent, waiting for her to continue.

"Sometimes I get tired of trying so hard." She swallowed around a spiny lump caught high in her throat. "Sometimes I wish I had someone I could trust to watch my back, someone I could count on to take care of me without trying to control me. To do what I want, what I need, without judging me. There are so many things I want. Maybe you could ... "

Caitlin squeezed her eyes shut, feeling horribly vulnerable, like some soft creature plucked from it's shell. She had said too much and there was no way to take it back. He was hugging her fiercely and it was too much, too dangerous. She pulled away, sandbagging.

"Maybe I'll just keep you as my sex slave instead," she said, her voice only shaking the tiniest bit.

"Yeah," he said, his laughter tinged with melancholy. "I'd be good, I promise."

He pulled the summerweight cover up over them, tucking it carefully around her chin and brushing stray wisps of hair from her forehead.

"I'm going to be useless tomorrow if I don't get some sleep," he said. He kissed her temple. "I'm gonna look into that shit we talked about, let you know if anything comes of it. OK?"

"OK," she answered like a child.

"Sweet dreams," he said.

"Sweet dreams."

She lay cold beside him until he slept and then started waiting for the sun to rise.

12.

Caitlin stepped into Wilson's dojo and struck a slinky pose in the doorway. His back was to her, *katana* held high above his head. When he turned to face her, his jaw fell open in cartoon surprise.

"Hi," she said.

Her hair was loose and streaming down her back, a shining curtain of liquid amber. Her simple black dress was highnecked and long sleeved, but its clingy fabric hugged every cut in every muscle, following the curve of her back and the swell of her ass until it reached the hem, less than halfway to the backs of her knees. Her long legs were sheathed in black seamed stockings and she wore nightmare heels of glossy patented leather. She sashayed over to where Wilson was standing, dumbstruck with his sword held at a forty-five degree angle in unconscious imitation of an erect penis.

She kissed his cheek, leaving a red smear.

"You ... " He swallowed. "You look like a beer commercial. Cheap. And ... and whorish."

"Glad you like it," she cooed, posing again.

"Get off my floor with those ... those shoes." He said the word shoes like it was a term for eliminatory functions. He dragged her out to the carpeted hallway.

"Do you mind telling me why you're ... ?" Wilson rolled his eyes. "No, don't. You are doubtlessly planing some sort of ludicrous foray into the sadomasochistic underworld in the name of 'research'. Am I right?"

"Correct as always, your majesty." Caitlin grinned. "So what do you think?"

"What do I think?" Wilson snorted "Of your preposterous get-up, or of the idea of haunting leather bars in vain attempt to add some sort of realism to your tawdry exposé?"

"Is it really necessary for you to be so negative?" Caitlin scowled.

He arched one half of his connected eyebrows.

"In all seriousness, Caitlin, you hardly need me to tell you that you are beautiful. And from what I understand, your outfit, while it may not be made of any fetishistic material, is thoroughly appropriate. The classic, seamed stockings are a nice touch, highly desirable to those with leg and foot fetishes."

"I'm going down to The Crypt tonight. There's some kind of slave auction and from what I understand, representatives from Absinthe's are going to be there, scouting new talent."

"Surely you don't plan on putting yourself up on the auction block," Wilson asked, horrified.

"No, of course not." Caitlin laughed. "I'm just a writer, an objective observer."

"Make sure it stays that way," he told her, frowning. "I would prefer if nothing bad happens to you."

"Wilson," Caitlin cried, throwing her arms around his neck. "You really do care."

"I ask myself why every day," he said rolling his eyes at the ceiling.

"Does this mean you'll drive me to the club tonight?"

"What?"

"I was hoping we could take the Jag." She fluttered her eyelashes. "It would look so much classier than pulling up in a cab."

"Absolutely not," he said. "I have far too much work this evening."

13.

Caitlin leaned across the seat of the cream colored Jaguar and tried to kiss Wilson as they pulled up to the curb on Hudson Street, just south of 14TH, but he blocked the maneuver with his forearm.

"Do not kiss me with that frightful red lard all over your mouth." He held her at arm's length and glared at her. "Are you sure you wouldn't like me to escort you, Lady? I would be most discreet."

"No!" She feigned a swipe at his head. "I'm not some kind of fucking damsel in distress! I have a black belt too, remember?"

"Suit yourself," he said.

"I always do," she answered.

She grabbed the handle on the door.

"Wait," he said, laying a hand on her shoulder.

She shot him a narrow-eyed glare.

"Here." He fished inside his loose-cut black shirt and withdrew a slender stiletto. Its eight inch triangular blade was matte black and a green turquoise eye glistened in the hilt. He laid it in her open palm, hilt-first.

"Remember," he told her. "Avoid bone. Go for the soft places."

"Thank you, Sensei." Caitlin smiled and slipped the blade into her purse.

Her feet were unsteady in her brutal heels as she made her way across the cracked pavement towards a flight of steps leading down under the street. A large, bloody-looking C on the wall at the head of the stairs was the only indication that she was in the right place. She felt brave and conspicuous, her blood singing with adrenaline.

The stairs were steep, turning to the right and leading her through a curtain of clear plastic strips, down to a high window surrounded by photographs and drawings of women in studded scraps of leather and men in muir hats with five o'clock shadows. Behind the scratched Plexiglas, a blonde woman sat thoroughly unimpressed with the spectacle of a trio of sequin-clad drag queens trading barbed flirtations with the bouncer. In her heels, Caitlin was taller than all of them. She paid, and the woman took her money without comment.

Inside, it was dim and crowded. Nondescript men prowled in wide orbits around the dominant women preening by the bar, occasionally coming close enough to mutter some request that seemed for the most part to be either rejected outright or ignored. An older man with a graying goatee lounged against a pillar with his arm around a blonde girl in a white lace g-string and a dog collar. An elegant transsexual lounged on a ratty couch while a hugely overweight bearded man pressed her long foot to his lips. A man in a white shirt and tie but no pants wandered aimlessly, kneading his semi-erect penis as if it were bread dough. His black socks and shoes contrasted starkly with his greyish calves.

Parting the crowd before him, a human pony cantered forward with a saddle on his broad back and a bit in his mouth. A giggling silicone queen with eyelashes like iron bars spurred him forward, swaying drunkenly in the saddle. In the center of the club, a petite, black haired woman dressed in a sheer bodysuit patterned to look like spiderweb was methodically tying a leggy blonde to a metal frame. The ropes crossed back and forth, over and under, forming a complex geometric design. It was hypnotic and absorbing and Caitlin was so busy watching the weaving ropes that she didn't notice Eric until he was standing right in front of her.

"Caitlin?"

"Eric," she flashed a tense smile. "I never knew you went in for this sort of thing. Does Sara know?"

He was not fooled.

"Mike's gonna shit." He looked back behind him and Caitlin followed his gaze to where Mike was standing, talking to a topless woman with enormous breasts and gold rings through her teacup-sized nipples. Helpless jealousy dug needles into her throat and she crushed it down, appalled at its intensity.

"What are you guys doing here?" she made herself ask.

"Working, what do you think? Trying to get some leads on this fucking Eiseman case." His nervous eyes kept bouncing back to his partner. "Caitlin, I'm serious, Mike is gonna lose his fucking mind when he sees you here dressed like ... " He gestured at her legs, trying not to really look at them. "Like that."

"Look," Caitlin said through gritted teeth. "I am so tired of male chauvinist attitudes disguised as chivalry. I am an adult and I have as much right to be here as anyone else. I don't need Mike or any other man to protect me."

"Christ, here we go." Eric threw up his hands and began backing away as Mike came towards them.

He looked worn and tired, his eyes shadowed with charcoal and the lines in his face like harsh slashes. She wanted to take him in her arms and kiss his unshaven cheeks, but she steeled herself and sent extra power to the forward shields.

"Hi," she said.

"What the hell are you doing here?"

Caitlin frowned.

"Research," she said. "What are you doing here?"

"What do you think? I'm investigating a homicide, same as every other day. It's my job, remember? The one you think is so fucking fascinating." His voice was low and vicious.

Stung, Caitlin turned away.

"Don't let me stop you," she said. "I'm not here to interfere with the workings of justice, I'm just a lowly writer."

"Listen, Caitlin." His voice was low and urgent. "It's not a good idea for you to be here. Go home."

Caitlin twisted loose from his grasp, eyes flashing, dangerous.

"Don't tell me what to do." She narrowed her eyes. "Whatever happened to 'You're so strong, you don't need me to protect you'?"

"Come on, Caitlin," Mike said.

"So what you're saying is, I can take care of myself as long as I stay home like a good girl. Is that it?"

"No, of course not." Mike shook his head. "But hanging around by yourself in a place like this, you're just asking for trouble."

"I'm a big girl and I can take care of myself as well if not better than you. What's this really about? Afraid I'll get in the way of your investigation? Or maybe you're afraid I might like it here?"

Mike rolled his eyes. "Why are you being so unreasonable?"

They stood, wounded egos huge between them, neither one willing to back down. Mike glared at her for another minute and then spun on his heel and walked away. Eric shrugged, mouthing the words, *I told you.* He turned and followed Mike out the door.

Caitlin stood still and full of anger and pain, wanting to run after him and apologize and hating herself for the impulse. She probably was being a little unreasonable, but she couldn't help it. It was a knee-jerk reaction whenever she got even the slightest hint that a man was trying to tell her what to do.

"It's about time someone told that guy to piss off."

A husky voice at Caitlin's shoulder made her turn, startled. A striking woman with blood-colored hair cut to pointed bangs on her forehead and high painted eyebrows stood poised with a cigarette in one black gloved hand. There was a silver ring in her nose and a leather choker around her long white neck.

"What do you mean?" Caitlin asked.

"That guy," she gestured with her cigarette. "He's a cop."

"Oh yeah?" Caitlin's stomach clenched and she felt shiny and obvious. A rush of exhilaration and stage fright filled her mouth with bitter saliva.

"He and his buddy have been hanging around, asking everyone questions about that girl that died." She took a long, suggestive drag on her cigarette and licked her dark lips.

"What girl?" Caitlin asked, deliberately nonchalant. "Do you have another cigarette?"

She nodded and offered a flat silver case.

Caitlin took one and before she could put it to her lips, a dozen flames sprouted all around her. She realized for the first time that they had an audience of hopeful men, clustered around them like a crowd of psychic vampires. Suppressing a shiver, she accepted a light from a thin, bespectacled gentleman to her left as if it were the most natural thing in the world.

"You mean to tell me that you haven't heard about the murder?" The corner of the woman's mouth curled slightly, her green eyes glittering.

"I'm from out of town," Caitlin said, the harsh smoke like steel wool in her throat. She smoked for less than six months back in her junior year at college and not since.

The woman raised her elaborate eyebrows.

"Funny," she said. "From your voice, I would have guessed Bronx Irish."

Shit. Caitlin dug her nails into her palms. *Think, girl!*

"Louisiana Irish," she said. "I'm from New Orleans. I'm told the accent is similar."

"A decadent town, I understand. Is there much of a scene?"

Caitlin took another drag off her cigarette, stalling.

"Actually," she said, feigning embarrassment. "This is my first time in a club like this." *Think, think, think.* "For the longest time, I was sure I was the only one in the world who thought about this kind of thing." She forced her voice into a warm, confessional tone. "Then when I found out about this place, it took me hours to work up the nerve to come. Now I'm here, but I have no idea how to get involved, or what to say to anyone. I'm sure I must stand out like a sore thumb."

Caitlin stood, silent, heart pounding in her throat. Her body pulsed with a heady cocktail of nervous energy and tingling, almost sexual fear.

The woman took another drag off her cigarette and smiled.

"God, I know how that is. I'm lucky, I had a brilliant Mistress for my first. She trained me and set me up with a job in one of the hottest dungeons on the planet. I don't want to name-drop," She looked to one side, and then the other. It was obvious that she did. "But I'm sure you've heard of Lord Absinthe."

"Absinthe?" Caitlin felt like cheering. "I understand he's very good," she said instead.

"The best." Her face had gone dreamy, remembering.

"Isn't he supposed to have people here tonight, for the auction?"

"Why?" she asked, a wicked smile spreading across her face. "You're not planning on going up on the block, are you?"

"If I were submissive, I might consider it. A chance to meet the legendary Absinthe would certainly make it worth my while."

"A dominant, eh?" The woman eyed Caitlin with renewed interest. "And this is your first time out?"

"That's right."

"Surely you've played in your own private life."

"It's hard to find anyone who is willing to indulge my fantasies. They are somewhat ... extreme."

"Really?" Leaning forward, the woman crushed her cigarette in a tin ashtray. She smelled of sandalwood and cloves and Caitlin could see the outline of her erect nipples through her sheer, intricately beaded flapper dress. There was a glint of silver in the dark pink flesh. "Do tell."

Another test, another level. Caitlin's mind and heart were racing. She was unused to flirting with women in any context, and it seemed an entirely more dangerous, more delicate operation. With men, all she really had to do was cross her legs and make them to do all the work. This was a whole new ballgame. She took a deep breath and a calculated risk.

"I like ... " She fished in her purse and extracted the stiletto. Reaching forward, she slid one hand behind the woman's neck and drew the point of the knife along the curve of her jaw, bringing it to rest in the soft place just under her chin. "Blades."

The woman's eyes widened and her nostrils flared. Her tongue snaked out and wet her lips, her gaze traveling from the knife to Caitlin and back again. She shifted on her stool, her legs coming slightly apart

"There's someone I think you ought to meet," she said.

14.

Mike and Eric sat in tiny delicatessen on Sixth Avenue. In the window a buzzing neon sign that was supposed to read "Loesman's" instead flashed, "L-man's", the dead letters dusty and grey beside their bright brothers. The place was tacky and familiar, a safe haven that had seen them through all the major events of the past ten years. The death of Eric's father. Mike's divorce. Every problem, big or small was thrashed out in this red vinyl booth by the window over hot pastrami and sour pickles.

Leering at the tired waitress, Eric stuffed french fries into the corner of his mouth while Mike stirred sugar into a cup of coffee.

"You can't let it eat you up, man," Eric said, waving a fry for emphasis. "You got more than enough shit to give you ulcers."

"You don't understand," Mike told him over the lip of the stained cup. "I feel like I'm fucking up and I don't even know how to stop myself. Like she's just too good to be true and I can't help but fuck it up."

He ran his fingers through his hair and turned his eyes up to the ceiling.

"I don't know what to do. I'm no good at this kind of shit." He swallowed another mouthful of the acrid coffee. "When it all went down with Maura, I thought I would never let myself be ... y'know, open ... with another woman. I figured I was just gonna be another one of these crusty old sons of bitches, 98 years old and eating TV dinners alone every night. Then, when I met her, I thought ... well, I don't know what the hell I thought."

"Mike, you've got to back off with this. You're making yourself crazy. She's just a kid. You can't expect her to make a heavy commitment." Eric waved at the waitress. "Lorraine, sweetheart, can I get some ketchup over here?"

"She's the same age Maura was when we got married."

"Yeah, right, and look how great that turned out." Eric smirked.

"Hey, fuck you."

"Relax, man." Eric showed his palms, the universal sign for peace. "I'm just trying to give you a little friendly advice. I'm telling you, this chick is a handful and a half. She don't take no shit from no one. Not you, not anyone. Now I've known you, what, ten, twelve years now. I know how you are. You like to take care of women."

"Wait a minute ... "

"Shut up and let me finish. Your way with women has always been to try and be everything for them. What you really want is to devote your life to painting their toenails. Am I lying?"

Mike smiled and shook his head.

"See?" Eric said. "Now you've met a real goddess and you want to keep her locked up. I'm telling you, it won't work. You can't tell a woman like that what to do."

"You're right, I know." Mike drained his cup and grimaced. "She's such a tough girl, but it still makes me crazy to see her running around with her ... I mean ... well, you saw how she was dressed. I know she don't need me to protect her, but these ... I don't know ... territorial feelings, they just come out of nowhere sometimes. I can't help it."

Eric nodded sympathetically and mimed pouring coffee at the waitress. She came around with the pot and filled their cups again.

"And I don't like the idea of her hanging around in that place, getting into all kinds of trouble. Not to mention the fact that there's some sick bastard out who get his jollies slicing up pussies." Mike winced and clutched his belly. "Christ, this coffee's killing me."

"Look, let's get the fuck out of here." Eric stood and slipped an arm into his jacket, writing in the air with the other hand. The waitress nodded and brought the check around. "Go home, try to get some rest. It's gonna be an early one tomorrow."

Mike nodded and dug in his wallet.

"Forget it, willya." Eric slapped down a ten dollar bill on the table. "You get the next one."

15.

Caitlin smiled, holding the woman's gaze for a moment longer. She applied more pressure to the knife point, just enough to raise the woman's chin and widen her eyes, then lowered the blade and slid it back into her purse.

"What's your name?" Caitlin asked, her victory hot under her skin.

"Justine," she said. She lowered her eyes like a shy child.

The tone of her body language melted from straight backed and haughty to demure and submissive in the time it took Caitlin to blink. She was really very beautiful, a delicate Erté girl with a graceful, flower stem body and narrow ankles.

"Mistress, if you will," Justine said. "I would like to introduce you to some friends of mine."

"Of course." Caitlin offered her arm and Justine took it, leading her through the goggle-eyed crowd, through a dark doorway and into a back room with a square stage in the center like a boxing ring surrounded by high couches. Caitlin refused to listen to the frantic music of her heartbeat, forcing herself to watch everything, miss nothing. On a platform under a glittering sign that read, "MEAT", three women lounged on a leather couch with a single male slave at their feet, his face hidden beneath a spill of thick red curls. Two of the women were kissing and whispering like schoolgirls while the other, a long-legged woman with a shock of radiant autumn hair, gave quiet commands to the slave.

Justine dropped to her knees beside the man and pressed her lips to the toe of the flame-haired woman's tall boot.

"Hello, Justine," the woman said with a fond smile.

The other two looked up and Caitlin saw that they were not two women, but a woman and a man in drag, both dark-haired and dark-eyed with inbred, aristocratic faces. They grinned and licked their chops like hungry jackals.

"Justine," they said in unison.

Justine kissed their offered feet and sat up on her haunches.

"Mistresses," she said. "I'd like you to meet a friend of mine."

She motioned for Caitlin to come forward.

"This is Mistress ... "

"Morrigan," Caitlin finished, extending her hand and forcing her lips into a smile.

The red headed woman leaned forward and took Caitlin's hand.

"Lady Belladonna," she said, her eyes holding Caitlin's for a long moment. "These mannerless hussies are Lady Nightshade and Lord Hemlock."

"Lady Hemlock," the boy said, taking Caitlin's hand and bringing it to his lips. His glossy lipstick left a smear on the back of her hand. "My ravishing twin, the Lady Nightshade and I were born 59 seconds apart. 59 torturous seconds during which I was separated from my one true love. But only 59 seconds, because even then, I could not bear a full minute without her. Of course, our traumatic birth was the only such occurrence."

He whispered something in his sister's ear and she giggled. Caitlin realized that they were both extremely drunk.

"She's so tall," Nightshade said to her brother as if Caitlin were not standing right there. "And she has the most beautiful hair. Tell her it's like melted gold, like Southern Comfort. Absinthe would wet his pretty leather pants if he saw that, wouldn't he?"

"My sister thinks you have very beautiful hair," Hemlock said, gesturing floridly.

Belladonna shook her head and motioned for Caitlin to sit beside her.

"Don't mind the twins," she said. "There's no speaking to them when they're like this, which is always."

She reached out and laid an elegant hand on Justine's bowed head, unapologetically studying Caitlin. There was a hungry intensity in the way she thrust her head forward like a curious predator. Caitlin refused to flinch under her excruciating scrutiny.

"Mistress Morrigan shares your fetish, Lady," Justine said, casting a quick glance at Caitlin. "I thought maybe ... "

"Of course." Belladonna stood and her male slave scrambled to gather up his Mistress' belongings. For the first time, Caitlin noticed a pale latticework of scars etched across the man's freckled back and chest.

"Lady Morrigan, would you care to join us in a short scene?"

Caitlin's heart froze. She forgot to breathe. A dreadful urge to laugh swelled in her chest and she was convinced that she would blow it all.

Oh fuck oh fuck oh fuck say something you moron don't just stand there with your mouth open fucking say something!

"I would be honored, Lady," Caitlin replied.

Justine walked ahead of them, head down and demure. Belladonna guided the girl up to the center stage and held out her hand to be helped up. Caitlin followed, silent, hoping to appear mysterious rather than ignorant.

The male slave scuttled up behind her and laid a black velvet bundle on the stage. Almost reverently, he undid the piece of red lace that held it together and unwrapped a collection of knives that would have made Wilson cry.

Belladonna motioned for Caitlin to join her on the stage as Justine unfastened her dress and let it fall to the floor. Underneath, she wore a wide leather belt that cinched her already slim waist down like the tiny center of an hourglass. A fine lace of scars covered her torso and thighs. Her pubic hair was shaved and a fat silver ring pierced the hood of her clitoris.

A crowd was beginning to form around them as Belladonna's slave laid out hanks of red and black rope and thick red candles. Belladonna herself was tying a red silk scarf over Justine's eyes and leading her to a strange piece of furniture that resembled a surrealist interpretation of a weightlifting bench.

Justine lay back as if preparing for a pelvic exam. Belladonna tied her delicately tattooed arms and spread her long legs, securing her ankles and knees to the painted metal frame.

"Help yourself," Belladonna said, smiling like a good hostess and gesturing to the glittering blades and spread open slave. "There is, of course, no blood allowed in this fine establishment."

Leaning close, Belladonna spoke into her ear.

"Perhaps another day."

Caitlin nodded and removed the stiletto from her purse, touching it to her lips. Belladonna flashed her a smile rich with subtle approval and selected an antique Japanese blade for herself from the collection of knives. Together they advanced on the bound woman, Caitlin slightly behind and casually watchful.

Laying a finger against her lips in a request for silence, Belladonna stalked around Justine's supine form. Justine's blind head moved slightly from one side to the other, trying to track their movements in the sea of club noise. Leaning in, Belladonna slid the point of the knife along the girl's inner thigh. She shuddered, her lips parted and blind face tipped up. Following suit, Caitlin touched her stiletto to Justine's hard pink nipple, tracing the curve of the tiny steel ring. Gooseflesh rippled across the girl's pale body as the knife points skated over her skin, dipping down between her legs and sampling the moisture there.

Caitlin felt calm and alien, an incredibly life-like replica of herself. She found herself imagining what it would be like to plunge the stiletto into Justine's vulnerable belly. The thought was oddly detached, emotionless, like the morbid curiosity of a child pulling the wings off flies. Justine looked unbearably delicious, fascinating, like some exotic bird or a rich dessert. Caitlin gathered her hair over her shoulder and trailed it across Justine's nipples, following it with the knife point. The girl gasped, straining against her bonds.

Belladonna smiled and handed Caitlin a burning candle. Holding the candle's twin, Belladonna crossed to the other side of the stage, cupping the flame behind her hand. She held it high above Justine's body, sending a red rain of hot wax down onto her breasts and belly. Caitlin followed suit, remembering how her sister Megan's half of their shared room had always been full of candles and how she used to stick her fingers into the flames, letting the wax drip down over her hands. Even at the dinner table, if there were candles, Megan would always play in the flame until their father would send her to her room, leaving Caitlin alone in unintentional preview of the Meganless future. Caitlin had always been the good girl, the one who always cleaned her plate and never played dirty games. Until now.

Caitlin looked up and saw that Belladonna had pushed the thick candle into Justine's mouth. She arched a russet eyebrow, nodding towards Justine's exposed vagina. Caitlin weighted Megan's body and dumped it into the black water in the back of her mind. With a deep breath, she spread Justine's slippery inner lips and slid the candle up inside her, unable to believe her own actions but equally unable to feel the kind of moral shock that her Catholic upbringing required. Burning at both ends like some perverse candelabra, Justine lay absolutely still, body singing with tense energy.

Caitlin stepped back and let out a deep breath. Belladonna ran the point of her knife in a long, sweeping motion from under Justine's chin to the cleft of her vagina, a ghost of a cut that would have emptied her of major organs with just a shade more pressure. Caitlin realized that she was holding the stiletto to her lips again. It smelled faintly like Justine.

Belladonna wrapped her fingers around the candle in Justine's mouth and motioned for Caitlin to do the same down below.

Mimicking Belladonna, Caitlin pushed the candle in further, then pulled it out. She could feel Justine's muscles clench around it as it slid out, almost as if she were trying to hold on. The male slave took the candle from Caitlin's unfeeling fingers and blew it out, wrapping it in a clean handkerchief. He whisked it away and when he returned, he held a pair of leather wrist cuffs and a curious thing that seemed to be a cross between a mask and a strap-on dildo.

Belladonna cuffed the male slave's hands behind his back and buckled the mask over his face. A round gag fit into his open mouth and a black dildo protruded from the other side, making him look vaguely like Pinnocchio. She unrolled a condom over the dildo and then motioned for Caitlin to join her up beside Justine's head. As the male slave positioned himself between Justine's legs, Belladonna pressed the point of her knife against the soft place below Justine's ear. On the other side, Caitlin did the same with the stiletto.

"Don't move," Belladonna warned.

She snapped her fingers and the male slave plunged the dildo up into the girl's vagina.

Justine gasped, her body rigidly still. The male slave fucked her like some ridiculous bird drinking nectar from a flower. Caitlin imagined how humiliating it would be to fuck someone like that, with your face bobbing up and down between their legs like those glass goony birds that drink colored water. His hands were locked behind his back, so his whole body rocked with each thrust. Caitlin didn't know if she wanted to laugh or scream. Justine's pulse thudded beneath the point of her stiletto.

Belladonna snapped her fingers again and the slave withdrew, his face glistening with transparent secretions. He slunk off to the side of the stage.

Justine was visibly shivering. Her mistress withdrew the blade and held it to Justine's lips.

"Kiss it," she said.

Justine kissed the flat of the blade, tongue sneaking out and tasting the edge. A tiny ruby bead formed on the tip of her tongue. Belladonna bent and kissed Justine, sucking her tongue into her mouth.

When she broke the kiss, she backed away and smiled at Caitlin. Taking a moment to carefully peel up the circles of cooled wax from Justine's breasts and belly with the sharp edge of the blade, she rubbed her palm over the round pink burns left behind on Justine's white skin, lingering before pulling Justine's blindfold off. The girl blinked and smiled as Belladonna set to work untying the ropes that held her down.

The girl stood carefully, unsteady as a newborn deer. She knelt and kissed Belladonna's feet.

"Thank Mistress Morrigan," Belladonna instructed.

Justine pressed her mouth to the toe of Caitlin's shoe.

"Thank you very much, Mistress Morrigan," she said.

Caitlin flushed and looked around for the first time. The crowd was full of eager faces, hungry eyes eating her up. She had never been regarded with such frank longing. She felt twelve feet tall and beautiful, sparkling with raw energy. She could make any man in the room eat from her hand if she chose and it made perfect sense. Inexplicably, it made perfect sense.

16.

"That was beautiful," Hemlock told her when she returned to the couch where he huddled with his sister. She could see his erection straining against the tight fabric of his dress. "You must come to Absinthe's where we can play for real money."

"You must convince her," Nightshade said, finger playing idly over the taut shape her brother's cock. "Tell her how important it is that she come and play at Absinthe's."

"You absolutely must," Hemlock repeated. "Otherwise you will break my sister's heart."

"He'll love her, I know he will. Tell her how much Absinthe will love her."

"Please," Belladonna interrupted. "You act like children in the supermarket, begging for sugar cereal with a prize in it." She took Caitlin's hand. "Here, let's sit for a minute."

Caitlin sat, trying to ignore the twins' whispering.

"Mama Belladonna will convince her," Nightshade said.

"Justine," Belladonna said. "Will you distract these brats."

The girl led the twins up to the stage. Caitlin watched as the two tied Justine on her stomach and striped her ass and thighs with short tailed whips.

"Listen," Belladonna said. "I would love to have a chance to play together under less restricted circumstances. Justine loves you and as excessive as the twins might get at times, you should know that they rarely like anyone besides each other."

Caitlin nodded, watching Justine grovel on the filthy carpet at Nightshade's feet. A low voice over the PA announced the beginning of the auction. Belladonna's male slave gathered up the equipment and the twins ran back to the couch, heels clacking and eyes red and wet under their sparkling eyeshadow.

"It's starting!" Hemlock called, taking Caitlin's hand.

Caitlin's head was spinning as she followed her strange new friends back into the front room.

The club was packed with jostling, leather-clad bodies. At the center of the room, a tall man in a powder blue tennis dress and a bad wig gestured grandly, appearing to be the MC of the evening. Belladonna parted the crowd before her and Caitlin followed in her wake, aware of the whispers all around them. There was a small cluster of reserved chairs to the left of a large wooden cross studded with eyelets. Smiling, Justine motioned for Caitlin to take her chair. Hot-faced and self-conscious, she sat and Justine knelt at her feet. As she watched the proceedings, she found herself stroking Justine's soft red hair. The girl leaned her head on Caitlin's knee and a strong wave of strange affection swept over her. She bit the inside of her cheek and made herself watch the auction.

The first group of slaves was male, and rarely had Caitlin seen a more diverse group. There were beefcakes and middle-aged marshmallow men. Each one came out onto the stage and executed a series of tasks, like showdogs, while the MC's gravely voice told the preferences of each one.

"This is David," he announced, as a very thin, bald man with a face like a baby monkey took the stage. "He is a contortionist who enjoys very strict bondage and body piercing."

The man grinned and wrapped one leg up around the back of his head. Belladonna smiled and held up two fingers.

"I have two hundred from Absinthe's," the MC said. "Do I hear 250?"

"Three," called a German woman with a thin dusting of white-blonde hair on her cheeks and a long cigarette holder.

Belladonna held up an open hand, fingers spread.

"Five hundred," the MC said.

Silence and Belladonna smiled.

"Five hundred once," the big transvestite called over the heads of the crowd. "Five hundred twice."

Another long silence and the German woman looked down at her shiny boots.

"Sold, to Absinthe's, for five hundred dollars."

The man came forward and knelt at Belladonna's feet.

Women were next and Belladonna bought a pair of Asian girls with bleached hair and gold rings in their noses. She seemed uninterested in the transvestite and transsexual category, so as the last one took the block, she stood and gathered her purchases around her.

"Justine," she said. "Get Lady Morrigan's phone number."

Then without another word, she turned to go.

Hemlock pressed his mouth to Caitlin's ear.

"Think about it," he whispered. "We'd love to have you."

He and his sister followed Belladonna and left Caitlin standing with Justine.

"Lady," Justine said. "I had a wonderful evening, and if you don't mind, I would like to have your phone number so that we can keep in touch."

Caitlin tore a sheet from her notebook and wrote her number, feeling as if she had been obscurely tricked.

"Thank you," Justine said, kneeling and kissing Caitlin's feet. Her mouth lingered, breath hot against Caitlin's arch. Her tongue flickered over the curve of her foot, sending nauseous chills through Caitlin's body. Justine stood.

"Good night," she said.

Caitlin stood and watched Justine walk away. Within seconds of her departure, the crowd coalesced into individuals, sweaty faced men with desperate eyes.

"Mistress," they all seemed to be saying at once.

She pushed her way through the clinging crowd towards the door.

"Mistress, excuse me."

Grasping fingers at her elbow. Caitlin kept moving, not looking up.

"Mistress, my name is John, and I ... "

Faster, not seeing, not hearing.

"Mistress, I really loved your scene and I was wondering ... "

She practically ran up the stairs, bursting out into the New York night like it was the most beautiful thing she'd ever seen.

17.

Mike let himself into his apartment, setting his keys, his pocket change and his shield in the ceramic dish by the door. With the mindlessness of habit, he checked each of the empty rooms for anything unusual or out of place. It was only after he was sure that nothing was amiss and everything was safe that he let himself collapse onto the sofa and unbuckle his shoulder harness. His head throbbed and bitter coffee gurgled in his stomach. He thought about getting up and maybe getting a glass of milk or something, but the distance between the kitchen and this sofa was just too vast. Peeling off his jacket and his sticky shirt, he found that the weird subterranean odor of that sleazy club had permeated the weave of the cloth. He pressed his hands to his face and realized that his skin smelled like that place, too. Disgusted, he stripped down in the middle of the living room. Socks and shorts, balled up to be stuffed into the hamper in the bathroom. Jacket, pants and shirt over the back of a chair, ready for the dry cleaners first thing in the morning. Even the dark silk of his fucking tie stank. He laid it over the chair and stalked off into the bathroom.

Peeling back the plastic curtain, he noticed that the tub was maybe one more shower away from needing to be scrubbed. He resolved to do it tomorrow night as he turned the spray as hot as it would go.

He closed his eyes and tried to get lost in the steam. The knotted muscles in his shoulders slowly began to uncoil. The constant, Rubik's Cube turning of the facts in the Eiseman case didn't stop, but it was reduced to a low background hum. He reached for the soap and came up with a pale sliver. It astounded him to realize that this was all the soap that was left. He had been meaning to get more, but the last time he had been in the shower Caitlin had been there too, and the size of the soap was the last thing on his mind.

He had to nip that thought in the bud before it got him thinking about how pissed he had been, about how she had looked with those rock video legs and her long body so tight under that clingy dress. About that defiant challenge in the tilt of her chin and the flashing acid green of her angry eyes. About the undeniable fact that as furious as he had been in that moment, he had wanted her, too and he still wanted her now.

"You're losing it, pal," he said into the spray, shaking his wet head.

He carefully coaxed a thin lather out of the tiny fragment and proceeded to scrub the clinging stench from his skin, trying to think of anything but Caitlin. He made himself go over the details the case, probing for inconsistency. The deeper he dug, the less sense everything made. Even though a case like this could bring a rain of glory and big fat attaboys to the detective who broke it, it could also be a cement block around the guy's neck if it went unsolved. Just thinking about it made Mike's head hurt.

Feeling sufficiently decontaminated, he stepped out and dried his tired body, catching a glimpse of his blurry reflection in the steamed mirror. He cleared a circle with his fist and squinted at himself. The skin around his eyes was bruise-dark and tender. Crow's feet at their corners looked deeply chiseled, not Santa-style laugh wrinkles, but the mark of unkind time, of too many pointless atrocities witnessed. He used to imagine that it was a tough face, maybe even a hero's face, but now it just seemed bitter and old.

His circle was steaming over again and he did not clear it. Instead he wrapped the towel around his waist and padded into the living room. Sinking back into the soft cushions of the sofa, he groped for the remote control to his stereo and turned it on, flipping the auto-tuner to a classic rock station.

The Eiseman file sat like a neglected child on the spotless coffee table, demanding his attention, but he couldn't bear to think about the case anymore. Instead, he pulled a thick white envelope with Caitlin's name on it from a drawer beside him and turned it upside down, spilling a torrent of photographs into his lap.

A dozen Caitlins smiled up at him. Caitlin at the Bronx Zoo. Caitlin eating a snowcone, her lips stained blue and purple. Caitlin astride her

Harley, flipping the bird to the camera. Caitlin wet, hair clinging to her damp, freckled skin, holding a towel up to her breasts and reaching with one hand to block the camera like an angry celebrity.

He picked up the phone and dialed her number.

"Hi," said Caitlin's voice. "This is me. You know what to do."

A sharp electronic tone and then silence.

"Caitlin," he said, holding the picture of her in the towel. "It's me. Listen ... " He took a deep breath. "I was an asshole, I'm sorry. I just ... I just care about you a lot, that's all. Call me when you get home, just to let me know you got home safe." He winced. "I mean ... I'm sure you're safe. I don't want to make it sound like I think you won't be safe. I just want to talk to you. You don't have to call me if you don't want to. I mean ... "

Another sharp tone cut him off.

"Shit!" He slammed the phone down.

He ran his hand through his hair.

"Great, now she thinks you're a real loser. Good job, dickhead."

He dragged himself to his feet and went into the kitchen after all.

"Talking to yourself," he said into the fridge. He opened a quart of milk and sniffed. "First you think a beautiful young girl like her is gonna go for a nasty old man like you, and now you're talking to yourself. What next?"

The harsh voice of the downstairs buzzer interrupted his monologue and he nearly dropped the carton.

"Yeah?" he said into the intercom.

"Mike, it's Caitlin. Can I come in?"

"Uh ... sure, yeah, of course."

He buzzed her in.

He danced through the living room, stuffing photographs into the envelope and smoothing back his damp hair. When her knock sounded on the door, he jumped and dropped the envelope, pictures spilling across the carpet.

"Fuck fuck fuck," he muttered. "Just a sec."

He gathered up the pictures and dumped them back into the drawer. A deep breath and then a quick glance in the mirror and he undid the three locks and the chain on his door and pulled it open.

"Hi," he said.

She stood in the doorway for a long moment, eyes hot green and full of some obscure hunger. She looked feral, dangerous. Then she stepped inside and snaked her arms around Mike's waist.

She kissed him like it was the only thing that would save her life. Her movements were urgent, aggressive, chewing up every thought in Mike's head. His earlier anger seemed irrelevant compared to the sweet warmth of her hips sliding against his stiffening cock. Eric's warning evaporated as if it had never been. He struggled to reach past her and push the door closed without breaking the kiss.

"Wait, hang on." He turned to lock the door and she slipped out of his grasp.

Never taking her eyes off him, she unzipped her dress and shed it like an outgrown skin. Shoes and stockings and garterbelt and panties all peeled away, not with the teasing art of a stripper, but with the economy of movement of someone interested in getting on with what came next. Naked, she stood before him, burning.

His hands were trembling as he reached out to her. Her skin was as hot as his was cool and the contrast was delicious. She demanded every ounce of his concentration, filling his world with the heat of her desire. He felt like a kid again, nervous, heart slamdancing in his chest. Her hands were impatient with the damp towel around his waist. He had never seen her like this and as much as it inflamed him, it disturbed him too. But it didn't matter, because he couldn't wait another second to be inside her.

She fell asleep afterwards almost instantly. Strange, considering her traditional insomnia. In the blue dark, Mike found himself staring at her, watching her smooth, empty face. He felt like he was looking for some clue or secret that had been missed. Some vital piece of information that would make everything else make sense. He felt as if he just looked hard enough, he would see through her skin and bone and into the vital dreaming Caitlin that had all the answers.

But in his heart he was deeply afraid of those answers.

18.

Caitlin, alone in an empty martial arts studio. Class would not begin for three hours, but her instructor was an old friend, and he never turned her away. Sweat soaked her *gi*, blinding her as she struck the bag again and again, alternating kicks and punches, left and right. The rough canvas ripped her knuckles but that pain was only one instrument in the symphony that filled her body with blood-red music. She could not see or hear. The only sound was the percussion of her heart and the solid thump of her feet and hands against the unyielding weight of the bag.

But even the cacophony of agony in her screaming muscles could not completely drown out the soft gasp that had escaped Justine's lips when the point of the stiletto had touched the delicate indentation behind her ear. Caitlin's mind would not be still; it ricocheted from one emotion to another with panicked intensity. Images of Mike and Justine rushed through her, blurring together into a frenetic orgy of sweat and blood and shining metal. Guilt rode close behind, dragging its weaker Siamese twin, shame. It was an unquestionable sin, this maddening desire that brought her mind back again and again to the sweet fragrance of Justine's submission. The thunderheads of a distant and wrathful God gathered like scab around the raw wound of this new found lust. Sinking her teeth into the soft meat of her lip, Caitlin doubled her speed, pushing herself, pushing herself, till pale green stars danced on the edge of her vision, till breath burned like knives in her chest, till spangled blackness swallowed all her thoughts.

"Caitlin?"

A voice from nowhere. Caitlin forced her head to turn toward the sound and saw a pair of bare feet. She realized that she was lying down. Her hands were dripping blood. Pin sized speckles of red on the mat. Smears on her forearms, on her *gi*. Her instructor knelt beside her.

"Here," he handed her a roll of cotton gauze.

She took the gauze, wrapping her bleeding knuckles. There was blood in her mouth, too, and she had to fight back a wave of vicious nausea.

"You want to talk about it?" her instructor asked, his face smooth and uninvasive.

Caitlin shook her head and struggled to her feet. There was a smear of fresh blood overlaying older stains on the bag's tough canvas hide.

"All right, then," he said.

He turned and walked away.

She gathered herself, breathing deeply, and began again.

Home again, her own place. Safe, sensible, everything where she left it. Her body was shaking, exhausted, but she felt strangely elated, sharply focused. She sat down at her desk and woke up the computer. She ignored the friendly greeting and keyed straight into her notes on the Eiseman case.

She let the events of the night before pour out through the tips of her fingers. The sun went down while she was writing and she didn't even notice. Her face was washed in pale light from the screen, eyes like holes. When the phone rang, she jumped, startled.

"Hi, this is me." Her own voice, too loud. "You know what to do."

"Lady Morrigan? This is Justine. If you're not busy ... "

"Hello?" Caitlin picked up the receiver and the machine screeched indignantly. "Hang on."

She thumped the off button.

"Are you still there?"

"I'm here," Justine said.

"Hi, what's up?" Caitlin winced at the moronic tone of her own voice. *What's up? Jeez.*

"Well, I'm just calling to see if you were interested in coming down to the Club tonight."

Caitlin's heart was throbbing in her chest like the empty space left by a pulled tooth. *So soon?*

"I'll be working until ten, but after that would be fine."

Good, she told herself. *Don't sound too eager.*

"Wonderful. Just dress caj, we'll primp at my place. Meet me at the Clit Club. Down 14TH from The Crypt, 10:15." She paused. "Morrigan, I'm so happy that you're coming."

Caitlin shivered, imagining the long curves of Justine's body under the steel tongue of the stiletto.

"I'll see you then."

She hung up the phone and backed away from it as if it might strike out at her like a praying mantis. Gooseflesh crawled over her skin and hot flickers of sexual energy flared between her legs. She wondered if she was becoming too involved.

19.

Caitlin walked down Fourteenth Street with her hands stuffed deep in the pockets of her Levis. Ghosts of ancient urine lurked in dark door-ways, reaching out like beggars as she passed, making her take shallow breaths. A pair of glitter-bright transvestites tottered by on impossible heels, micro-minis barely covering the lowest curve of their boyish asses.

The Clit Club needed no sign. It was marked by a loose arrowhead formation of young trendy-looking women. At the head of the crowd was a woman in 50's butch-drag with a clipboard, sending them in by twos and threes.

Caitlin scanned the crowd, searching for Justine. Feeling as if a huge, flashing sign above her head was screaming, "I fuck men!", she sidled up to the woman with the clipboard.

"Excuse me," she said. "I'm looking for a woman named Justine ... "

Justine appeared from the doorway and slipped around her to kiss Caitlin's cheek. She wore a tiny leather dress, her waist cinched with the same wide belt Caitlin had seen the night before. Her boots were knee-high and thick heeled. Their heavy straps and buckles reminded Caitlin of some kind of medical braces.

Justine took Caitlin's arm and pulled her toward the entrance to the club.

"I thought you said dress casual," Caitlin said.

Justine smiled.

"This is casual," she said. "You should see me when I dress fetish."

Justine's apartment not far, a converted warehouse down Little West Twelfth Street, next door to what had to be the mysterious House

of Absinthe. On the outside, the Club looked just like every other
building on its block, heavy steel doors and long rusted racks built for
meat-hooks and bulky sides of beef. Like the Clit Club, it seemed to
require no sign. It was only a quarter to eleven, but the sidewalk was
packed with leather-clad bodies. Justine led the way through the crowd,
her chin held high with the stiff-backed *hauteur* that Caitlin had seen
when they had first met.

"Hey, Justine."

A handsome leatherman with a neatly trimmed auburn mustache
and a muir hat cruised up to them as they navigated through the crowd.
He was clad in a few thousand dollars worth of new leather and had a
pretty blonde boy on a leash.

"Hank." Justine turned her cheek to be kissed.

"What do you say, Justine," the man said, his voice low and intimate, insinuating himself between her and Caitlin. "Can you get us in?
For old times sake? I'd make it worth your while."

She shook her head and slipped around him, taking Caitlin's hand.

"You know I can't do that, Hank." She shrugged. "Sorry."

The boy pouted and crossed his sculpted arms. It was obvious that
the promise of getting in to the Club was the only reason he was on the
end of a leash in the first place.

"Aw, c'mon," he said. "What ever you need, you got it."

"I can't help you," she said, turning away.

They worked their way to the door of Justine's building.

"Hey, Justine," A woman's voice called.

"Shit," Justine said, struggling with her key in the lock. She pushed
the door open and ushered Caitlin inside, slamming the door behind
them.

"God I hate that." She leaned against the wall. "Everyone and their
mother is my best friend, begging me to get them in."

An enormous black man in an expensive suit sat behind a desk
reading a hardcover book in another language. German, maybe. He
looked up when Justine came in, but went back almost immediately to
his reading.

"Hey, Jonathan," Justine said.

The man waved absently.

"Why me?" Caitlin asked as they walked down the curving hallway.

Justine frowned.

"What?"

"Why me?" Caitlin asked again. "I mean, I counted like seventeen women out there that make me look like what's left over after I have too many beers and forget to flush."

Justine laughed.

"Not only that," Caitlin said. "But I told you, I really don't have a lot of experience."

"Don't sell yourself short," Justine told her. "Any used-up old whore who's tired of sucking cock can pick up a whip and call herself a professional dominatrix. But some just don't have it and other people ... well, they just do. Like they were born with some twisted gene that marks them as one of us. Those kind of people can spend their whole lives in vaguely unsatisfying vanilla relationships, and then one day pick up a whip or a piece of rope or knife and realize that they're home."

Caitlin listened hard, wishing that she had her tape recorder. She resolved to hide in the bathroom and write it down as soon as they got upstairs.

"I can tell that you're one of those people. Even before we did the scene together. I could tell by the way you held your body, the way you let that guy light your cigarette. So many people like you and me end up getting discouraged or deprogrammed by lovers who just don't get it. Belladonna encouraged me, trained me, took me under her wing. It made all the difference in the world to me then. It makes me feel good to think I might be doing the same for someone else."

Caitlin felt a pang of guilt for deceiving this beautiful and honest woman who was genuinely trying to help her. Then an image rose in her mind, an image of Justine in bondage with the unforgiving point of the stiletto against the place where her life ran close to the surface and it made her wonder who was really being deceived.

"*Allo*, Justine," a voice called, accompanied by heavy footfalls in the long hallway.

"*Bon soir*, Monsieur Renaud."

A squat, pink faced man sidled up and kissed Justine's hand.

"I trust your session with Lady Regina went well," Justine said.

"As always," the man answered. "But please, you must introduce me to your beautiful friend."

"This is the Lady Morrigan," she said. "Morrigan, this is Henri Renaud."

Caitlin held out her hand to be kissed.

"Please," Henri said. "Tell me that she is dominant."

"I can speak quite well for myself," Caitlin said. "And yes, I am."

Henri's already pink face flushed even brighter.

"Of course," he said, bringing her hand to his lips. "I hope that we will be able to have a session together."

"That's enough," Justine said. "We need to make ourselves beautiful for Morrigan's debut at the club."

"An easy task, I'm sure." He bowed his head and turned to go. "I will see you inside."

Justine looked at Caitlin, smiling tightly as if restraining laughter. She took her hand and led her to a elevator inside a wire cage. Pushing the complaining metal gate aside, she pulled Caitlin in and slammed it behind them. She hit the button marked 3 and burst out laughing.

"What?" Caitlin smiled.

"I told you, you're a natural," she said.

The elevator came to an abrupt halt, throwing the two women against the gate and each other. Justine peeled the gate back and they stepped out into a dark hallway punctuated with red doors. Her apartment was number 19.

Justine slid a long, old fashioned key into the lock. She pushed the door open and any other questions Caitlin might have asked evaporated.

Justine's apartment was a museum. Every inch of the deep purple walls was covered with glittering masks and animal skulls, swords and axes, prints by Gustav Klimt and H.R. Giger. There was a human skeleton dressed in fragments of medieval armor and a bald mannequin wearing a leather ball gown studded with broken glass and pieces of bone. A small fireplace held a pile of human femurs burning with coiled flames painted an ethereal pale green against the black back of the niche.

"Wow," Caitlin said.

"Funny, that's exactly what everyone else says." Justine laughed. "Can I get you something to drink?"

Caitlin's eyes would not be still. Every where she looked, she saw something new. She saw a series of Man Ray photographs in tiny silver frames and a vase of dark purple hybrid roses. The windows were covered with old X-rays, pelvises and skulls and ribcages making pale grey stained glass for a morbid church.

"Water, I guess," she said, just to say something.

Justine disappeared behind a velvet curtain. Caitlin heard the sound of a refrigerator being opened and the clink of ice in glasses. She returned a minute later with two chunky-cut goblets. Caitlin took one and drank deep, feeling suddenly parched. The water was icy cold and had a faint taste of lemon.

"Can I use the bathroom?" Caitlin asked, setting her glass down on a coffin that doubled as a coffee table.

"Down the hall, first door to your right."

The bathroom was as amazing as the rest of the apartment. There was a huge claw foot bathtub with a black lace shower curtain that went all the way around on an oval brass rail. There were glass shelves crammed with arcane cosmetics in blue and green glass bottles. Caitlin sat on the toilet with her notebook in her lap, trying to remember Justine's words. When she thought she captured them close to true, she skipped a few lines and wrote quickly.

> I am on the verge of something huge. I feel like
> a kid running down a steep hill, sometimes it's
> hard to tell if I'm running or falling.

She made a quick list of some of the more outrageous items in the apartment, just for color, then snapped the book closed. She wiped, flushed, and pulled up her jeans. The tiny cake of soap was rose scented, and reminded Caitlin of her mother.

"We want to get downstairs by midnight," Justine said as Caitlin reappeared. "Don't want to miss Absinthe's arrival."

"Of course," Caitlin answered.

"So," Justine was grinning like a kid. "You want to look at some clothes?"

It was like every little girl's dream, dress-up for grown ups. Justine had a huge closet ten feet deep and four rows wide. The clothes were organized by material, one row of latex, one of PVC, one of leather, and the farthest to the right seemed to be all costumes, Victorian lace and uniforms and antique gowns from the twenties and thirties. The entire floor was covered with shoes.

"You pick," Caitlin said. "I wouldn't even know where to start."

"Well, what material do you like?" Justine asked. "Do you like a heavy fetish look, or more classic?"

"You choose," Caitlin said, hoping for the best.

"OK, fine." Justine smiled and plunged in. "You'll just have to trust me. Your choices are gonna be a little limited, because of your size, but I'm sure you're used to that. Go ahead and strip."

Caitlin began to undress, studying her body in Justine's full length mirror with a critical eye. Her body was sleek and muscular, but she feared that it was just too big, too masculine, not curvy and lush the way she always wanted. Her stepmother Irene had always told her that she was a late bloomer, ludicrous, considering she was already six feet tall her first year in high school. At 18, she had resigned herself to life without breasts. Or at least, a minimalist interpretation of breasts. Irene had that certain Irish body type that was all boobs and no butt. Caitlin's ass and legs were the only thing that she knew was good. Not much hips to speak of, but a tight, round ass and endless legs that usually meant she didn't get many catcalls until she was walking away.

Besides, her body was not just a decoration and she was very proud of that. Even if she looked like a boy with her clothes off, it didn't matter because she could kick anybody's ass who had something to say about it. And all those lush, pin-up girls out on the sidewalk could eat their pretty little hearts out, because she was inside, getting ready for her debut at the hottest dungeon on the planet.

"I don't see you in latex, or PVC," Justine's voice said from the depths of the closet "It's too science fiction, too artificial. I see you in something more organic. Something that flows ... like your hair. Wait ... "

There was a rustle of hangers and she appeared with a black sheath dress of luscious satin. It was cut on bias and flared slightly at the bottom, like a fluted champagne glass. It smelled antique, like flowers fallen away to dust.

"Wow," Caitlin said running her fingers over the slippery fabric.

"You say that a lot," Justine said. She handed Caitlin the dress. "Try it on, but take your panties off. You have to be naked under this dress or it just doesn't work."

Feeling shy under Justine's frank scrutiny, Caitlin pulled off her plain cotton underwear and slipped the dress over her head.

Amazingly, it fit her perfectly. The cool satin clung to her body without a ripple, settling against her skin like it had always been there. When she moved, the fabric caressed her, intimate as a lover.

"It's beautiful," Caitlin said, spinning like a little girl in a brand new Easter dress.

"You're beautiful in it." Justine said.

There was a long chunk of awkward silence and Caitlin could feel hot blood flowing like lava in her cheeks. She forced her mouth open to speak, to fill the thick air between them.

"Do you have some shoes?" she asked.

Justine laughed.

"Do I have some shoes?" She covered her mouth with the back of her hand. "Well, I have a few pairs. Your feet are pretty small for your height. What are you, a nine?"

"And a half," Caitlin said.

Justine dove back into the closet, crawling on her hands and knees through the sea of shoes.

Caitlin struck slinky poses in the mirror, listening to the rustle and thump of Justine's search.

When she reappeared from the depths of closet-land, she was holding two pairs of heels, one a subtle black-on-black brocade and the other tall spikes with thin ankle straps. She handed Caitlin one of each, along with a pair of satin opera length gloves.

"You'll want these too," Justine said, taking Caitlin's hand in hers and examining the rough scab crowning her knuckles. "For now."

Caitlin slipped the long gloves on, feeling vaguely embarrassed. Then the shoes, one of each, left knee bent to accommodate the taller heel. In the mirror she turned first one way, then the other.

"What do you think?" she asked.

"Go for the spikes," Justine advised. "They're more fetish."

She handed Caitlin the mate of the taller shoe. Leaning against the mirror, Caitlin balanced on one foot, gloved fingers struggling with the tiny silver buckle.

"Please, Mistress," Justine said, kneeling. "Allow me."

She fastened the buckle and pressed her warm cheek to the top of Caitlin's foot. Caitlin found herself staring down at the back of Justine's neck just under the pile of blood-colored hair. The curve of her back was a pure arch, culminating in the inviting swell of her ass, and Caitlin imagined what it would feel like to bring her palm down hard on that gentle curve. A slick fist clenched between her legs, shocking her, bringing her blood closer to the surface.

Justine looked up, eyes nothing but wide black pupil. She pressed her mouth to Caitlin's foot, warm tongue flickering across the row of toe-cleavage that showed above the edge of the shoe.

Caitlin watched herself reach down and twine her fingers in the girl's hair, pulling her up to her knees.

"There will be plenty of time for that later," she told Justine, caressing her face like you would a favorite cat. "Right now, concentrate on being beautiful enough to be seen with me."

Justine smiled and looked down.

"Yes, Mistress," she said.

20.

Justine led Caitlin through a labyrinth of long halls and narrow stairways, down a different elevator and through a door guarded by a man who looked like he came from the same cloning vat as the one downstairs. He checked Caitlin's name on some list and nodded, stepping aside to let them pass. Caitlin's feet were already bemoaning her footwear selection as they made their way down the hundredth hallway to a plain metal door at the end.

On the other side of that door, on a cluster of green velvet chairs, sat Belladonna, the twins, and a vaguely Asian-looking woman with her face half hidden in rippled shadow.

Belladonna rose and took both of Caitlin's gloved hands in hers.

"Morrigan," she said pressing her cheek to Caitlin's. "So glad you could make it. Of course you remember the twins."

"It's that girl with the hair," Nightshade said to her brother. "Let's kiss her."

The two laid sticky mouths on Caitlin's face, hands clutching at her like infants grabbing at a shiny toy. Hemlock was dressed as befitted his gender, shirtless with tight leather pants and snakeskin boots. His sister was dressed identically.

"So good to see you," Hemlock said. His soft voice reminded Caitlin of Kaa the Python in Disney's *Junglebook*. "I hope you'll be with us for a long time. My sister and I both wanted desperately for you to be admitted. We hope you'll play with us this evening. Will you do that?"

"Don't pester her, Hemlock," the third woman said, stepping forward. The twins slunk away, whispering as the woman offered her hand to Caitlin. "I'm Hellebore."

She studied Caitlin from behind wire rimmed glasses, nostrils flaring slightly as if she were testing the air between them. She was dressed in sober black, classic and subtle with a single silver ornament pinned at the throat. The brooch was heavy and almost crude, it's shape strange and deceiving. Intestinal coils curved and spiraled, organic and yet unlike any anatomy found in this humble universe. And above it ...

The woman's face was an asymmetrical nightmare of distorted features. Her left eye was dark and serene while its sister was a pale, bulging monstrosity, roving rebelliously along its own illogical path. The cheek beneath was concave, a knotted curve of malformed bone. Her mouth was full and sensuous, beestung lips hideously sexy beneath such ugliness. Her long braid was pure, glossy black.

"First impressions are very important," Hellebore said. "I sincerely hope that you will live up to expectations."

She returned to her seat and a strange stillness held the room in silent tableau. It was Justine who finally broke it, coming forward to kneel before Belladonna and pressing her mouth to her Mistress' foot.

"Hello, Justine," Belladonna said, smiling at the simple distraction.

Caitlin stood aside and struggled not to wrap her arms defensively around herself. She was almost in. Her skin shuddered under the delicate touch of the satin dress.

"Where are Colin and Melissa tonight?" she heard Justine ask.

"I gave them the night off," Belladonna answered. "Though Lord knows what they're going to do with themselves with no one to tell them what to do." Her laugh was low and rich. "I suppose I will miss them, but I have you to keep me company. And the beautiful Lady Morrigan."

She motioned for Caitlin to sit beside her. Justine knelt at their feet.

"Even if she isn't a member of the master race," Belladonna said. "We forgive her, don't we, Justine?"

Caitlin frowned.

"The master race?"

Belladonna laughed, fingers playing in Justine's hair.

"Redheads, of course."

Caitlin wanted to laugh but it was all she could do to peel back her lips in an approximation of a smile. Chilly unease nested low in her belly.

"Morrigan," Belladonna whispered. Her breath was warm and violet-scented. "I don't want you to dislike Hellebore. She is a strange and fascinating woman, but more than a little xenophobic. Once she warms up to you, ask her to invite you down to her shop. She owns the most fabulous rare book store, down on Broadway and Tenth Street. You would just love it."

Caitlin nodded, filing that little info-byte for future consideration. She wanted to ask what had happened to the woman's face, but didn't.

"Is she dominant?" Caitlin asked instead, glancing over to where Hellebore sat alone and brooding.

"You know," Belladonna said, warming to the gossip. "In all the years I've been here, I've never seen her participate in anything. Her scene, I think, is purely voyeuristic."

Caitlin nodded. She felt unable to focus on anything. Her heart was racing.

Somewhere in another room, a clock sounded.

"Midnight," Nightshade and Hemlock called in unison.

"Where is he?" Hellebore asked, strange features unreadable.

"He'll come when he comes," Belladonna replied.

Caitlin wondered if they were talking about Absinthe. She followed dumbly as everyone stood and filed towards a doorway draped in black lace. Belladonna produced a long leash like a magician's trick and clipped it to the ring on Justine's collar. With a gracious nod, she handed the leather loop on the other end to Caitlin. She took it, feeling like an understudy with no time to rehearse.

The curtain was peeled aside and Caitlin got her first glimpse of the Club.

21.

Caitlin had no idea what to expect. When she passed through the curtain, she found herself in a huge, high-ceilinged warehouse. She felt small and intensely fascinating, like some rare beetle. All around her, faces with eyes like colored glass. Chic, custom made leather outfits hugged surgically-augmented bodies. Women too beautiful to be three-dimensional posed with men in complex harnesses or suits that cost more than her entire wardrobe.

She walked beside Belladonna with her chin square, poor-girl pride unrelenting in the face of money. Everything looked excessive, like a dessert with too much whipped cream and strawberries and chocolate chips and cherries and sprinkles.

The space around them was dotted with Victorian couches and lit with thick black candles. Smooth beauties both male and female wove skillfully though the crowd in spite of the chains that hobbled their ankles and bound their wrists to trays of champagne or cigarettes or sweets.

Little dramas seemed to be constantly unfolding in every corner. On a plush couch by the bar, a regal black woman sat with a young man bent over her knee. She gripped a fistful of his long blonde hair and brought her open hand down again and again on his narrow ass. He moaned and ground his hips against the stiff black taffeta of her ankle-length skirt.

A trio of leggy women in skin tight latex posed and pouted like high-tech heroines in a cyberpunk stroke-film, barking harsh commands to the man who knelt before them. His paunchy, middle-aged body glittered with rows of needles and bright drops of blood.

Two pigtailed girls were bound face-to-face with their plaid skirts hiked up and their white cotton panties around their knees. A spectacled man with a thin yellow cane struck their plump thighs and hot pink asses with neat sets of three. They squealed and writhed, fresh young cheeks damp with tears.

A thickly tattooed woman hunched intently over a medical examination table, her broad hands sheathed in tight latex gloves as she pierced the labia of a lush starlet. On the far wall, a fat woman was being whipped by an elegant butch in full SS regalia. The victim's soft white flesh was crossed with deep, bleeding welts. Close by, a pair of older men in full leather sat smoking expensive cigars while a naked and eager boy polished their motorcycle boots to a mirror-gloss.

In the back of the club was a glassed-off, white tiled room with a drain in the middle of the floor. A tiny Asian girl hung from the ceiling, her legs spread wide. A red rubber enema bag was filled with champagne and hoisted high above her head. The nozzle was inserted and the bag emptied. When the nozzle was removed, revelers in red and purple latex held up elegant crystal goblets to catch the stream of bubbly flowing from the slave's dusky asshole. A toast was proposed and everyone drank to each other's health.

Overwhelmed suddenly, Caitlin allowed Justine to subtly lead her to a plush chaise lounge where she let her shivering legs collapse under her. The girl produced her silver cigarette case from somewhere in the artfully arranged shreds of non-clothing that graced her slender body and offered one to Caitlin. She accepted and let the girl light it for her. She could not allow her strange new emotions or childish moral judgments to interfere with her observation. She must see everything, record everything.

As she smoked she continued to let the impressions of the room wash over her. She began to detect another, more subtle game of dominance and submission being carried out in shadowed corners. Deals were being discussed over welted flesh. The low hum of social and financial power was heavy in the air, woven through every conversation. Business cards and air kisses were exchanged along with bodily fluids. Those with less power displayed themselves shamelessly before those with more. Doms struck menacing and haughty poses, hoping to attract the attention of millionaire masochists, while subs groveled and struggled to outdo each other in displays of endurance and humiliation. Caitlin could recognize a few famous faces and there were even more faces too powerful to be famous.

Through the cloud of exhaled smoke, she watched the crowd. They had gone quickly back to their own activities once Hellebore and the others had entered and dispersed, but they seemed subdued, watching the curtained doorway from the corners of their eyes. All around her, whispers surging and receding like a secret tide. Then, suddenly, all sound and movement ceased and the room went hushed and expectant like the crowd waiting for a suicide to jump.

She pulled Justine close and whispered in her ear.

"What is it?"

Before the girl could answer, the lace rustled and peeled back strip-tease slow and the crowd drew a collective breath as Absinthe himself sauntered forward, accompanied by a single slave girl in an intricate leather chastity belt.

He had the easy confidence of a man used to having his picture taken, a decadent swagger and a luscious sneer that was pure performance art. He was small boned, almost child-like, but he seemed to completely fill any space he entered. His body was smooth and ageless, his face androgynous in its cold perfection. His hair was midnight water, indecently long, falling to just below his girlish waist. His eyes were arresting and strange under arching black brows, their pupils wide and glistening, their irises like fragile rings of amber. In some light, they seemed almost scarlet. He wore a purple velvet frock coat, skin tight leather shorts and high black boots with spike heels. His pale chest was bare, nipples rouged with dark makeup.

Caitlin watched him as he worked the crowd. He greeted each of his guests with the frightening attentiveness of a campaigning politician, checking to be sure every need was met, allowing ample time for each one to lavish gifts and worship on his worthy person before moving on. He flirted outrageously, unleashing both barrels of his formidable sexuality at point blank range. Sex oozed from every pore. No one was safe from his burning eyes and subtle teasing. Even the most uncompromising dominants seemed to eat from his hand. Slaves fought like dogs over the tiniest crumbs of his attention.

He stopped to exchange pleasantries with a knot of excruciatingly polite Japanese men in dark suits. Their voices were low and cultured as they respectfully praised the slave's obedience, jet eyes like hooks. He stopped to examine a line of beautiful naked slave boys, wrinkling his nose and waving a dismissive hand to show that none impressed him. The slaves' owner, a dark-eyed woman in a beige suit, bowed her head, her face reddened with anger and shame.

He made his way towards Caitlin like a cruising shark, tighter and tighter circles. Her heart pounded in her throat as she watched him, trying to swallow him whole, distill his essence, capture him for later display. A thousand metaphors clustered around his image. She could smell him, an intoxicating brew of sex-sweat and corruption, of warm leather and the sharp metallic tang of blood. Or semen. Or both.

She struggled to prepare herself, but without warning he was behind her, inches away, and she was intensely aware of him, as if every cell of her skin was screaming under the aggressive assault of his aura. Though she could not see him, she could feel his hand reaching out to her, and she did not turn to face him. His fingers stilled in the air between them, and she knew he could feel her awareness. There was an excruciating charge between them as he waited for her to turn, but she wouldn't let herself acknowledge him, determined that the first move should be his. She nearly screamed as his long nailed fingers touched her hair.

"Lady Morrigan," he said. His voice was higher than she expected, honeyed and oddly devoid of accent. His nails caressed her scalp, sending armies of gooseflesh over her body. "May I?"

Without waiting for her answer, he sat beside her, his slave kneeling at his feet. The girl's skin was shockingly white even in this pale crowd and her glossy scalp seemed more hairless than shaved, as if it had been chemically depilitated. Her high forehead was devoid of eyebrows and hugging her boyish hips was an elaborate leather chastity belt held closed with a heavy silver lock. The girl looked up at Caitlin with shadowed eyes and quickly looked away.

"You are more beautiful than I could have imagined," Absinthe said, speaking close to Caitlin's ear. "I knew I made the right decision, allowing you to be admitted."

He stroked her hair, twining long, shining locks around his fingers and she bristled. She wondered how much of this fawning she was required to tolerate. Fuming silently, she ground her teeth together, struggling to remember how hard she had worked to get here. Telling him to go fuck himself, or worse, wiping the sleazy grin off his face with the back of her hand, was probably not a good strategy. When he brought a golden fistful of her hair to his lips, she pulled away and stood, drawing herself up to her full height, an intimidating six-seven in the spike heels.

"With all due respect," she said, smoldering anger held back on a tight choke chain. "I hardly know you, and I cannot tolerate being pawed by a total stranger, no matter how famous."

The entire club was silent. Caitlin stood terrified and elated at the center of a whirlpool of eyes, defiant and convinced that she was about to be bounced out of here forever. She tried to tell herself that it didn't matter, that she had all the information she needed, and was about to turn and leave of her own accord, when Absinthe stood and bowed his head, mock-contrite. Being forced to look up to meet her gaze did not seem to threaten him in the least. His arrogance was unshakable.

"Point well taken, Lady," he said. His amber eyes were dilated, nocturnal. They reminded Caitlin of the eyes of lemurs or bushbabies. "I forget my manners in the face of your beauty. Will you forgive me?"

Caitlin cocked her head, unsure if she had heard correctly. She could not risk asking him to repeat himself, so she nodded and tried to appear as though it were not that important.

"Please," Absinthe said, beckoning her to follow him. "Come have a drink with me. Give me that, at least."

He held out his hand, eyes quietly maniacal, full of subtle humor like the one bad boy in a church choir.

She glanced at Justine, but the girl would not meet her gaze. She reached out and took Absinthe's hand, remembering Crow's warning. His palm was smooth and hot against hers.

He led her to a secluded table by the empty fire place. Justine and Absinthe's slave trailed behind them, both used to living beneath notice.

"Morrigan," Absinthe said, gesturing for her to have a seat. "An unusual name. A Celtic goddess if I'm not mistaken."

Caitlin sat, Justine at her feet.

"That's right," she said. "You don't run into a lot of people named Absinthe, either. It's a drink of some sort, isn't it?"

"No, you don't." Absinthe grinned, petting the smooth, hairless head of his slave. "And yes it is. Would you like some? It's an acquired taste, but I assure you, it's one worth acquiring."

He snapped his fingers and a shaven-headed boy appeared with a tray of delicate glasses full of yellowy-green liquid. He took two of the narrow goblets and a dish of cubed sugar, setting them on the table.

Caitlin took a glass and examined it's contents. Absinthe took the other and held it high in toast.

"To the beautiful Mistress Morrigan," he said.

"To the ill-mannered but charming Lord Absinthe," Caitlin answered, clinking her glass to Absinthe's. She was about to drink but he shook his head and she paused, glass still raised. He picked up a sugarcube between two long nails and pressed it to her lips. Her mouth hardened against the sugar's rough edge, then relented and let it in.

"Like this," he said, clenching a sugarcube between his teeth and sipping from his glass. Caitlin followed suit, pulling the liquor through the sugar and into her unsuspecting mouth.

It was appalling, like some quack tonic from the turn of the century formulated to induce miscarriage. Viciously bitter, medicinal almost, with undertones of licorice and chlorophyll. The sugar surrendered to the bitterness without a fight, but she could imagine the flavor without the sweet intervention and shuddered. She choked it all down like a good girl and was immediately sorry. Her stomach clenched. Her head spun. She felt suddenly hot and dizzy. Then the feeling subsided and diluted, leaving her only slightly buzzed and mellow. She noticed that Absinthe had taken her hand and was caressing her palm with his thumb as though he were preparing to read it.

"I am not always a selfish lover," he said. "I don't want you to hate me."

"I don't hate you," Caitlin said. Her mouth and tongue felt strange, hypersensitive. "I hardly know you."

"I hardly know myself." He finished his drink and set the empty glass down beside Caitlin's.

A long moment of charged silence spun out between them. His eyes were acutely focused and she would not look away. Something was stirring inside her, rising like a charmed snake from the secret depths of her soul. The heat between them was more than sexual, it was a struggle for dominance and intimidation where neither would back down. An unmistakable challenge that was as compelling as it was disturbing. It was the grown-up echo of her confrontation with Mike in the Crypt, but purer somehow, sweeter. The moment unfurled, endless as the fire deepened. Then, in a single, inexplicable twist of seconds, the burning friction of their wills transmitted into a sudden understanding. A strange, unspoken acknowledgment of commonalty that excited and horrified Caitlin.

"You are exquisite," Absinthe said. She felt a curl of heat between her legs as strong as if he'd touched her there and she could tell by the tense posture of his body that he felt it too. Slowly, without looking away, he reached down and caressed his slave's throat. "Isn't that right?"

"Yes, Master," the girl answered.

"Your slave is very well trained," Caitlin observed, deliberately leading the conversation into safer waters, convinced that she had passed into some new level and unsure how to feel about it. The tension between them did not die down, it merely idled like a smooth running motor.

"Her name is Jez," Absinthe said as if discussing a lapdog. "Greet Mistress Morrigan properly, Jez."

The girl pressed her lips to Caitlin's shoe.

"Very pleased to meet you, Mistress Morrigan," she said.

Caitlin broke eye contact to study the girl, her alleycat ribcage and angular cheek bones, her concrete colored eyes and bruised lips. The softly gleaming skin of her scalp looked oiled. The skin that covered her narrow bones was slick as rubber, almost unnatural. Her voice was soft and androgynous. She didn't even seem old enough to drink.

Something about the girl's defensive posture reminded Caitlin of her sister.

Other, more subterranean memories writhed just beneath the murky surface of her mind, but she forced them down and returned Absinthe's smile. She could not allow herself the luxury of reflection.

"I want you to have everything," he was saying. "I would like to do a scene with you."

Caitlin pulled Justine close, taking meager comfort from the girl's familiar smell.

"That would be fine," she said, only half sure of what she had agreed to. His eyes were deep, full of secrets.

"Beautiful." He motioned to Hellebore, who Caitlin hadn't even noticed sitting less than ten feet away. "Mind Justine, would you?"

Hellebore took Justine away and Caitlin watched them go with visible regret, feeling as if she had lost her native guide in the dark heart of an alien jungle.

She tried to stand but felt overwhelmed with waves of curious vertigo. Her lean, disciplined body was not used to decadence. She sat back, feeling molten, outrageous, like some lush denizen of a more romantic era. She watched with slow fascination as Jez pressed her lips to Absinthe's fingers. She wanted to kiss them both. Their mouths were slick and lollipop red, irresistible. Absinthe's hands were in her hair again, pressing it against his lips. His voice was hypnotic in her ear.

"I can't help myself, Lady," he whispered. "It's the distilled essence of sunshine's memory."

She was lost in a maelstrom of sensation. The world seemed to be nothing but a glossy river of soft hair flowing over her, black and blonde, coiling strands intertwining. Her own familiar scent mingled with the carrion sweetness of Absinthe and the spicy-strange helpless perfume of Jez. She felt abstract, full of possibilities.

Absinthe's mouth hovered inches from hers, lips slightly parted, waiting, and she reached for it, tongue questing for the source of his hot butcher-shop breath. There was blood in her mouth, blood and the sensuous meat of his tongue moving over hers. Hands wandered, ownerless, over the length of her body. She shuddered, groaning into the charnel darkness of Absinthe's mouth.

Some distant voice in her mind demanded to know exactly what she thought she was doing, but she could not answer and found that she didn't care.

Teeth slashed at her tender mouth, drawing her own blood and she rocked her hips, swallowing reflexively. Absinthe withdrew and licked his lips, leaving Caitlin cold and dizzy, suddenly aware of the attentive eyes all around them. Absinthe helped her to her feet and she staggered like a drunken prom queen. The voice inside her head muttered something about journalistic objectivity, but it was silenced as Absinthe slid an arm around her waist and brushed her hair back from her face, whispering.

"You are beautiful, delicious."

He was manacling Jez to a chain hanging from the ceiling, spreading her legs. Caitlin was kissing Jez's soft face, teasing her. Everything was strange and bright, inevitable. Jez was bleeding from intricate cuts across her chest and belly and Caitlin tasted the girl's blood in her throat, a singular flavor that made her jaw ache with inexplicable resonance. She remembered Justine and the knife in her hand and there was a new blade in the unfeeling grip of her remote fingers, a long, gleaming razor. Absinthe licking the blade, kissing her. Jez was sobbing, ecstatic and trembling and they were soothing her with gentle hands, letting her down.

"Morrigan," Absinthe's voice was inescapable. They were sitting back at the table by the fireplace, suddenly, like a cut in a film. "I want you here with us." His hand rested on her thigh. "You are so fresh, so full of passion. You make the simplest task into a work of art. I want you to stay with me."

"Of course," she said, appalled to realize that she was stroking his bare chest. She pulled her hand away. Jez was kneeling at their feet.

"I don't care if you're inexperienced," he told her. "Experienced woman are jaded and stale, nothing affects them. This place needs an infusion of new blood, new desire."

He took her hand and brought it to his lips.

"I would like to make love with you tonight."

"Mmm." Caitlin shut her eyes and tipped her head back. When she opened them, she saw a man dressed as a harlequin, his shiny red and white suit glistening with diamond shaped shards of mirror. He wore a silver mask and as he turned towards her, Caitlin saw that he was not wearing red at all. He was naked, bloody mirror fragments embedded in his white skin.

She turned away and saw the monkey faced contortionist from the Crypt sucking his own dick as a group of older women gasped and applauded.

Behind him and to the left, the twins had a pale, black-haired boy chained to the rough brick wall. Nightshade was holding a long jewel-encrusted hat pin and a small gilded box. Hemlock stood beside her, stroking the boy's sharp bones. Reaching into the box, he extracted an enormous, fiercely struggling cockroach and deftly impaled the insect on the pin. Nightshade took the boy's cringing penis in her tiny hands and pierced it crosswise with the length of the pin, trapping the flailing roach. As Caitlin watched in disbelief, the spasming legs and feelers of the dying insect brought the boy to a horrified, sobbing orgasm.

Caitlin's head was spinning. Each tableau her eyes settled on seemed more surreal than the one before. She pressed her face into the inky curtain of Absinthe's hair, imagining black and gold intertwining like sun and shadow.

"Take me out of here," she said.

Part Three

INSIDE

22.

Consciousness came to Caitlin like a slowly dripping liquid. Her first thought was that it was still night. There was hair in her face that was not her own. Her head was full of malicious insects. She didn't know where she was. It took long aching minutes to remember the events of the night before.

Absinthe's private rooms were all black velvet and purple candles. The decor looked as if it had been selected by suicidal teenagers with too much eyeliner and very rich parents. Justine's beautiful dress was a crumpled heap a few feet away from the inside-out frock coat. Caitlin realized that she was still wearing shoes and gloves.

A smooth skull nuzzled against her breasts and she realized that she was holding Jez in her arms. Her curved back pressed against Absinthe's chest and belly. The girl looked up at her, her eyes clear and wide awake. Caitlin felt a shiver through her guts, an ambiguous sensation. Like a half-empty bottle from last night's binge, Jez seemed to Caitlin both achingly desirable and weirdly repulsive. What she found she really wanted was to pull the girl closer and kiss her soft bruised lips and ...

Her mind refused to finish that thought. Instead, she extracted herself from the flesh tangle and sat up on the edge of the bed, holding her fragile head in her hands. Her bladder was horribly full. Stripping the long gloves inside out and tossing them away, she leaned down to wrestle with the ankle straps on Justine's shoes. She was knotted with frustration by the time Jez knelt before her and unhooked the tiny buckles. The slave helped her into the bathroom and stood silent and unobtrusive as she pissed.

"Do you like living here?" she heard herself ask as she wiped and flushed.

"Of course," Jez answered. "I'm lucky."

"Lucky?" Caitlin leaned over the black sink, splashing cold water on her face. She could not bear to look too closely at her reflection in the tinted mirror.

Jez nodded and held out a black towel. Caitlin dried her face, feeling a sudden intense longing for something that wasn't black.

"Jez," she said. Her head was pounding, the pain making her reckless. "Did you know a girl named Eva Eiseman?"

Jez eyes flew wide and she looked back over her shoulder to where Absinthe sprawled across the bed. There was bright fear in her face.

"Please, Lady," she whispered. "Don't ask about Eva. It's not safe."

Caitlin was struck with intense pity for this strange child. She seemed so young, with her lost eyes and pale, vulnerable throat marred by lurid bite-marks. Caitlin shuddered, thinking of Eva and her bitten neck. She felt a thin thread of fear coiling in her belly. For all his charm and passion, Absinthe was still the first on her list of suspects. In the heat and fury of all her new emotions, she could not allow herself to forget. But more than the thought of a murderer's kisses, something else was troubling her. Somewhere in the back of her mind, Caitlin could remember the taste of Jez's sweet flesh between her own teeth.

Seeming to understand without speaking, Jez took Caitlin's arm and led her back into the bedroom.

Her jeans and t-shirt were piled incongruously on a black velvet chair, folded neatly with her socks and boots on the floor below. She dressed quickly, watching Absinthe's sleeping face with one eye as she buttoned her jeans. There was blood crusted on his chin. He looked like a little boy, exhausted after a birthday party, or Christmas.

Jez knelt before her and kissed her grungy boots.

"It was good to meet you, Lady," she told her. "I hope to get a chance to play with you again."

She stood and leaned close to Caitlin.

"Be careful," she whispered.

23.

"My God!" Wilson exclaimed, standing in the doorway of Castle Bergin and covering his mouth and nose with one hand. "You smell like an abattoir. Where have you been, slaughtering goats?"

Caitlin pushed him aside and strode down the hallway.

"I want you to check up on something for me," she called behind her.

"I refuse to allow you to remain in this house until you take a shower," Wilson said. "Do you hear me?"

"Fine, fine."

She detoured to one of the palatial bathrooms and began to strip, unmindful of Wilson standing in the open doorway.

"Lady," he said, horrified. "What happened to you?"

She turned and was confronted with her full length reflection in the bathroom mirror. Her neck and shoulders were covered with bite marks. She stared, twisting before the mirror. She seemed to remember blood and teeth and freight train passion, out of control. The images brought a flush of heat followed swiftly by chilly guilt.

Wilson was furious.

"Who did this to you?"

"It's OK," she said, fingers tracing the swollen bites. "I guess you could say it was … consensual."

"Consensual? Have you lost your mind?"

"Yes, consensual and yes, I have probably lost my mind."

Caitlin turned on the shower.

"I spent the night with Absinthe," she said.

"What?"

She ignored him, easing her way under the needle fine spray. She winced under the stinging water, preparing for the inevitable lecture.

"Wonderful," Wilson said. "Is this some sort of elaborate suicide? Perhaps you should go down to the 10TH Precinct. No doubt they'll find that the marks on your neck match those found on the corpse of Eva Eiseman. Or maybe you were merely attempting to deliberately infect yourself with the AIDS virus. I hope you at least had the sense to practice some type of safe sex, though the concept of dental dams for vampires seems to be somewhat impractical."

She couldn't track his words; her thoughts were chaos. His voice faded to a low drone while the events of the night before replayed over and over in her mind. She struggled to make some sense out of it all, to extract useful information from the whirlwind of sensation. But it all seemed too much suddenly, she felt overwhelmed. Her neck hurt, a thudding, and thoroughly unromantic pain that flared sharp when she ran her fingers over the revised topography of her skin. Sinking down in the tub, she hugged herself, feeling vulnerable, bathed in confusion and contradiction.

"Caitlin?" Wilson slid the frosted glass open a crack, trying to avert his eyes from her nakedness. "Um ... are you OK?"

Something about his simple, awkward concern broke through her fragile self-control and she started to cry.

"I don't fucking know," she sobbed. "I'm tired, I'm sore and I'm hung-over. I just ... just need to think, to ... sort things out. I feel so crazy, I don't know."

"Hey, don't ... um ... " Wilson looked over his shoulder as if expecting someone to show up and save him from this girlish display.

But he didn't need to worry. The storm of tears ran its course, passing as suddenly as it came. Once the gush of emotion was out of her, she felt lighter, full of the sort of shaky relief that followed a bout of vomiting. Whatever poison had curdled inside her, it was out now, and she was ready to deal with what came next. Even Jesus Christ had his moment of doubt, and that never stopped him from taking care of business. The idea of Jesus surrendering his martyr's flesh to Absinthe made her smile a little as she pushed clinging wet hair from her face.

"I'm OK, really," she said, struggling to her feet. Her voice was still a little raw. "Listen." She cleared her throat. "How about that favor? Can you find out about a rare book store on Broadway and Tenth Street. It's owned by one of Absinthe's inner circle, a woman who calls herself Hellebore."

Wilson eyed her distrustfully, testing to see if another outburst was waiting to ambush him. When he seemed confident of her stability, he sneered.

"Oh, of course, I would love to. Everything that I'm working on pales to irrelevance in the face of your sexual adventures."

Caitlin smiled into the spray, cheered by the one thing in her life that never seemed to change. Wilson's attitude. She turned to him and pulled a puppy-eyed face.

"Please?"

"Oh no, don't even try." Wilson crossed his arms over his chest. "I'm not even looking."

But she knew he would.

24.

Mike was staring into the brackish depths of his department coffee, debating a second round of Excedrin, when Absinthe appeared in the squadroom, swept in by a rush of feminine laughter. Trish Connelly was beside him, her thick cheeks blushed and her eyes lit with girlish humor as he leaned close and whispered in her ear. He was dressed conservatively, excruciatingly tasteful in his dark suit. His hair was pulled back and neat, eyes bright as burning metal. Mike disliked him immediately.

All eyes watched as Connelly led him through the maze of desks and into the fishtank.

"So you think this is our guy?" Eric asked, lounging against the wall beside Mike.

"Works for me," Mike said, chasing three more Excedrin with the last of the coffee after all. He had a feeling he was going to need them.

"Well, he better, 'cause there ain't nobody else."

"You gonna have a go at him?" Mike asked, tilting his head towards the closed door.

"Hell yeah," Eric answered, flashing teeth. "I wanna let him sweat for a little while first, though."

"Make him cry, Detective."

"Damn right, I will. Teach that boy about real S&M, NYPD-style."

Mike laughed.

"Put him over your knee and spank him."

"No way," Eric said. "He'd enjoy it too much."

Eric glanced over Mike's shoulder at the file open on his desk. Eva Eiseman sprawled before the camera's unflinching eye.

"Y'know," Eric said, shuffling through the file. "I hope to God you're right about this Absinthe guy."

Mike nodded and was about to speak when he was interrupted by Connelly's three-pack-a-day voice.

"Yo, Kiernan," she called, waving him over.

Mike and Eric exchanged curious glances and Mike shrugged.

"What's up, Trish?" he asked, feeling Eric's eyes on him as he crossed the squadroom.

"You know this guy?" Trish poked a callused thumb at the closed door.

"No, why?"

"Well, he knows you," she told him. "He says he won't talk to anyone else."

"You gotta be kidding."

"Do I look like I'm kidding?" Connelly asked.

Mike looked back over his shoulder to where Eric stood. Eric shrugged but there was subtle resentment in his eyes.

"Guess not," Mike said.

———————◆———————

Inside, Absinthe lounged in a plastic chair, managing to look perfectly comfortable in what had to be one of the least comfortable rooms on earth. Mike studied him for a few minutes through the one-way mirror.

"I don't know about this," he said.

"Aw go on, ya baby," Connelly said, slapping his shoulder with a meaty hand.

When he opened the door, the first thing that struck him was the smell, blood and sex and sweet corruption, mingled with the rich stink of pheromone. It raised his hackles and kicked his dislike up another notch.

"Detective Michael Kiernan," Absinthe said, acknowledging him with a regal gesture that set Mike's teeth on edge.

"Let's get right down to business," Mike said, refusing to let his irritation show. "We don't want to take up too much of your time."

"How considerate." Absinthe smiled, a predatory display. "Although I suspect that you would in fact like to take up all my time. In jail, that is."

Mike found himself staring at Absinthe's teeth, superimposing their distinctive contours over the bruised crescents in Eva's pale flesh. The main objective, short of eliciting confession, was to convince him to submit to dentition analysis. If he was innocent, he should have no reason to refuse, but leading up to the request would require extreme care.

"What makes you think we want to put you in jail?" Mike asked.

"I'm a suspect, am I not?"

"Are you telling me you should be?"

Absinthe laughed, a musical sound that flowed like cream.

"Well," he said, eyes bright with perverse amusement. "Isn't this fun? All around the mulberry bush, the monkey chased the weasel."

Mike slapped a photo of Eva's dead face on the table between them. He followed it up with the shot of her mutilated vagina. Close up, the laceration was appalling.

"Do you recognize this girl?" he asked, watching Absinthe's face, gauging his reaction.

Absinthe's eyes flicked down to the photos, lingering on the photo of her vagina and then back up to Mike. His smooth features revealed nothing.

"Of course," he said.

"Can you identify her?"

"Eva Eiseman," Absinthe said, as if discussing wine.

"Can you describe your relationship with the deceased?"

Absinthe took out a packet of obscure Egyptian cigarettes and shook one loose. His hand paused halfway to his lips.

"May I?"

Mike shook his head.

"No smoking in here," he said. "Board of health fascists, you know the deal."

Subtext: *I'm your pal. If it were up to me, I'd let you.*

"I see." Absinthe slid the cigarette back beside its mates. "Then I'd best make this brief. Addiction is a terrible thing, you know."

Mike said nothing and Absinthe arched a dark eyebrow before continuing.

"Eva came to work for me back in December of last year." Absinthe smiled. "She was my Christmas present."

"What exactly was the nature of the work she did for you?"

"She was my slave," Absinthe said as if that explained everything.

"Can you be a little more specific?" Mike asked.

Absinthe's mouth twisted lasciviously.

"If you'd like," he said.

Mike reined in his annoyance and waited for him to go on.

"She provided various personal services."

"Sexual services?"

Absinthe's strange eyes locked with Mike's.

"That's right."

"And how much did you pay her for these services?"

Again, that insidious laugh.

"Let's just say it was volunteer work."

"So you had a personal relationship with the deceased?"

"Look," Absinthe said. "She was my slave. Either you understand or else you never will."

"Fine," Mike said. "Were you aware of Eva's real age at the time you ... employed her?"

Absinthe's mouth hardened in the corners.

"She presented us with false identification. I was not aware of her actual age until after her death."

"What sort of ID did she give you?"

"A driver's license."

"What was the name on the license?"

"Silverstein," Absinthe said. "It seemed genuine. I only learned of her real name from the newspaper accounts."

"Can you tell me your whereabouts on the night of June 10TH, around, say, 10 PM?"

"Am I a suspect?"

"No one is accusing you of anything," Mike said, showing his palms. "It's just routine questioning."

"I was with one of my other slaves. I gave the girl an enema and then whipped her. She was able take it for almost ten minutes before she lost control of her bowels. I have it all on videotape if you're interested."

Mike kept his face neutral, refusing to react.

"What time did you finish this ... activity?"

"Just before midnight," Absinthe answered. "I always go downstairs to the club at midnight. I spent the rest of the night in the company of approximately a hundred customers and friends who would be happy to verify this it you find it necessary."

"Can you list a few names?" Mike asked. "Including the name of the slave you mentioned earlier."

"You know, Michael," Absinthe drawled. "This is really becoming quite tedious." He stretched like a cat and leaned his chin on his fist. "And frankly, I'm dying for a cigarette. Perhaps you and I could go somewhere more comfortable. Have a few drinks and discuss things in a more informal atmosphere."

"I really don't think that would be a good idea," Mike said, suspicious of this sudden chumminess.

"Wouldn't it?" Absinthe smiled, just a hint of teeth. "I think you'd find we have a lot in common."

Absinthe leaned forward and pulled a long coil of golden hair from an inner pocket. It was three feet long, tied with a violet ribbon.

"She really is an exceptional creature, isn't she?" Absinthe toyed with the soft lock. "Surprisingly tight for a woman of her stature."

Mike's throat constricted, ice congealing in his belly. He swallowed a burning mouthful of stale air and fought to keep his reaction subterranean.

"Who are you referring to?" he made himself ask.

"You really don't know?" Absinthe chuckled softly. "Some detective you are."

Absinthe leaned in, relishing Mike's anger, reaching casually through the crack in his facade.

"I know it's hard for you to accept." So understanding, like a snake consoling his prey before swallowing it whole. "It would really be so much better to talk about it in private." He tilted his chin towards the one way glass.

Denial hit like a hammer, warring with horribly vivid images of Caitlin spreading for this arrogant freak. *It couldn't be true. It had to be true.*

And under it all, memories of coming home to find Maura red faced and sweaty with some terrified asshole behind her trying to put on all his clothes at once.

The pain was huge and total, striking with deadly accuracy at the heart of his damage. His expression was iron, a dead poker face, but he knew if he opened his mouth, it would all fall down.

Then the door behind him opened and Absinthe's smile widened.

"Grace," he said, nodding to an arctic blonde in an impeccable suit. "Detective Kiernan, my attorney, Grace Dunn."

"We've met," the woman said, extending a flawlessly manicured hand.

Mike let out slow breath between his teeth and shook her hand. It took tremendous effort not to crush her cool fingers.

"Counselor," he said, his voice icy. There were few people he cared for less than Grace Dunn and it seemed hideously appropriate that she should be representing one of the few.

"Well then," Absinthe said, "I'm afraid I'm going to have to end our little conversation."

He pocketed the lock of hair and extracted a thin leather card case.

"In case you change your mind," he said, pressing a card into Mike's unfeeling hand.

———

Eric was waiting outside when Mike came out.

"Was that Grace Dunn I just saw walk in there?" he asked.

"What?" Mike passed a hand over his eyes. "Oh, yeah."

"Christ, it fucking figures." Eric rolled his eyes. "There goes our case. That bitch could get Satan off on a technicality."

Mike didn't answer and Eric frowned, laying a hand on his shoulder. "You alright?"

Mike shook off Eric's touch, silent.

"What'd he try? To fuck you?"

Silence.

"Turn you down?"

More silence.

"Hey, Mike," Eric said, cocking his head to catch Mike's eye. "It's me, remember?"

Mike shut his eyes and shook his head.

"Just drop it, alright?"

Another long stretch of tense silence. Finally, Eric nodded and reluctantly let it go.

25.

"Lily Le Bidois," Wilson said, gesturing with the butt of a sandwich filled with wet, unidentifiable ingredients. "Age, 48. Hair; black, eyes; brown. 5'11", 145 lbs. Born with an unspecified malformation of the bones surrounding the right eye. Owner of Dark Books on Tenth and Broadway. Daughter of Marie Le Bidois aka Miranda Bathory, octoroon actress known for her sexpot roles in classic B movies like *Vampire's Embrace* and *Countess Dracula*. She committed suicide in 1964, but not before passing on her lifelong obsession to her 16 year old daughter. Including items inherited from her mother, she now owns the single largest collection of writings and artifacts relating to the history of sadomasochism."

Caitlin blinked and struggled to assimilate the new information. After the two hour ritual of hair washing and braiding, she had collapsed on Wilson's bed, watching the hypnotic scrolling of raw information over his hunched shoulder. She had drifted off to the familiar keyboard sonata and when she woke up he was gone. Following the clicking of keys, she found him in the kitchen with a laptop and a cellular phone. He stuffed the remainder of the sandwich into his mouth.

"Coincidentally," he said, speaking around the sodden mouthful. "1964 was the year that the payments began."

Caitlin frowned.

"Payments?"

"Payments." Wilson nodded. "Massive fund transfers from Bank of Tokyo every six months. Fifty thousand in 1964. The last one, three weeks ago, was 750 thousand."

Caitlin whistled appreciatively between her teeth.

Wilson grinned.

"Tracing the transfer back to its source is proving to be quite an electronic goose chase. It's clear that whoever is funding Lily Le Bidois' obsession does not want their involvement to be made public."

"So you think she's got some kind of investor?"

"No, I think someone is investing in her silence."

Caitlin sat down beside him and peered at the screen. Its liquid numbers told her nothing.

"How do you mean?"

"Lily Le Bidois was born on Christmas Eve, 1948. Nine months before that, Miranda Bathory was in Japan, searching for a ritual blade that had been used by a sadistic blood-drinking samurai. On Lily's birth certificate, the father is listed as 'unknown'. I would not be surprised if her father was Japanese, a poor but noble man whose brief indiscretion with an American actress came back to haunt him after he had made his millions."

Caitlin threw her arms around Wilson and he flinched like a child being hugged by an overzealous aunt.

"You are just too brilliant," she told him.

He smirked.

"Well then, I shudder to think of the outlandish display of affection about to be visited upon me when I tell you what I found out about the House of Absinthe."

"Please, don't make me beg."

"Well Absinthe himself is an electronic nobody. That is to say, he could be anyone. His name is not on any leases or bank accounts. None of the club's financial records are in his name or under any other conceivable pseudonym. He doesn't own the place."

"So who does?"

"Ms. Lily Le Bidois, of course."

Caitlin whooped and kissed Wilson's forehead. He pushed her away and she grabbed hold of his wrists, using her own momentum to pull him to his feet. She snaked one arm around his waist and dragged him into a manic waltz.

"I should have know it," she said, laughing. "Oh this is just too perfect. The thing about the Japanese dad and the scream queen mom is delicious. The deeper I get, the bigger the picture becomes. The lines of power, who's controlling who."

He gripped her shoulders and stopped her movement.

"Listen," he said, serious. "These people are big. Imagine the most powerful person you ever met. These people own him. They own the person who owns him. You're totally out of your league." Wilson pulled away and frowned. He turned his back and began rooting in the refrigerator. "I'm just warning you. Not only is one of your new acquaintances a murderer, they are also rich enough to get away with it."

Wilson tossed her a can of Coke and pried another off the plastic harness for himself.

"I know, I know." Caitlin shook her head. "I'm being as careful as I can. They don't know anything about me."

Caitlin opened the soda, spritzing her hand with a fine mist of sweet liquid. She licked the side of her fingers.

"You gave them no information at all?"

Caitlin squeezed her eyes shut, sucked air through her teeth. In her mind, she saw herself handing her phone number to Justine.

"Stupid," she hissed.

"What did you, give them a tissue sample?"

"I gave my phone number to one of the slaves."

Surprisingly, Wilson did not berate her for her thoughtlessness. Instead he shook his head. "When?"

"That first night at the Crypt."

Wilson squinted, thoughtful.

"Well, they seem to have accepted you in spite of your journalistic inclinations."

"Maybe they don't know ... "

Shaking his head, he cut her off.

"Do not underestimate your opponent." He tossed back a wisp of hair. "Assume they know everything. These people could destroy you without cracking a sweat, yet they've chosen not to. Not yet."

Caitlin shook the last drops of soda into her mouth.

"Look," she said. "I have never felt this close to something so huge. I can't stop now."

"Did you listen to anything I just said?" Wilson crushed the can, exasperated.

"I'll be careful."

"Fine, whatever." He sat back down, fingers flying. "Why let a silly little thing like reality get between you and greatness?"

He said it low enough that Caitlin could pretend she didn't hear him. She could not tell him about the way her body was singing to her in a voice she never knew she had. There was so much more that he could not possibly understand. So many strange emotions and tender, newborn sensibilities. Such a weird sense of belonging, of having lived a life of restrictions that were suddenly lifted. Even she was not entirely sure what was happening to her, but she was sure that her prior outburst was nothing but birthing pains, her mind stretching to accommodate her new emotions. Not really new, just newly awakened. A little scary, but unquestionable right. If Wilson didn't get it, that was his problem. Sometimes that just made things easier.

"I want to track down this absentee father," he said, already half-lost in cyberspace. "If I stumble on anything new, I'll post it."

"Thank you, Wilson." She kissed his scratchy cheek and he waved absently as if she were a fly.

"Thank me when it's over. If you still can."

26.

Caitlin sipped at a weak, syrupy vodka and cranberry and watched a pair of big-haired gothic boys draw on each other's faces with eyeliner. The bar was tiny and predominately red and black, cattle-car shaped with a cramped stage on one end. The band was morose and cadaverous and the off-key whining and flabby synthesizer notes were making Caitlin's drink taste worse. Justine was late, but Caitlin felt more invisible here than she had at the Crypt so she waited, watching.

When Justine finally arrived, she arrived. She swept in the door in a full length white lace dress with a thin veil trailing behind her. Her hair was piled high on her head, glittering with pearls, and her make up was high contrast, raccoon eyes and matte black lips against the chalk of her skin.

With her were a man and a woman. The man was dark and intense with close-set eyes and a sharp widow's peak that reminded Caitlin of a comicbook character from her childhood called the Submariner. His black coat was severe and Edwardian in cut and he wore white spats over his shoes. He was carrying a guitar case and saying something that she couldn't hear, but from the twist of his lips, she could tell it was bitterly sarcastic. The woman could have been Justine's sister, delicate and longboned with waist-length red hair and narrow, white wrists. She was also dressed in pale, flowing lace with long, pointed slippers on her feet.

Justine bowed her head and kissed her companions' fingers, then made her way toward Caitlin.

"Morrigan," she said, leaning in and kissing Caitlin on the lips. The smell of her body, sandalwood and female sweat, was intoxicating.

Caitlin's hands slipped around the contour of Justine's insect waist and she held the girl close, breasts and bellies pressed together. Shuddering, Caitlin pulled away.

"Hello, Justine," she said.

"Sorry I'm late, Mistress."

Caitlin smiled inside, letting it slowly drift towards the surface.

"What time is it?" she asked.

"It's 10:43," Justine said, consulting her tiny silver watch.

"And what time were you supposed to meet me?" Caitlin asked.

"10:30, Mistress." Justine looked down at her shoes.

"That's thirteen minutes late."

"I'm sorry, Mistress."

Inside, Caitlin was giggling fiercely. She felt simultaneously nervous and elated. Words spilled from her lips before she could stop them.

"Well, Justine, I'm afraid you're going to have to take thirteen spanks to make up for the thirteen minutes you made me wait, one for each minute."

"Here, Mistress?" Justine's eyes were wide.

Caitlin couldn't believe her own mouth, but it felt obscurely right.

"Yes, here." Caitlin felt her lips curl in a glassy smile. "Be happy I don't make you take them out on the street."

Justine flushed.

"Yes, Mistress."

She laid her flat hands and forehead on the bar, her ass high. Caitlin pushed up her long, rustling skirts, revealing her bare legs and white lace panties.

"Count them," Caitlin said, adrenaline racing under her skin.

Yanking the panties down, Caitlin brought her hand down sharply on Justine's left cheek.

"One. Thank you, Mistress."

Caitlin bit the inside of her lip to keep her wild smile in check. She loved the way the crowd focused intensely around them, eyes full of shock and awe and desire. She loved the pink blush that spread over Justine's skin as the blows added up and the way that the girl arched her back like a cat in anticipation of Caitlin's hand.

"Thirteen. Thank you, Mistress."

She pulled Justine's panties back up over the hot flesh and let her dress fall. Justine knelt and kissed Caitlin's boots.

Caitlin pulled her to her feet and kissed her lips, aware of staring faces all around them. The girl's mouth was soft and her skin was disturbingly smooth, so unlike the stubbled roughness of men. She tasted like cloves and sugar, her tongue darting lightly over Caitlin's lips. Caitlin struggled to keep a handle on the slippery heat of her strange new emotions. She felt brave and alien, her heart lurking high in her throat. When she broke the kiss, she looked down into the dilated pools of Justine's eyes and felt like she could do anything.

While she had been otherwise engaged, the useless band had disappeared and Justine's friends had set up on the stage and burst out into throaty electric chords. Caitlin recognized the song as "God of Thunder" by Kiss. The red haired singer's voice was high and sweet, operatic almost. She closed her eyes, remembering those *kabuki* demons from a million years ago. They had been one of Megan's favorite bands and for almost a year, her sister's mad drawings had been full of leering gladiators with black-and-white faces and long coiling tongues. Megan would sometimes lock herself in their bedroom and wring those old misogynistic ballads from her cheap guitar until their father would pound his fist against the door and break the lock. That guitar had a tacky orange sunburst and a strident, nagging voice and it died three days before its owner, murdered by their father's scarred and angry hands. He smashed it like an over-zealous rock star, its dying feedback slicing through the fingers that Caitlin had stuffed into her ears to block out his screaming. His face was deep red, whiskey soured blood raging in his unshaven cheeks, and he was yelling, reciting the familiar litany of how she was squandering her God-given gift with that useless noise. *For fuck's sake, Megan, don't you see how you're breaking your father's heart?* If it had been an ordinary night, Megan would have turned her sullen face away, silent, and he would have yelled until he was tired and then staggered back into the livingroom to resume his slow suicide. But that night, she had stood defiant and said in a calm voice far too adult for sixteen year old lips,

'I am not your second chance. I play what I play because I have to. If I ever stop then I'll be an empty shell like you. Don't try to rub my face in your own failure.'

He beat her then, with the same limber hands that had coaxed such beauty from the gently curving body of the long buried fiddle. Ten years it had spent cold and untouched in its wooden box just as his Rose lay cold and untouched in hers, and as he beat his best loved daughter, he cried helpless, drunken tears that both frightened and disgusted Caitlin. He smashed Megan's mangy, sad guitar and in the morning, did not remember doing it.

Caitlin bit down on her lip, swallowing the unwanted memories. She realized that she still had her arm around Justine's waist. She was afraid to take it away, because that would draw attention to the fact that it was there in the first place, and also because she was enjoying the gentle pressure of Justine's body against hers. She stood stiff and still and listened to the band, ridiculously aware of her every breath and Justine's.

They had to leave before the end of the set to be at Absinthe's by midnight. Justine blew kisses at the band as they made their way through the black-clad crowd and they grabbed a cab out on Broadway.

In the back of the cab, they leaned against each other, giggling and imagining what fetishes the people on the street were hiding.

"Diapers," Justine said, pointing to a power-yuppie with an expensive tie talking on a cellphone.

"Saran Wrap," Caitlin said, singling out an enormous fat woman struggling with several bags from Dean & DeLuca.

"Golden showers." Justine pointed to a sourfaced old lady.

"What's that?" Caitlin asked, watching the woman adjust her plastic scarf around her thin blue hair.

"Getting peed on," Justine explained. "Or peeing on someone."

"Oh yeah." Caitlin smiled. "She definitely drinks pee." She pointed to a scrawny bleach-blonde in purple spandex. "German Shepherds."

"Enemas." Justine pointed to a prim white haired nurse.

"Giving or getting?"

"Giving, I'm sure."

Caitlin laughed. She was amazed by the variety of human sexuality. The most outrageous thing she could come up with was old news to Justine. She could turn around and say something that was twice as bizarre.

"Castration," Justine said, pointing to a squat, toad-like man in a leather trenchcoat.

Caitlin was about to say no way, nobody could be into something that extreme, when she realized that it was her editor.

"Holy shit," she said. "That's Joey The Eel, my editor. He's a pig."

They were stopped at an intersection and Joey D'Illio was waiting to cross the other way. Caitlin slouched down in the seat, giggling.

"Really?" Justine started rolling down the window.

"No, no," Caitlin covered her face with her hands. "Oh Jesus."

"Come here, you pathetic piece of shit," Justine called. "Show us your miserable, diseased little excuse for a cock so we can cut it off!"

The light turned and the cab pulled away, leaving him staring after them with his jaw hanging open.

The two of them howled with laughter, collapsing against each other.

"Oh my God," Caitlin sputtered, clutching her aching belly. "I can't believe you did that."

"Fuck him," Justine said. "He doesn't deserve you."

"Well that's all well and good," Caitlin told her. "But I gotta eat, y'know."

"Bullshit," Justine said, eyes flashing. "You shouldn't have to degrade yourself by even speaking to a low life like him." She took Caitlin's hand. "Listen. I got a session tonight, a regular. He usually wants to watch another woman dominate me. Strictly flogging and boot fetish, sort of an all-girl Amazon kind of thing, real easy. He'll have a heart attack when he sees your legs. Five hundred bucks apiece, what do you say?"

"Five hundred?" Caitlin shook her head. "I don't know, though. I wouldn't even know what to do."

"Yes you will." Justine's eyes were wide and solemn. "I know you have it inside you. I'll give you the particulars and all you have to do is follow your instincts."

"I'm just not sure."

Justine shook her head.

"I've been in the scene for six years," she said. "Give me a little credit for being able to tell a natural dominant when I see one. I wouldn't even suggest it if I didn't think you could handle it. Now you know I'm one of the last people on earth to try and tell you what to do. If you really don't want to, then I'll never mention it again. It just breaks my heart to see a true dominant forced to suck up to worthless shit-heads like that guy just to make ends meet when there are submissives out there who would fight over the privilege of paying your rent."

Caitlin met Justine's gaze and, looking down at her trusting face, she was filled with wonder and a strange sense of coming home.

"Alright, then," she said.

Justine whooped and threw herself on the floor of the cab, pressing kisses to Caitlin's scuffed cowboy boots.

The rest of the ride was short, but it didn't take long for the seed of nervousness to root and grow long strangler vines in Caitlin's belly.

"Now listen," Justine was saying. "This scene is a piece of cake. We'll be in the main room for Absinthe's arrival, then we have plenty of time to relax before meeting Lawrence at 1:00. I'll tell you the premise when we get inside."

She paid the cabdriver and pulled Caitlin through the crowd. All around them, envy and desire, a volatile ocean. She felt like a rock star, like a goddess. Feeling hyper-aware of her jeans and plain black t-shirt, she held her head high as they hustled past the bouncer and inside.

"No sex, right?"

"No sex," Justine said. "He likes it if we act like we might be lovers, but we don't have to make out or get naked. You don't mind acting like my lover, do you?"

Caitlin blushed.

"No," she said.

Justine took two glasses of champagne from a naked boy with a silver tray and handed one to Caitlin.

"You've never really been with a woman before, have you?"

Caitlin took a sip of the effervescent liquid, covering her confusion. She thought about the slave girl Jez, her soft, compliant flesh. From what she could remember, the slave had kept her chastity belt on all night. Did that really count? How did one measure intimacy in a world where ordinary intercourse is so rare?

"You're not from New Orleans, either." Justine studied her over the rim of her glass. "I can't figure you out at all. I think you're hiding something, but I don't want to know what that might be. I like the mystery better."

The clock on the mantle announced midnight. As the last chime dissipated, the lace rustled and Belladonna entered with two red headed slaves. Behind her were the twins and Hellebore.

Belladonna smiled and came forward, extending jeweled fingers to be kissed. As Justine pressed her lips to her Mistress's hand, Belladonna leaned in and kissed Caitlin's cheek.

"Morrigan," she said, violet breath hot on Caitlin's neck.

"Belladonna," Caitlin answered. "Good to see you."

The twins sidled up and kissed Caitlin simultaneously.

"Lady Morrigan," Hemlock cooed. "You are beautiful as always."

"Ask her if she'll play with us tonight," Nightshade whispered, stroking Caitlin's hair with sticky fingers.

"Will you play with us tonight, Lady?" he asked.

She glanced at Justine who was looking at her feet.

"I have an appointment at one," she said.

"That's a million years from now," Hemlock pleaded.

"Surely she could play now, just for a little while," Nightshade said.

"Oh, I don't see why not," Caitlin said. It couldn't hurt to have a little practice before yet another test.

"She'll do it, my love," Hemlock said, his eyes bright, dancing.

"Wonderful," Nightshade said, clapping her little hands like a child.

"You are a far more tolerant woman than I," Belladonna said. She leaned in and spoke low in Caitlin's ear. "They have been obsessive over you for days. You will make their evening, no doubt."

"I will keep Justine until you are finished," she said. The girl had already fallen into hot whispering with the red haired slaves.

"Fine," Caitlin said, but the twins were already pulling her away.

27.

Mike paced the length of his apartment, his mind a lunatic mosh pit of conflicting emotion. The depth of his anger and betrayal was vast, profound, utterly unmanageable. He and Caitlin had exchanged no vows of fidelity, yet he was so deeply stung by Absinthe's smug accusations that it had been all he could do not to smash that pretentious pretty-boy's face in.

Back when he had walked in on Maura's side dish, his hatred had been laced with thick veins of contempt for the pathetic yuppie bastard. The entire exchange had that don't-shoot-officer feel of a small-time criminal getting ready to explain that he was just holding the dope for his brother. When he told the guy to get the fuck out, the little prick had nearly wet himself with relief, flattening his body to the wall in order to slip past without brushing against Mike in the doorway.

But this was different.

Absinthe was unapologetic and arrogant, deliberately tapping into the core of emotions Mike had not even acknowledged to himself. It made him crazy and he hated himself for being so easy to unhinge.

Because from the first time with Caitlin, he'd found himself feeling an irrational, hindbrain impulse that said in no uncertain terms: *Mine.*

It was an emotion that was not interested in logic or realistic expectation. It was not open minded. It dug knife-edged claws into his gut when she sparred with male students in her karate class, when she talked high-tech computer shit with that snotty little wiz kid friend of hers. It made him want to kill the hapless geek behind the counter down at the corner bodega for staring at her ass while she searched in the cooler for her favorite brand of iced tea. It made him want to grab a double handful of polyester Hawaiian shirt, pull the fucker's greasy face real close and say: *Mine.*

Until now, he had kept this emotion back on a tight choke chain, suffering in silence, afraid to even admit how deep his feelings ran. Unbeknownst to him, it had been weightlifting and sharpening its claws down in that locked room inside his head. When Absinthe had sprung the latch, it came roaring out like a fucking freight train, ready to flatten everything it its wake. Including himself.

To even think of that sleazy cocksucker putting his hands on her filled him with homicidal rage. His imagination was merciless, torturing him with vivid pictures of her going down of her knees for him, opening herself to his mouth and his cock. And why? The cynical whisper inside his head answered without hesitation: *For the same reason she's fucking you. Information.*

That couldn't be true. She must feel something for him. Feelings this deep couldn't be one way. That slimy prick must have done something to her. Tricked her somehow.

"Motherfucker," he said to the empty room, fists clenched tight enough to hurt.

Like a teenager's first crush, the conflagration of his obsession grew huge inside his heart, painting larger-than-life portraits of the object of his rage. Absinthe became godlike in the face of this hate, an inhuman archetype of purest evil. It was not only him, but guys like him, a whole nefarious army with Absinthe as its general. Around and around inside his head, this uncontrollable hatred chased its tail, getting bigger and stronger with every turn. Like a breeder reactor out of control, it burned hotter and brighter with no end in sight and no place to go.

Images of Absinthe with Caitlin gave sudden way to images of Absinthe's pretty face disintegrating under the impact of six .38 slugs in glorious Technicolor. Twenty years of intimacy with the consequences of homicide dissolved in the face of this virulent impulse. Only once in his life had he fired his gun at another human being in the line of duty. It had not been beautiful. It had made him sick. But this. This was so hideously pure, so primal and naked that it obliterated everything in its path.

Absinthe's card was a cool white rectangle against the dark wood of the table, beckoning.

That soft, reasonable voice inside Mike's head told him: *Call him. Agree to meet him, make him tell you everything ...*

And then kill him.

He paced. Glared at the phone, silent and seductively available with Absinthe's card beside it. He looked away, continued to pace. He had left a dozen messages on Caitlin's machine, but she wasn't home. Where the fuck was she, anyway?

With him, his mind answered.

He shook his head. Absinthe was just trying to fuck with him. He didn't want to go accusing Caitlin until he was absolutely sure.

He picked up Absinthe's card and put it down, then picked it up again. Holding it, he paced.

It took nearly ten minutes for him to break down and call.

Corner of Jane and Water. Mike in jeans, squinting with his hands stuffed into his pocket. Sweat beaded under his shoulder holster, soaking through his unseasonable denim jacket.

This was the place. An abandoned hotel, its dull brick hide extensively defaced with scrawling graffiti. Blind windows scabbed with splintery boards. Rusted padlock hanging loose, rendered impotent long ago by squatters. Mike could imagine that this must have been a classy joint once, wrought iron still prim and beautiful, ornate despite years of corrosion. Above the door, gargoyles crouched, their faces worn and featureless, anonymous in their dotage.

Smelled like setup city.

Mike's fists clenched and unclenched. The prick refused to talk to him, had some flunky arrange this meeting. For all he knew, the same flunky was waiting inside to neatly deprive him of his life while that snotty little queer had tea with 200 friends, untouchable. No one even knew he was here.

Bullshit. He wiped sweat on his sleeve. If that was the case, then he would just have to convince the flunky that it was in his best interest to inform his employer of Mike's sincere desire to meet in person. Images of Caitlin drove him up the piss-stained steps, muscles tight as piano wire.

Inside was dim and stinking, vomit and dry rot lurking like thick shadow. His eyes were wide, skin alive to every breath of fetid air in the rotting lobby. Beneath his feet, moldy carpet like dead skin, rich with insects. He could make out a pattern of ferns on the stained wallpaper. In the murky dimness, they looked like the bones of aliens.

Above his head, the skewed carcass of what must have once been a beautiful chandelier. Stripped of its crystal, it hung like a monstrous spider, all angles and bare wire.

On the other side of the wide, echoing room, a charred desk and the broken honeycomb of mailboxes. Mike could hear his own breath and the angry pulse of his heart.

From the shadows beyond the desk, a sharp rasping sound and a flare of shivering light. A match, illuminating the aristocratic contours of jaw and cheekbone, the glittering pits of bright eyes. Absinthe.

He dipped his mouth to the flame, lighting a cigarette behind his hand.

"Hello, Michael."

The sound of his voice was blood in the shark tank of Mike's rage.

"Get out where I can see you," he spat, fists still clenching and unclenching.

Again, that rich, low laugh, sexy as a woman's, infuriating.

"I'm not going to hurt you, Michael."

Absinthe dropped the smoking match and stepped out into the middle of the room. A hole in the gilded ceiling let down a spill of light and Absinthe stepped into this pallid brightness like an actor stepping into the spotlight.

Mike bit back on his fury, refusing to play this game.

"Tell me," he said.

Absinthe smiled, all teeth and shadows.

"I used to live here," he said, gesturing grandly. "Things were very different then."

Mike bit down on his lip, tasting blood.

"Look," he said. "I really don't give a fuck, OK. All I care about is Caitlin, so what ever you have to say about her, you better say it now."

Absinthe smoked, his pale exhalations wreathing his face.

"A purposeful man." Absinthe cocked his head. "I admire that."

He stepped out of the light and the tension in Mike's body cranked tighter.

"Let's not stand around in the lobby like heathens," Absinthe said. "Care for a drink?"

Mike blinked. This encounter was becoming more and more surreal with each passing minute. He found it difficult to maintain his fury in the face of such lunacy.

"The bar is through here," Absinthe said, turning away and heading off towards a dim arch gaping like an open throat.

Mike held his ground, eyes widened. No fucking way was he gonna follow that reptile into a dark room. Probably ten guys in there with infrared goggles and assault rifles.

He went in anyway.

It was not entirely dark inside. There was a single candle stuck into the mouth of a beer bottle casting fitful shadows across a scarred table and up onto Absinthe's face. He was sitting on a milk crate, smoking as if waiting for an acquaintance at some swank cafe. There was a paper bag at his feet.

"Come, have a seat," Absinthe invited, smiling like a good host.

Mike scanned the empty room again and again. There was a dark doorway down at the other end of the desecrated bar that worried him, but otherwise nothing. Just broken glass and dusty old rat turds. He was about to ease down onto the other milk crate when Absinthe bent down and reached into the paper bag.

Mike jumped back, gun in hand before he even realized it.

"Keep those hands where I can see 'em," he spat, drawing a bead between Absinthe's wide amber eyes.

A slow smile spread across his lips as Absinthe pulled his hand from the bag. He was holding two bottles of beer, their brown glass skins slick with cold sweat.

"You needn't be so jumpy," he said as if the threat of imminent death did not apply to him. He set the beers on the table. "Please, sit. Have a brew. Relax."

Three, five, then ten heartbeats passed. The long muscles in Mike's neck and shoulders were clenched like fists, his gut sour and grinding. Reluctantly, he holstered the gun and sat.

"You overestimate my hostility," Absinthe said, drawing in a last drag of bluish smoke before grinding the butt out under his boot heel. "I don't want to kill you or even hurt you. I just want you to cease your pursuit of our mutual ladyfriend."

He produced a church key and opened the two bottles. The hiss of gas escaping was huge in Mike's disbelieving ears. For a long moment, he could do nothing but stare at the thin steam swirling around the open mouth of the icy bottle. Blackened Voodoo was the name on the label. *Didn't that just figure.*

"You got some balls," Mike said, anger on a short leash.

Absinthe shrugged, took a swig from his beer.

Mike could feel the leash fraying, red rage slowly eclipsing logic.

"I don't know who the fuck you think you are, but I don't think you have any business telling me not to see my own fucking girlfriend."

"But you see," Absinthe said, gesturing with the bottle. "She is now my 'fucking girlfriend' as you so eloquently put it. You could never possibly understand. Caitlin is an extraordinary woman. Far too complex for your pedestrian desires."

"You don't know shit about her." Mike clenched his teeth, struggling to remain cool.

"I know more about her than you could ever dream of in your tawdry little Penthouse fantasies. You love the way she controls you, the way she owns your heart and your cock, your fear and your desire. But you don't know why. I do. I can open doors for her. Show her things. Nurture her dominant soul. Give her what she needs."

That was it. Free now and overwhelming, rich anger flooded Mike's senses like the best drug in the world. He reached across the rickety table and grabbed a double handful of Absinthe's silky fag-shirt, hauling him to his feet. It was so liberating, almost sexual in the intensity of its release. Before he could stop himself, he felt his fist connect with Absinthe's pretty, upturned face and it was so good, so pure.

"You lying sack of shit. I should kill you just for saying her name."

From the doorway behind them, a nearly naked waif, pale as a ghost, nothing but wide grey eyes shadowed with sleeplessness and pain.

"Please ... " A voice as thin and ethereal as its owner. "Don't hurt him."

This strange new presence neatly punctured the perfection of Mike's rage. He let go of Absinthe's shirt.

Blood trickled down Absinthe's chin, webbing his teeth as he smiled.

"There will be no more harassment of me or my staff by the police. Regarding the death of Eva Eiseman and my alleged involvement, I think we can safely consider the case closed."

"Fuck you we will." Mike felt sick, his head thumping with adrenalinated blood.

"If investigation continues, I will be forced to press charges against you for assault and attempted murder."

Absinthe righted his fallen milk crate and took another beer from the paper bag. As he uncapped it, he tilted his head up towards the glossy eye of a camera crouched up under the ceiling, calm and spiderlike.

"You son of a bitch."

"After all." Absinthe smiled, licking blood from his split lip. "This man invited me to an abandoned building and then pointed a gun in my face. Physically assaulted me. Called me all kind of nasty names. And why? Because his girlfriend loves the way I fuck her. I swear your honor, that's exactly the way it happened. Isn't that right Jez."

The little wraith slipped up beside Absinthe, eyes bright with unshed tears.

"That's right, sir."

"Now if you'll excuse us." Absinthe drained his beer and turned away, taking Jez by the hand. Jez cast a strange, wistful look over one bony shoulder before they both disappeared into the darkness, leaving Mike alone with his pain.

28.

In the back of the club were rows of steel doors. At the center, a muscular woman sat crosslegged in front of a pegboard full of keys with big plastic tags.

"Evangeline," Hemlock said, bowing deep at the waist. "Is number 13 available?"

"Of course." The woman pulled down the key and tossed it at Hemlock's chest. He caught it in both hands.

"Ask her if Jeremiah is in session," Nightshade said, tipping her head towards her brother.

"Jeremiah's free, but he has a 12:30." The woman answered, impatient. Her dark eyes were narrow, barely tolerant.

"Send him in," Hemlock told her, taking Caitlin's hand and Nightshade's.

Room 13 was tiny but sumptuous. Eyelets studded the frame of a wide leather bed and the low ceiling above it. Oil lamps provided fitful illumination, tossing long shadows over walls painted to resemble bruise-colored marble. An intricately carved dresser revealed drawers full of pain-inducing paraphernalia of every type Caitlin could imagine, and then some. There were wicked constructions of spikes and metal rings whose arcane purpose she could only guess at. An enormous, gilded mirror caught Caitlin's reflection and threw back a goddess with gold dust in her hair, uncompromising even in street clothes. It was a terrifying illusion.

"When you do sessions here, nine times out of ten, it'll be in these rooms." Hemlock spread out his arms like a tour guide. "Unless the customer wants public humiliation. We are not customers. We never have to pay."

Caitlin felt uneasy and constricted. Her eyes kept flitting back to the mirror, watching herself cross her legs, tilt her head. She wondered how she was going to ask them about Eva.

Hemlock was whispering to her, telling her she was beautiful and then there was a sharp knock on the door and Nightshade let in a naked boy who Caitlin assumed was Jeremiah. He was blonde and green eyed like her, pretty, with a girlish mouth and freckled skin. He knelt down, silent and waiting.

"Jeremiah," Hemlock said. "This is Mistress Morrigan."

"Tell her to spit on him," Nightshade whispered.

"Spit in his face," Hemlock said, almost too soft to hear. "He loves that."

Caitlin frowned. Then, with a mental shrug, she gathered saliva in her mouth and spit. It struck the boy's cheek and slid down along the curve of his jaw. His cock twitched.

"Tell Mistress Morrigan what a slut you are," Hemlock commanded.

"I'm a slut, Mistress," the boy intoned. "A worthless whore to be used only for the pleasure of my Mistress and Master."

Nightshade pulled a riding crop and a repulsive lipstick from a drawer. She held the slave's face still while she smeared pink across his mouth.

"Tell her how you love to suck cock." Hemlock smirked and caressed his leather crotch.

"I love to suck cock." The boy was trembling as Nightshade wrote the word "SLUT" in big lipstick letters across his hairless chest.

Caitlin could not stop herself from grinning wildly. Her heart was beating so fast it hurt.

"Maybe we should send him out on Ninth Avenue and see if we can make a few bucks," she said, pitching her voice low to keep it steady.

Hemlock and Nightshade turned to her, eyes brilliant like broken glass.

"Yes," Nightshade said, clapping her hands together and laughing. "We'll send him out to suck cock for money."

"A dollar a dick!" Hemlock shrieked.

"Oh too perfect!"

Nightshade handed the crop to her brother and dug in her pocket for a single silver dollar.

"Here," she placed the coin in Caitlin's palm.

"It's too good a deal to pass up," Hemlock crowed, huge grin twisted in one corner as he gave her an exaggerated wink.

Caitlin paused, her mind hatefully blank.

Think!

"Right," she said. "Get to work, slut, and make it good, or you'll get a beating, too."

Hemlock flicked out with the crop, its leather tongue snapping at his ass cheeks and between, while Nightshade dug in a drawer and came out with a dildo and a studded leather harness. The boy crawled on his hands and knees towards her as she bucked the harness around her narrow hips, giggling. Hemlock reached into a clear fishbowl full of condoms and tossed a bright packet at the slave.

"Make him put it on." Nightshade screwed her lips into a pout of distaste. "Who knows what kind of diseases a slut like that might have."

"Yeah," Hemlock said, giving the boy a fierce stinging slash with the crop. "I wouldn't let your filthy lips touch my sister's cock. Who knows how many big greasy dicks have been in that mouth."

The slave picked up the condom and tore the plastic with his teeth, sliding the rubber sheath over Nightshade's belligerent candypink dildo and then taking it deep into his mouth. His dick was half-hard, glistening with a single drop of clear fluid. Caitlin watched with weird fascination as the drop elongated, stretching towards the carpet, then snapped.

Hemlock was digging in the drawers now, coming out with tiny metal clamps connected by a chain. Dangling the clamps noisily off one finger, he bent down and stroked the boy's silky fine hair, whispering nasty encouragement.

"Is he doing a good job?" Caitlin asked, feeling full of jittery hilarity.

"He's obviously had lots of practice." Hemlock said, caressing the boy's bulging cheek.

"Let's put him over the horse," Nightshade suggested, pulling the rubber dick out of the boy's mouth and trailing saliva across his face.

"Yes, let's."

Nightshade pulled a padded horse out into the center of the room and hauled the boy to his feet, Hemlock encouraging him to action with sharp licks from the crop. Laying him over the horse the long way, Nightshade locked his wrists and ankles to cuffs on the four wooden legs. Hemlock slunk up behind him, slipping teasing fingers into the cleft of the boy's ass.

"Clamp his nipples," he said, handing Caitlin the sliver chain.

Intrigued, Caitlin examined the nasty little device. The chain connecting the rubber-tipped clamps was about eighteen inches long. She reached out and ran her hand over the leather padding of the waist high bench that they were calling a horse.

"Why don't we clamp one nipple, then run the chain under this horse and over to the other nipple. That way if he struggles, it will pull on his tits."

Caitlin stood in the brave silence of her suggestion, trying not to shiver under the predatory focus of their gaze.

"Of course," Hemlock cried, startling her. "How perfect."

"Yes, let's do that." Nightshade patted the boy's head in an almost reassuring manner.

Caitlin bent down and clamped a tender pink nipple, ran the chain underneath the horse and clamped the other. The chain jingled cheerfully and the boy made a sound like a kicked dog.

"Hold still," Caitlin said, thinking of Justine, blindfolded with the knife insistent at her throat.

Nightshade slid her dildo back into the slave's wet mouth and Hemlock continued his ruthless teasing, fingers alternating between gentle caresses and brutal pinches, punctuated by occasional flicks of the crop across his ass and thighs and even the tender curve of his vulnerable balls.

Caitlin watched, feeling bodiless, like a video camera. Watching the mingled emotions of frustration and lust and pain and desperation rush like storm-driven clouds over the slave's contorted face made the world seem so much bigger than she had ever guessed. It was like discovering that you had a third eye that you never noticed. Once you see it, you can't go back to not seeing it. She was suddenly full of nameless desires and inexplicable emotions, as if she had entered a second puberty. A flush of heat like hot wax moving just under her skin shattered her illusions of having left her body behind.

The slave was groaning deep in his throat, useless hands clenching and unclenching, twisting against the cuffs that held them. Nightshade pulled her dildo free and came around to where her brother stood.

"Cocksucking whore," Hemlock spat, slapping the boy's ass with the flat palm of his hand.

"Lady Morrigan hasn't had a turn," Nightshade said, dismayed.

Caitlin's belly knotted. Was Nightshade going to suggest that she put on that ridiculous contraption and let the slave suck on it? It seemed ridiculous, absolutely out of the question, yet imagining what it might be like gave her a nasty sort of thrill.

"Yes," Hemlock agreed. "We have been awfully selfish!" He slapped the slave's ass again. "Tell Mistress Morrigan that you deserve her strictest paddling."

"Please, Mistress," the boy said. "I need your loving discipline to correct my wayward tendencies."

Caitlin wiped her lips on the back of her hand, feeling simultaneously relieved and disappointed and more than a little intrigued by the prospect of paddling that fine, upthrust ass.

"You don't sound very enthusiastic," she said. "Are you sure you really want it?"

"Please Mistress," the boy sobbed. "Punish me in any manner you see fit. Please. I know that I am not worthy of your firm hand, but I only want to please and amuse you. I'll gladly accept any punishment that makes you happy."

He turned big green puppy eyes towards her.

"Anything, Mistress."

Caitlin took a deep breath and spit into the boy's face. He gasped and ground his hips against the leather.

"Tell me you want it," Caitlin said, accepting the smooth wooden paddle Nightshade pressed into her hands, studying its satiny finish and streamlined oval shape.

"More than anything Mistress. I am your toy to use in any way that pleases you, Mistress."

Caitlin hefted the paddle's weight, testing, feeling ridiculous and powerful and contradictory. The boy was moaning and thrashing against his bonds and the twins were staring with sharp, vampiric eyes as Caitlin walked slowly across the room. She stared down at the boy's ass. His cheeks were smooth and firm and the crack was furred with fine golden hair. She could see thin red licks from Hemlock's crop and the pale ghosts of previous beatings criss-crossing his ass and thighs.

"Stop whining!" she said, running an experimental hand over the warm curve of his ass. "You'll have plenty to cry about in a minute."

The slave went still and silent, his flesh nearly humming with expectant energy. Caitlin closed her eyes, searching for her center. When she exhaled, she opened her eyes and brought the paddle down on the lower curve of his left cheek.

The sharp crack sounded huge in the quiet room and the slave whispered, "Thank you, Mistress."

The spot where wood connected with flesh began to blush, white filling in with pink, then a deeper red, tinged with purple around the edges. Smiling to herself, she gave his other cheek a matching swat. He raised his ass higher, groaning softly and thanking her again.

She quickened her pace, left then right, until the whole of his ass was cherry red, throwing off heat like a glowing coal. Looking down at that burning flesh, Caitlin felt her own kind of warmth, a slippery heat that coiled deep inside her. It was the strangest sensation. She felt as if she were huge, enormous. Her head seemed to brush the ceiling, her fingers could wrap all the way around his fragile body. If she wanted to, she could snap his spine with one hand. He was crying out with each new blow, sobbing and thrashing, and Caitlin imagined the innocent wood was a conduit through which every ounce of her aggression and passion could flood the deep vessel of the slave's exposed psyche. He had given himself over to her completely, his body no longer his own. She imagined she was sculpting with a knife of pain, each blow defining him until he was hers alone, a creature of her creation, living and dying in the moments between the cracks. She felt intimately connected, as if the paddle were an extension of her own body and the rhythm of it was almost like the rhythm of fucking, hypnotic, arm back and then down hard, wood cracking against willing flesh and the slave crying out in mingled pain and pleasure. Sweat stung her eyes and the muscles of her arm ached and it felt so good, so liberating.

With the next crack, the boy screamed and tossed his head back, hips bucking hard enough that Caitlin paused, curious. Then he shuddered and every muscle in his body went slack.

Caitlin pushed her hair back from her face. Her breath was tight in her chest and she felt weak and elated. She stepped back, unsure of what was supposed to happen next.

"Did he have an orgasm?" Nightshade asked, and Caitlin turned her head, jolted back to reality. She had forgotten that the twins were there.

"I don't know," Hemlock answered. "Let's check."

He unbuckled the restraints and pulled the boy down to his knees. There was a silvery sheen of semen on his flat belly.

"Ew, look at this horrible mess!" Nightshade exclaimed, pointing to the cloudy smear on the smooth leather.

Hemlock slapped the boy's face.

"Clean that up, you pig!"

The boy licked the puddle of his own sperm with relish. Hemlock smacked his incandescent ass and pressed his face down against the leather.

A soft tone sounded from somewhere in the wall.

"Oh no, it can't be over," Nightshade said, distressed. "I wanted to give him an enema!"

"Don't fret, my darling," Hemlock said, his voice low and soothing. "We'll play more later."

The boy kissed all of their feet before he left, but Caitlin couldn't help noticing that he gave the most attention to hers.

———

Exhausted, Caitlin lay on her stomach on the leather bed, her head pillowed on Nightshade's thighs. She felt weirdly drained, as if every blow had poured energy from her body and into the slave's. Nightshade and Hemlock were twisting locks of her hair into bracelets around their wrists and giggling.

"How long have you been here, at Absinthe's?" Caitlin asked.

"What a silly question," Nightshade said, tilting her head against her brother's.

"Forever, of course," Hemlock said, separating a strand of her hair into sections and twining it into an elaborate braid.

"Did you know a girl named Eva Eiseman?" Caitlin asked, forcing nonchalance. She had no idea if this was the right time to ask, but she seemed unable to stop herself.

The fingers in her hair stilled.

"She wants to know about Eva," Hemlock said.

"Should we tell her? Look how pretty she is."

"I don't know. It might not be safe."

"I think we should tell her," Nightshade said, caressing the back of her neck.

"We were with her the night she was killed," Hemlock said, low voice full of the rich intonations of gossip. "She was an arrogant girl, headstrong, willful. She used to be Absinthe's favorite, before Jez."

Caitlin shut her eyes, focusing intensely enough to make her head throb, memorizing.

"She was in love with Jez. She told us they wanted a night on the town together. Normally that sort of thing is not permitted, but we were feeling indulgent. We, my sister and I, let them out that night."

Hemlock paused and the room was silent for long, ticking seconds. Caitlin raised up on her elbows, brows arched.

"Of course, we made her earn it, didn't we, darling." Hemlock stroked his sister's cheek and Nightshade smiled, remembering.

"It was quite the decathlon of endurance we put her through," Nightshade said. "Sensory deprivation, electricity, even. But she was determined and so we let her have her little adventure."

"We knew she would try to run away," Hemlock said. "But we also knew that she wouldn't get far."

Caitlin searched Hemlock's bright eyes for some revealing emotion, but saw nothing but her own curved reflection.

"Do you have any idea what happened to her?" Caitlin asked finally.

Nightshade and Hemlock exchanged wary glances.

"Who would do such a terrible thing?" Nightshade asked, looking away.

"We don't like to think about it," Hemlock said. "It's too upsetting."

"Let's talk about something more fun," Nightshade said, running her hands down Caitlin's spine.

"Yes, let's." Hemlock pressed his mouth to Caitlin's shoulder.

A soft knock on the door, then and Justine slipped quietly inside. She was dressed in some odd tattered uniform like something out of a "women in prison" movie.

"Excuse me, Master. Mistress," she said, bowing her head demurely. "It is nearly time for my session with Mistress Morrigan."

Caitlin nodded, inexplicably relieved.

"Of course," Hemlock said, pressing an alcoholic kiss to Caitlin's lips. "You were superb. Fabulous. A rare bird, Lady Morrigan."

"Maybe she'll play with us again soon," Nightshade said, pressing sticky lips to Caitlin's throat. She snuffled like an animal, inhaling the fragrance of Caitlin's skin. "She smells so delicious, I could just eat her up. She's so fresh."

Caitlin extracted herself from the twins' embrace as if untangling herself from the coils of a lazy but potentially dangerous serpent. They hardly seemed to acknowledge her absence, tongues flashing and whispers soft and dreamlike. Hemlock's fingers wandered up between his sister's open legs and she sighed, a sound too intimate to listen to from the outside. Justine took Caitlin's arm and closed the door on their incestuous passion.

29.

Justine hustled Caitlin into a dressing room done up in black and copper. Laid out on one of the low tables was the ensemble that Justine had put together for her. Something like a futuristic military uniform as designed by a horny comic book artist. Caitlin stripped quickly and examined each item with bemused disbelief as she slipped it on.

Thigh high, spit-shined leather boots with spiked heels and killer gloves, wrist length and snug to the curve of her knuckles. A high collared leather jacket that buckled tight to her waist and a leather g-string with silver studs of varying sizes, flat circles graduating to squat cones and finally tall spikes at the center, over her hidden labia. She had to stand with her legs slightly apart to avoid injury. She glanced in the full length mirror and was amazed at what she saw.

She saw a dominatrix. If she had seen her own picture in one of those fetish magazines, she would have believed that this was a tough woman, a woman who knew what she wanted and expected it NOW. There was no fear in that woman, no self-doubt. She laughed.

"What is it, Mistress?" Justine asked.

Caitlin nodded towards her own reflection.

"I can't believe it's really me."

Justine bowed her head to hide a smile.

"Soon you won't believe you were ever anything else."

She held up a pair of matte black metal handcuffs.

"Are you ready?" she asked.

For the second time in one night, Caitlin stood anxious in front of a door to one of the tiny rooms, wondering what was going to happen. Justine stood before her, handcuffed hands behind her back, hair hanging in her face. She looked back over her shoulder and winked.

"Give him a couple more seconds to stew ... " she whispered.

Caitlin nodded. She went over and over the premise that Justine had laid out, sure that she would make some awful mistake. It was not the same as playing for fun. This man was paying good money for this and if she did something wrong, he would be angry and demand a refund. Caitlin was sure she could not survive that humiliation.

But at the same time, the premise intrigued her. Justine had been concise and businesslike in describing it. A future society in which women rule and men are slaves kept alive only for the purpose of producing sperm for artificial insemination and doing jobs women consider beneath them such as housework. Caitlin was a cop. Justine a criminal. Her crime, preforming oral sex on a man. Her punishment, limited only by Caitlin's imagination. If she got stuck, Justine would prompt her, Bre'r Rabbit style. *Please don't whip me, please don't make me lick your boots, please don't throw me in the briar patch.*

But Caitlin felt strangely confident. In a curious way, this play-acting was very much like chronicling the adventures of Victoria Steele, her hardboiled heroine from the latest round of McNovels. Bookem Books had sent her a"bible" for the series that read very much like Justine's premise. What Vic Steele looks like, how she acts, where she lives, even how often per book she has sex and in how many ways. Within these strict guidelines, you are free to do what ever you can think of in six weeks.

Smiling slightly, Caitlin began to tell herself a story, one in which the drop-dead gorgeous redhead, the tough-as-nails and always uncompromising Vic Steele is posing as a dominatrix.

Justine half-turned, speaking softly.

"Showtime," she said.

———

The man crouching naked inside the room was utterly unremarkable. Late thirties with pale brown hair swept back from his soft, ordinary face. His eyes were dark and furtive like the eyes of a small scavenger.

Caitlin took a deep breath and pushed Justine into the room ahead of her. The girl crumpled prettily to the carpet.

"Kneel properly," Caitlin ordered and Justine scrambled to her knees, spine straight and head bowed.

"Citizen," she said, pitching her voice deep and authoritative. "You have been accused of a monstrous crime. The crime of performing oral sex on a subhuman male. How do you plead?"

"Guh ... guilty, Mistress." Justine whispered.

"I can't hear you," Caitlin bellowed. She wanted to laugh out loud, but she kept her mouth stern and unamused.

"Guilty, Mistress," Justine answered like a young recruit answering his drill sergeant.

"Slave." Caitlin snapped her fingers. "Get me a dildo."

The client gaped stupidly at her, his thin penis twitching.

"I am addressing the subhuman!" Caitlin barked and the man jumped as if stung, scrambling to the bureau and digging out a large rubber dick. He crawled across the floor and laid the ridiculous sex toy at Caitlin's feet.

"Citizen," Caitlin said. "I want you to demonstrate to me exactly what took place during your encounter with the subhuman male."

Justine's eyes went comicbook-wide. She was really very good at this.

"Please," she whimpered. "Have mercy, Mistress."

"Do not speak to me again." Caitlin kicked the dildo with the toe of her spiked boot. It rolled and thudded against Justine's knee. "Begin now."

Caitlin let herself smile just a little as Justine took the dildo in her shaking hands and proceeded to fellate it with reluctant lips. In the corner of her eye, she could see the client breathing like a hard-worked horse. She let the moment spin out a while, silently amused.

"Enough," she spat.

Justine bowed her head and laid the shiny dildo on the floor.

"The punishment for such perversion is fifty lashes."

Justine threw herself down at Caitlin's feet, sobbing.

"Stop sniveling and take your punishment like a Woman!"

Caitlin's blood moved hot under her skin. She felt a burning sort of exhalation. It was working and more than that, it was wonderful, unlike anything she had ever felt. The closest comparison was the rush she felt when the words flowed like a river from the tips of her fingers. It made her feel strong, unstoppable as a force of nature.

She tied Justine's cuffs to a heavy iron ring set into the wall and ordered the client to fetch a supple, many-tailed flogger. She laid into Justine's delicately scarred flesh with relish, laying out long candy-pink welts and it felt so good, heady as sweet liquor in her belly. Justine was counting and crying and the client was panting, sweat glossing his unremarkable face.

"Fifty," Justine cried. "Thank you, Mistress."

Unbound, the girl collapsed and crawled across the floor to press kisses to Caitlin's shiny boots. Reaching down to clutch the narrow curve of Justine's jaw in her gloved hand, Caitlin tipped the girl's flushed face up to hers.

"Because of the seriousness of your crime, I am afraid corporal punishment will not be enough to correct your perverted ways."

Justine struggled to bow her head, but Caitlin held firm, keeping her face turned up.

"For a period of time designated by me," Caitlin said, stroking the girl's hot cheek. "You will serve as my personal slave, performing all the menial tasks reserved for subhuman males. If you are going to fornicate with males, then you must live like one yourself until you understand the error of your ways."

She bucked a dildo harness around Justine's hips and a heavy collar around her long white neck. The dildo was bright fleshy-pink and protruded comically.

"While you wear these accouterments, you are no better than a subhuman male. When I feel that you have learned your lesson you will be reinstated to full Womanhood."

Justine pressed her forehead to the floor.

"I understand, Mistress."

Caitlin stalked away and sat in a high backed chair.

"Your first duty as a slave will be to clean and polish my boots." She snapped her fingers again. "And be quick about it."

Justine turned to the bureau and took out a soft cloth.

"No," Caitlin scolded. "Use your tongue."

Caitlin heard a soft sound from the client, and when she let herself see him out of the corner of her eye, she saw that he was masturbating furiously. She guessed this must be a good sign, but it was still hard not to laugh.

Justine threw herself into the task of bathing the shiny leather of Caitlin's boots with her long, flexible tongue. Caitlin took a hardcover book titled *The Correct Sadist* from the table and opened it, pretending to read while she secretly watched the client. She could have been staring right at him and he wouldn't have noticed. He was utterly absorbed in watching Justine and pulling on his skinny erection.

Caitlin picked up the dropped cloth and tossed it at the client. He grunted with surprise as it struck him in the chest.

"Do not allow one drop of filthy, subhuman secretions to stain my carpet," Caitlin said, biting back a grin.

He bobbed his head and held the cloth over his leaking purple dick.

"Continue," Caitlin ordered and Justine went back to work.

The same soft tone that had ended her play with Jeremiah sounded from within the walls and seconds later, the client came silently, his beet-red face twisting as he caught the spurting semen in folds of the cloth. Justine sat back on her haunches and winked.

The client extracted his neatly folded street clothes from a drawer in the bureau and dressed quickly without eye contact. He dug out his wallet and pressed a crumpled wad of bills into Justine's hand.

"See you next week, Justine," he said without turning around as he scuttled out and slammed the door.

Caitlin just stared at the door for a long time, amused. She found her mind wandering back to Jeremiah and the exuberant kisses lavished on her feet. She jumped a little when Justine wrapped her arms around her ribs and tucked a folded lump of money into the top of her jacket.

"150 each, baby," she cooed, lips inches from Caitlin's ear.

Caitlin shuddered and pulled away.

"I thought you said it was 500 each."

Justine laughed.

"150 tip," she said. "That's on top of the five."

"Six hundred and fifty dollars for that?" Caitlin was dumbstruck.

"550, actually," Justine replied. "The house takes a 20 percent cut of the fee, of course, but the tip is all ours."

For an elastic minute, Caitlin could not force words through her frozen lips. It had to be wrong. A sin. The implications of that kind of money made her head spin. 550 dollars for one hour of preposterous playacting. Unbelievable. Fabulous.

Justine's face was mock solemn and in her eyes she saw an echo of Absinthe.

"I just made 550 dollars," Caitlin told her.

Another long silent minute and then mad laughter burst out of Caitlin like a infant's first real breath and she pulled Justine into her arms.

"550 fucking dollars," she sang.

Justine smirked in her embrace.

"So are you happy?" she asked, seemingly content to be tightly held.

"Yes," Caitlin answered, still grinning. "You were great."

"No," Justine pulled away. "*You* were great. I told you, you're a natural."

Caitlin shrugged. She made her voice breathy and low, her lips a sexy sneer. "Piece of cake, baby," she drawled.

Justine had probably never read Vic Steele, but she laughed anyway and Caitlin laughed too, and she felt like Queen of the World.

30.

Back in the fray and flush with her new success, Caitlin let Justine massage her feet while men with subtle ties and gleaming manicures introduced themselves with much more class but no less hunger than the men from the Crypt. One dark-eyed boy with a power chin and a celebrity smile asked respectfully if he might join Justine on the floor before her. She shrugged as if it hardly made a difference and he flushed, sinking, smitten to his knees.

Caitlin realized, as he reverently removed her other boot and pressed his mouth to her stockinged foot, that she had seen him before. He was one of those TV hunkpuppets from a popular teen drama. Instead of laughing, she closed her eyes and smiled, losing herself in the luxurious sensations. She could feel her objectivity sloughing off like an outgrown skin, but she didn't want to pull its thick, unfeeling substance back over her sensitive new flesh.

The hours seemed to pass differently inside this place. Each mouthful of wine, each kiss seemed to go on and on and the music of the lash was an inescapable rhythm. A beating heart that drove the players to follow its tempo as they danced their carefully sadistic waltzes. There was only one flaw, one itching dissonance that brought Caitlin's eyes back again and again to the ticking clock.

"Where is he?" she asked, finally, surprised that she had spoken aloud.

"Oh, you know," Justine said. "He comes when he comes."

She looked away, pressing her lips to Caitlin's foot.

Caitlin frowned, but said nothing.

She was staring into the poisonous green depths of a fragile glass of absinthe when Hellebore spoke her name.

"Morrigan," she said. "Absinthe would like to see you in his chambers."

Hellebore's twisted visage didn't ever seem to get boring. Everytime Caitlin saw her, the malformed chaos riveted her gaze, transcending politeness. She had to force herself to look away, to wonder at the meaning of this summons. Frowning, Caitlin stood and dismissed the heartthrob, leaning down to kiss Justine's forehead.

"I'll be back," she told the girl.

"I don't think so," Justine said, her voice almost too small to hear.

"What?" Caitlin turned Justine's face up to hers. "What do you mean?"

Justine shrugged.

"We all have our masters," she said.

Caitlin held the girl's face a minute longer, then released her.

"Hellebore," she said, keeping her eyes on Justine. "Tell him I'm otherwise engaged."

Justine looked up, eyes bright with surprise and joy. She pressed her lips to Caitlin's boot.

The polished depth of Hellebore's good eye reflected another sort of surprise, laced with subtle approval. She nodded and turned to go.

31.

Practicing Tai Chi in her livingroom, Caitlin struggled to center herself, to order her whirling thoughts. The events of the night before were like bullets lodged in the soft tissue of her brain, shiny and cold, inescapable. There was no doubt now. She was in deep, deeper than she ever could have imagined. Breathing slowly, she fought her tormented imagination, reaching for the calm thoughtlessness at her center. When the phone rang, she spun towards it, breath caught in her chest. Her machine was full of unplayed messages that she hadn't bothered to erase, so she reached over and picked up the receiver.

"Hello?" Her heart was still pounding.

"How could you?" It was Mike. His words were thick and slurred. He sounded drunk.

"What ... ?"

"DON'T ... " He paused, silent. "Don't play dumb with me, Caitlin." She tried to speak and he cut her off.

"Did you really think I wouldn't know?" His voice was dark with molten rage. "Did you genuinely believe that you could fuck our primary suspect and I wouldn't find out?"

Sick vertigo tumbled in her belly. She could not speak.

"How could you let that freak touch you?"

Caitlin narrowed her eyes, anger and shame and indignation swirling together inside her, forming a toxic brew.

"I don't know where you got that idea," she said.

"He fucking told me, that's where."

Slow fury in her veins. Bastard had no fucking right, but that was a whole other argument.

"I am not under investigation," she said, feeling sullen, violated.

"Maybe you should be."

"What for, wounding an officer's pride?" Caitlin could feel her new-found Mistress persona unfolding, straightening her spine, setting contemptuous fire in her voice. "You don't even know the half of it."

"It's true, isn't it?" His voice was suddenly soft. If only he had kept yelling. Guilt folded her in its familiar embrace.

"I kept hoping maybe he was lying, just trying to fuck with me, but he isn't, is he?"

Caitlin closed her eyes.

"No," she said. The word was a razor blade in her throat. Her voice cracked.

Silence over the line and Caitlin could not have filled it if her life depended on it. The click of the connection being severed was huge, like the meaty finality of a guillotine blade, cutting her off with appalling permanence. She stood with the dead receiver in her hand until the bland mindlessness of the dial tone gave way to the indignant honking of a phone off the hook.

She made a low choking sound and yanked the phone out of the wall. It tumbled out of her shaking hands and she screamed and started breaking things.

When her anger had spent itself, a strange cold calm rushed in to fill the empty space. She methodically swept away the fragmented evidence of her rage and sat down to make herself beautiful for the Club.

32.

Sitting with Belladonna by the bar, Caitlin watched the lace curtain, her face an expressionless shell over her seething emotions. The idle wash of Belladonna's catty gossip bathed her in mindless sound. She heard only fragments.

"I mean it's not as if he's never done anything like this before ... not showing up for a whole night like that. Who knows when he'll be back."

Belladonna's monologue ceased abruptly and Caitlin turned her head towards the new silence.

"Hellebore," Belladonna said, voice cool and poisonous.

Hellebore was standing still and dour with her good eye locked away under a thousand feet of ice.

"Morrigan," Hellebore said, turning away. "Come with me please."

Belladonna arched an eyebrow. Caitlin gathered herself and rose to follow.

"I'll see you later," Belladonna said, her eyes making it quite clear that any and all new dirt must be shared at once. Caitlin nodded, thinking suddenly of Wilson and the hierarchy of information.

Hellebore led her soundlessly to Absinthe's chambers. Instead of wasting her energy interrogating the woman, who would undoubtedly refuse to answer any questions anyway, she began to focus on her anger. Absinthe had no right to go fucking around in her personal life. And how the hell did he find out about her relationship with Mike in the first place? The more she thought about it, the angrier she became.

By the time Hellebore opened the door of Absinthe's rooms and stepped aside to let her in, Caitlin was furious. She felt as if blue sparks would fly from her eyes and her fingertips, as if she could break down the walls with a wave of her hand.

Absinthe was lounging in bed, skinny body draped in a dark silk night shirt. His lower lip was scabbed and swollen. Jez sat behind him, brushing the tangles from his hair. He fussed at the girl and complained like a petulant child.

"Ow," he whined. "Must you pull so hard?"

Caitlin smiled, feeling the heat of her anger struggling behind her clenched teeth. If Mike did that to his mouth, then he got away lucky compared to what she would do.

"Allow me," she said, holding out her hand for the brush.

Jez glanced up and looked away, fearful and silent. She let Caitlin take the brush from her shaking hands. Her grey eyes flashed with some secret lightning as she scuttled away and knelt at Absinthe's feet.

Caitlin ran the brush gently through Absinthe's hair, mindful of the knots, taking time to smooth each one with minimal pain. Her knuckles strained up against her skin as she gripped the brush's silver handle. She could feel him starting to relax against her.

"What did you tell him?" she asked, her lips inches his neck.

"What?" She could feel him go tense and wary.

"You heard me."

"I don't know what you're talking about."

She sank her fingers into his hair and gripped it tightly.

"Yes, you do," she said.

"Let go of me." She could hear anger rising in his voice.

"Answer me," she said.

"Let go." He began to struggle, his fingers scrabbling uselessly against hers.

She held onto his hair for a moment longer, then let go. He stumbled away from her, his face flushed, eyes flashing. He trembled, body coiled tight like an angry mink.

"Don't ever do that to me," he spat. He was breathing hard, almost panting. She leaned closer, pressing her advantage.

"How did you know Mike Kiernan and I were involved?"

He narrowed his eyes.

"I don't have to tell you anything."

Caitlin threw the brush as hard as she could at a mirror above his head. It shattered dramatically. He flinched as silver splinters rained down around them.

"Yes, you do," she said, her voice low and reasonable.

His eyes were as bright and sharp as the mirror fragments littering the carpet. Glass crunched under her shoes. There was less than a foot between them.

A part of her was screaming to stop, telling her that she was ruining everything, but there was heat in his strange eyes as she reached out and touched his bruised cheek and she knew that something irreversible was happening. It was not anger that flushed his skin and quickened his breath. It was desire.

"Hellebore told me," he said, showing his teeth.

"What?" She closed the space between them.

"About you and Michael Kiernan."

Caitlin smiled.

"How did she find out?"

He licked his lips.

"I don't know."

She gripped his cheeks between thumb and fingers and sat, straddling him. His cock flexed against her pubis. He shivered.

"Are you sure?"

"Yes," he said. "I'm sure."

Her mouth was inches from his. She let go of his face and let her hand slide back under his hair. As she wrapped her fingers in the fragrant tangles, a soft sound echoed in his throat and she felt him give in. It was a powerful, almost physical sensation, the hot combat of their wills escalating, burning brighter and stronger until she broke through to this exquisite surrender. His sudden vulnerability was the most intensely erotic thing she had ever experienced. She understood suddenly, how a man must feel when a woman opens herself up and lets him in for the first time. The heat between her legs was intolerable. She pressed her mouth to his with a hunger deeper and more frightening than she could have ever imagined.

The torn skin of his lips broke open under her vicious kiss and blood slicked her probing tongue. She forgot her anger, forgot the fight with Mike. Her fingers tore through the flimsy silk, exposing his hot flesh to her hands and teeth.

When she was able to think again, she remembered Jez.

Absinthe was lying beside her, holding one of her hands in both of his, breathing softly. She wiped sweat from her eyes and scanned the room. It took several passes before she saw the girl wedged into the far corner near the bathroom. Her face was utterly blank, like a lifelike sculpture of herself. It took a moment for her to notice Caitlin. When she did, she burst into tears.

She pulled her hand away from Absinthe and went over to where the girl huddled, sobbing.

"Jez," she said softly. "What is it."

She shook her head, inconsolable. Caitlin took the girl in her arms and Jez clung to her with a strange desperation.

"I love you," Jez said.

Caitlin stroked the girl's smooth scalp, distracted and fascinated by the vulnerability of her skin, the delicate angles of her bones.

Absinthe propped himself up on one elbow, grinning lasciviously.

"My beautiful ladies," he cooed. "My Mistress and my slave." He held out his hands to them. "Come back to bed."

Caitlin looked down at Jez. There were still tears on her face, but her expression had become weirdly calm. They went together back to Absinthe's bed.

33.

After that, it all just seemed to flow from some inner place for Caitlin. The Frenchman who had kissed her hand in the hallway that first night began pestering her for a scene until giving in and beating his leathery ass with a studded rubber paddle was pure bliss. She dressed in Justine's gowns and allowed herself to be taken shopping by eager clients. Prowling through shoe stores with a cat smile and a haughty toss of her hair, she would turn up her nose at pair after pair while some erstwhile Walter Mitty would follow with his credit card clutched in sweaty fingers. She stood for fittings at Body Worship and the Noose while busy hands measured and draped and sheathed her long body in butter-soft leather and glossy latex. It seemed that there had never been any other way. She felt pampered and spoiled, special. Finally, she was the favorite one, unique and appreciated, as if there had never been a new baby sister so full of talent and brilliance. There was just Mistress Morrigan, the only child and star of everyone's show.

She was walking down Broadway on a thick summer afternoon with a bottle of expensive juice in one hand and a shopping bag from Patricia Fields in the other when she realized she was on Tenth Street. She had just ditched the client whose obsession had financed her latest shopping spree and she was walking without destination when she found herself by the subtle doorway of Dark Books.

There was a buzzer. She peered through the murky glass and saw nothing but shadows. Draining the last of her juice, she set the bottle down on the sidewalk and rang the bell before she could change her mind.

A harsh tone responded to the voice of the bell and she pushed the door open.

Inside was a museum. Bookshelves reaching to the cathedral ceiling, crammed with richly bound volumes of every description. Glass cases displayed odd leather and metal devices as if they were gold and diamonds. In one case, an clockwork flower of pitted metal whose spiked petals blossomed outward with the turn of a screw. Beside it was a beautifully tooled chastity belt and a leather collar for the penis, ringed on the inside with fine golden nails. Paintings and woodcuts showed women and men being deliciously tortured by fantastical beasts. The air inside the shop tasted ancient, like the dead breath released from violated tombs.

Hellebore was there, sitting on the floor before a low table. There was a heavy book open before her, its fragile pages scrawled with disturbing shapes in ancient, faded ink. She wore white cotton gloves that made her look absurdly like a Disney cartoon.

"Condanna," she said. "1725. A very dark lady. Most of her work was burned. This diary and a single torn canvas are all that survived."

She gestured to a ruined painting sealed under glass. Caitlin could make out a figure, a young boy with raven's wings sprouting from his well-muscled back. His hands were bound, his eyes and nose hidden beneath black cloth. Only his lips were visible, so full and finely rendered, they seemed to be waiting for a kiss. The rips across the canvas looked like gaping wounds in the boy's delicate flesh.

"It's very ... unsettling."

Hellebore carefully turned the page of the frail book. The next page was a study of several long-limbed figures in fabulously intricate bondage. Underneath, frantic, sharp-edged handwriting. Italian, maybe, or Spanish.

"She knew," Hellebore said. "She devoted her life to the quest for the perfect slave, the ultimate submissive. She understood the way it really works."

"The way what works?" Caitlin took a step closer.

"I'm very busy right now," Hellebore told her without looking up.

Caitlin refused to be brushed off.

"You have a really amazing collection. I'd like to come by some time when you aren't so busy, maybe hear a little bit of history on some of these things. Who knows? It might teach me something about myself."

Hellebore looked up, dark eye unreadable, pale eye wild in its lunatic travels.

"Are you in love with Absinthe?" she asked.

Caitlin was so shocked by this question that she found herself answering truthfully.

"No, I don't think so. I think I'm more in love with the person I become when I'm with him."

Hellebore seemed to savor this answer like a wine-taster, nodding thoughtfully.

"He's changed," Hellebore said.

Caitlin frowned. Unsure of how to respond to this, she held her tongue.

"Jez has changed him and you have changed him. He is not himself. He behaves erratically. He makes irrational decisions. He has become fixated and obsessed with Jez and now with you. He talks of nothing else."

Caitlin nodded, unsure of what to say. She thought of Absinthe's sudden submission that first night, of his unending hunger for humiliation. She wondered if anyone else besides Jez knew of the King's newest diversion.

"But you," Hellebore continued, closing her ancient book and sliding it into a heavy plastic cover before stripping off the silly gloves. "You are a rare woman. You have potential that even Absinthe cannot imagine."

She turned her ravaged face away, hiding in the inky shadows and Caitlin felt a curious, cold relief.

"I'll see you at the club tonight," Caitlin said.

Hellebore waved a dismissive hand.

Caitlin pressed her palm against the smoky glass of the door, allowing herself one last glance back at the archives and their meticulous keeper. Hellebore looked up, her good eye like glass in her cold face.

"Things are changing," she said. "I know you feel it."

Without answering, Caitlin pushed the door open and escaped into the hot city, knowing that Hellebore was right. Things were changing.

Weeks passed in the liquid dreamtime of the Club and Caitlin did not go back to her apartment. She spent her days exhausted in Absinthe's arms and her nights abusing clients or taking lessons from Belladonna or the twins.

"Always aim below the tailbone and above the lowest curve of the cheeks." Belladonna would explain, stroking the luscious ass of a little dark haired renaissance angel named Bettina with a richly tooled flogger. "Do not allow the tails to wrap around the hips. When you are through, you should have an almost V shaped pattern of diagonal welts, like this."

The variety of implements for the administration of pain amazed and delighted Caitlin. Whips and paddles, crops and straps and bamboo canes, even innocent objects like hair-brushes and wooden spoons. Each had its own distinctive temperament, its own unmistakable signature. She mastered them all, each in turn.

The twins showed her how to properly insert a bardex enema nozzle and taught her the ins and outs of play piercing. But it was Little Nightshade who taught her that most difficult and dangerous of skills, use of the much misunderstood bullwhip.

"When norms think of sadomasochism," she said, the long, oiled length of glossy leather flicking out softly once twice and then a vicious crack that rang in Caitlin's ears. "They automatically think of the bullwhip." Crack, again, that gunshot punctuation. "But in reality, it's one of the rarest implements, the true queen of pain. Tell her, Hemlock."

Caitlin was the perfect student, and it was not long before she had surpassed her teachers in cruelty and creativity. The other dominants were mixed in their opinions of the new girl. A good handful disliked her without reserve, hating her for her closeness with Absinthe and the way that submissives flocked around her like she was gold and emeralds and sweet sugar. On the other hand, there were women like Mistress Freya, a dark eyed goddess who had been there longer than anyone else. She took an immediate liking to Caitlin and taught her to tie knots like a sailor. Her knowledge of the human anatomy and how to stretch its limits was invaluable in teaching Caitlin the art of erotic restraint. She kept the catty ones under control and those who persisted had to deal with Absinthe.

He would watch her from his high backed velvet chair, boots propped up on a crouching slave and Jez sprawled across his lap. No matter where she was or what she was doing, he always seemed to be watching her with those unnatural eyes. His secret submission was never forgotten. Its flavor was in every touch, every glance.

———————

In bed alone on this latest of a string of long, Jezless nights, he pressed kisses to the soft skin of her wrist and spoke against her flesh.

"Sometimes I wish we could leave here."

Caitlin tried to soothe him, but his eyes were manic, his gestures jerky and strange. More and more nights were like this lately, Jez off with some millionaire in a ten thousand dollar tryst set up by the ever-present Hellebore, and Absinthe as clingy as a child, full of strange talk and stranger desire.

"You could leave," he whispered, face pressed into her throat.

"Now why would I want to leave?" Caitlin stroked his tangled hair. "I just got here."

He continued as if he hadn't heard her.

"I think even Jez could leave. You're both so much stronger than I am."

She wanted to tell him no, of course that wasn't true, but it was and they both knew it.

"I'm a hot house flower," Absinthe said, almost too soft to hear. "A creature of this world. Do you have any idea how long I've been doing this?"

"No," she answered, ritualisticly, they way she did every time.

"Every session, every submissive, they take a little bite out of your soul. They take and take and leave nothing but emptiness behind."

He looked up into her face, eyes wide and hungry.

"I am more open with you than I've ever been, but I have nothing left to show you. There's nothing left inside me now. The mask is all that's left. Absinthe." He made a soft spitting noise. "Absinthe is all that's left."

He pulled away from her, straightening his narrow back and brushing hair out of his eyes.

"You love it here because it's so new and so free, but that freedom is a lie. What do you think your newfound worshipers would do if they ever saw me spank you. They would hate you. They would tear you apart. The roles we play here are as strict as the roles of housewife and whore. Inflexible."

No tears then, just empty eyes staring into the shifting depths of a glass of absinthe.

"Can't we go somewhere? You, me and Jez." He drank deep and dropped the glass to the carpet. It rolled away, unbroken. "I could leave with you, if you'd have me. We could be a family. We could go somewhere ... "

Then he would press his hungry mouth against her throat, hurt her until she hurt back and love would begin again, vicious, like the first time.

———————————

Caitlin could feel her old life dissolving as if it were a dream from which she had been awakened too fast. During a public humiliation scene staged in Central Park for a group of German businessmen, she was nearly arrested with Justine and Bettina. For the first time since the argument, she found herself thinking of Mike, remembering how it used to be.

Sagging in the plush limousine with the girls' leashes in her gloved hand, she felt suddenly overloaded, maxed out. She thought of Absinthe's despairing words, of submissives that eat your soul and of every hungry, clutching client in the last few weeks. Like the crash after a sugar rush, this sudden wave of depression had her craving the simple pleasure of Mike's embrace and that craving was followed by an even colder guilt.

She promised herself that she would go home in the morning, see if he had left her a message, maybe even call him. Underneath, she was sure that Mike was a part of the old world and that the woman she used to be and the woman she was now could not, by the laws of physics, occupy the same space at the same time.

34.

Mike and Eric in Callahan's, drinking. Eric was engaged in a rambling monologue directed at the bartender, the bottle of Dos Equis in front of him, God, and anyone else who would listen.

"So I'm cruising down 14TH and here's this sweet little uniform looking all in distress and shit and of course I gotta stop. Detective Horsecock at your service, sweetheart. Next thing I know, I catch this Chelsea Ripper thing like a bad case of the fucking clap. I got reporters crawling all over me. I swear to God, I can't even jerk off without eight guys asking me how it feels. If I don't get some kinda break in this bitch soon, I'm gonna end up shooting somebody. I don't sleep. I can't remember what my wife looks like. It's crazy."

His eyes were dull and bloodshot in cradles of swollen flesh. Threads of silver seemed to have sprung up over night in his thick black hair. His face was cut in several places from shaving in the third floor men's room with hands that shook from too much coffee.

Mike could not look into his friend's haggard face. Instead, he looked down into the depths of a shot of Irish whisky, guilt a bitter chaser whose flavor coated and infected everything. He had looked his partner dead in the eye and told him that Absinthe was covered, that they should look into some other angle. Watching Eric starving for leads in this case, chasing the faintest ghosts and sifting through the most hopeless crumbs, was physically painful, knowing that he had sacrificed his friend to save his own ass. But it was as if his sin of omission had taken on a life of its own. The longer he let it eat him, the less control he seemed to have over his own actions. Not a day passed that he didn't replay the fight with Caitlin over and over in his mind, inventing brilliant comebacks and scorching declarations that could not be denied. He dreamed of fucking her, of making her beg him to take her back. Masturbating in bitter solitude, he imagined taking her by force, guilt and shame drenching him like his own lonely sweat.

He could not keep his mind on his work. Forcing himself to care why some asshole drug dealer shot some other asshole drug dealer had always been hard. Now it was nearly impossible. Cases began to run together in his mind. The endless parade of shootings and cuttings and bludgeonings was nothing but blurred scenery behind obsessive thoughts of Caitlin.

He remembered the first time with her, how he had been so nervous and so amazed that yes, she really did want him. He thought of her voice, of the way she would sometimes laugh when she came.

"Why are you laughing?" he had asked, not sure if he should be insulted or flattered.

"Because I feel so happy," she told him.

So many memories. How she used to pick things up with her long toes. How fierce and beautiful she looked sparring with the other students at the dojo. Lying in bed with her, he had told her about Maura and she had been thoughtful, understanding.

On their first date, she had asked him if he was the good cop or the bad cop.

"I'm the bad cop," he told her

The silent bartender refilled Mike's shot glass and traded Eric's empty for a fresh one.

"I tell ya, Bobby," Eric said, shaking his head.

The bartender nodded, coolly sympathetic.

"It'll go down," he said, running his rag over the murky surface of the bar.

"Yeah." Eric drained the bottle in two long swallows and set it down empty. There was no hope in his voice at all. "Sure it will."

Mike threw back his new shot and motioned for it to be filled again. The bartender poured with one eyebrow high, but remained silent.

Staring into the whisky's golden depths he thought of Caitlin's hair, its rich perfume, the way it framed her face with its unappologetic luxury. He thought of the severed curl tied with the violet ribbon, glinting against Absinthe's pale fingers. Washed in thick, maudlin sorrow, he emptied the shot glass.

With the liquor's heat came a plan, a shining idea born whole and sudden from the grey surf of his vast depression. He was suddenly certain that if he could just see her, face to face, then he would know for sure if there was anything left. If there was even the tiniest flicker of that lost connection, if he looked into her eyes and saw even a drop of love ... well, he would take it from there. Until then, there would be no peace for him. He pulled himself to his feet, slightly unsteady but full of conviction.

"You want a cab, Kiernan?" the bartender asked.

Mike shook his head, laying a crumpled wad of cash on the bar.

Eric turned to his partner, seeming to see him for the first time.

"You OK, man?" he asked, frowning.

"Ask me tomorrow," Mike said.

He stood for a moment longer, then walked away.

35.

Caitlin was exhausted as she fumbled in her bag for her keys. The sun was rising over the spiked skyline to the east and its dull orange rays made her head throb. She didn't see Mike until he reached out and touched her shoulder.

Immediately defensive, she spun away, eyes wide and ready to fight. When she saw it was Mike she relaxed but only a little. His suit looked days old and he needed to shave. He smelled like overboiled coffee and car deodorizer and rank liquor-sweat.

"Caitlin," he said. His voice was low and thick.

She watched him, body tight, eyes wary.

"What do you want?"

"I just wanna talk to you for a second."

She turned away, heart manic under her ribcage.

"I don't think this is a good time," she said. She felt nauseous, exhausted. This wasn't the way she had imagined it. She needed time to think.

"It's important," he said

He stood with feet planted wide, belligerent, like an angry kid.

"If it's really important, then call me later today, after we both get some sleep, OK?"

She stepped up to the door, keys now found and in her hand.

He reached out and grabbed her arm, fingers rough and clumsy. His face was inches from hers, breath hot and ripe with the perfume of hard liquor.

"No, it's got to be now."

She froze, shocked into stillness, her body rigid with indignation. There was a tight, animal smile locked across her face. This was madness.

"I'm sorry." He let her go and staggered back, covering his face. "I can't ... It's just ... "

"Mike," Caitlin said, her voice icy. "Go home, you're drunk."

"Yeah, I'm fucking drunk." New anger flared in his glassy eyes. "What the fuck would you do if the woman you love ran off with some perverted fucking murderer who makes a total asshole out of you in front of the entire fucking world."

Caitlin felt cold fingers squeezing the breath from her throat. He was ranting, saying something about transfer and reassignment, but all she could hear was *woman you love*. She felt dizzy, weightless.

He was crying, shaking his head, and it was appalling, something that should only been done in private not displayed on the early morning street for anyone to see. His face was contorted, monstrous, dehumanized somehow in its anguish. It reminded her of her father.

"I love you," he was saying, the words melting into each other and burning her like napalm. "I just fucking love you."

He wiped tears and snot on the back of his hand, a pitiful, child-like gesture.

"I though maybe you loved me, too." He took a step closer to her. "Don't you? Under there somewhere, don't you feel anything?"

Caitlin couldn't answer. She felt fossilized, as if her warm, breathing body had been stealthily replaced by unfeeling stone.

"I gotta know," he breathed, taking another unsteady step. "Do you love me at all? Even just a little?"

There was a single, crystalline point in the flow of seconds where Caitlin felt the presence of a vital crossroad. He was close enough to touch, and if she wanted, she could draw him, unresisting, into her arms and say that one tiny word of affirmation. She could take him up to her apartment and lay him down in her bed, take off his jacket and his shoes, kiss his forehead and let him sleep. Then maybe talk about it, try to work it out over coffee later, when things made more sense. Go back. If she could only force her lips to speak that single, simple word.

But she could not, and she felt the moment pass, felt the opportunity slip away forever into the land of the might have been. Maybe there really was another universe in which she had pulled him close and said, *yes, I do love you.* But in this world, Shroedinger's cat was dead, hopelessly, irreversibly dead, and she felt an aching sense of emptiness and loss.

"Go home, Mike," she heard herself say.

"I gotta know," he said, grabbing her arms. "Tell me."

"Get off me," she hissed, pulling away, but he would not give up.

"I know you do." He was pinning her against the wall and there was bad, crazy hunger in his eyes. "Say you love me."

She struggled grimly, but in spite of his drunkenness, he still had almost a hundred pounds on her and he was crushing her wrists, pressing the length of his body against her. And, despite her anger, she still didn't want to hurt him.

"Say it," he whispered, gripping a handful of her hair and turning her face to his. "Say you love me."

Something snapped in Caitlin, and she was washed in sudden calm. She went still and dead in his arms and when he relaxed his grip, running his fingers up over her breasts, her hands broke loose and flashed out, one gripping his throat and the other, his balls. With the lower hand, she twisted viciously and with the other, she applied slow pressure, forcing him to his knees.

She let herself go down to her knees with him, her grip unrelenting. His face was purple, killing mad like a cornered animal, twisted with hard pain. She gave one last brutal squeeze and pushed him away. He collapsed, clutching his wounded manhood and wheezing helplessly.

There was no joy in victory, only a huge coldness, like the vast black vacuum of deep space. She stood over him and saw in the heaving and defeated curve of his back, the ruin of her old life. Mistress Morrigan had destroyed the last remaining fragment of a life that belonged to Caitlin Anne McCullough. There was no longer any going back.

She watched as he dragged himself to his feet, coughing and retching. He looked at her and if she had seen hate in those eyes, she could have sealed herself off forever, but instead she saw huge and hopeless pain that seemed to fill the world with its vicious dimensions. And underscoring that pain, a heavy backbeat of shame and self loathing. When he turned and walked away with his body curved in on itself and utterly defeated, she was almost grateful.

36.

The air conditioning was on the fritz. Clunky fans halfheartedly stirred the hot, leaden air. Limp detectives fanned themselves with crime scene photos. Ties came off and sleeves were rolled up. Sweat flowed, tempers flared, and the shift had just begun.

"Please, God," Nolan begged, eyes turned up to the ceiling. "Let that fucking phone ring."

The other detectives grunted in agreement. The same dark prayer was in everyone's mind. Let somebody die in this sizzling slice of the big bad city. Or more specifically, let somebody get murdered.

"It's too fucking hot to kill anybody," Demski said, rolling a wet can of Coke over his forehead.

Carrera was the only one who didn't look wilted. Her damp hair was pulled up off her neck, her caramel skin glossy with sweat, but instead of detracting from her beauty, it simply made her look unbearably sexy, as if she had just tumbled out of bed. Her thin blouse was nearly transparent with perspiration, revealing the outline of her lacy bra.

Eric was in no mood to appreciate this fact. He was feeling hot and surly, running on fumes. His desk was buried in paperwork. He could smell his own armpits. The Chelsea Ripper case was still primary in his mind and he chewed at it every day with increasing desperation, but death went on the Rotten Apple and no one in Homicide could afford monogamy.

Mike was late. When he arrived he looked terrible, eyes bleak and shadowed.

"Yo, Buddy." Eric peered at his partner over the mountains of paperwork. "You get hit by a truck on the way to work or what?"

Mike shook his head, silent.

The bureaucratic quagmire in front of him began to suck Eric back down before he could pursue the point.

The shift continued on its merry way, bringing the usual parade of meaningless cruelty and astonishing stupidity. It was nearly midnight when Eric approached his brooding partner.

"Hey, Mike," he said. "Take a ride with me. I wanna talk to this Parker chick again."

Mike looked up as if startled.

"Who?"

"Ginelle Parker," Eric said. "Her boyfriend threw her baby out the window, remember."

"Oh, yeah, right." He ran his hand over his eyes, distracted. "Bring Nolan."

"Fuck Nolan," Eric said. "You know you're the only boy for me."

"I don't know, man," Mike muttered. "I'm just not feeling up to it."

"Come on, Mikey." Eric dangled the keys to the Fury in front of his eyes. "I'll buy you a pastrami sandwich."

Mike smiled, just a little. The contrast against the deadness of his shadowed eyes made it that much more painful. It hit Eric again how bad his partner looked. It had been weeks since they had really spoken. This Ripper thing had eaten everything in Eric's life. It was time to get out from under it.

"We'll go to L-man's, OK?"

"I don't know, Eric."

"Come on, man, don't make me beg."

"I just ... "

"If I take Nolan, he'll be trying to feel me up every two seconds and we'd probably both get killed."

Mike's smile grew a fraction of an inch.

"Yeah, alright, let's go."

37

The slaves were being prepared for the evening's festivities. Heads were being shaved, bodies bathed and oiled. Justine, like the other professional submissives, took turns seeing to the care and maintenance of Absinthe's fulltime slaves. It fell on her that night to care for Jez, not that she ever needed to be shaved. Her scalp was always smooth and shiny, her forehead round and blank without even the tiniest hint of eyebrows. Rumor had it that Absinthe had all her hair electronically destroyed.

Justine washed Jez carefully, soft cloth working around the tight leather of the chastity belt. She could just imagine how funky Jez must be under that thing. No one she knew had ever seen her without it. She was rubbing scented oil into Jez's pale flesh when the girl leaned heavily against her as if she could barely support her own weight.

"I need ... " Her voice was tiny, breathless.

Justine frowned.

"What is it?"

"Morrigan," she whispered. "Where is she?"

"I don't know, honey," Justine said.

"It's all falling apart." Her eyes rolled fearfully towards the partially open door. "You see how he is."

Justine hushed her, pulling her closer.

"Don't talk like that," she said, stroking the girl's smooth head.

"I don't want to be with him anymore. He's different. I'm afraid he'll never let me go."

Jez covered her face with her hands.

Justine's heart was pounding in her chest. Jez's fragile shoulders trembled as she cried, clinging to Justine like a child. She was reminded of the way her three little sisters had clung to her the night she told them she was running away from home. Soft spoken banality spilled from her lips as she held the girl close, feeling larger than life. She was so pretty, so sweet. It broke Justine's heart to picture her bright spirit crushed under Absinthe's demanding obsession. He had become more erratic, more self-absorbed than ever. It had been a fertile field for the whispered seeds of gossip. There was no end to the speculation, and people had a tendency to talk freely in front of slaves as if they were animals, incapable of understanding. Justine had heard more than her share of rumors, but hearing Jez's soft, stifled sobs made it all that much more real.

"Call Morrigan," Jez said, voice cracking. "She'll know what to do."

"Jez," she said. "I can't do that. What would I tell her?"

"Please." Jez's grey eyes were heavy with clinging tears, mouth trembling. "Just call her. I can't do it alone. If I don't get away from him soon, he'll kill me."

The door burst open and Justine nearly jumped out of her skin. Absinthe stood, silhouetted in the doorway. His expression was lost in shadow. She pushed Jez away, as if the girl were a bloodstained murder weapon that could prove her guilty of some atrocious crime.

Absinthe stepped into the room, cool light spilling across his face, and Justine realized that he really was crazy.

"What's wrong, Justine?" he asked, moving slowly towards her, eyes full of dark humor.

"Nothing, Master," Justine said, looking down. Her face burned with pulsing blood.

"Nasty girl," he said, smile crawling over his lips. "Playing with Daddy's toy."

He grabbed Jez by one arm like a dropped doll and Justine flinched.

"Good little girls don't play with Daddy's things."

Of all the scenes that Justine had endured in her career as a professional submissive, the Daddy scenarios were the hardest. They dredged up buried things. Absinthe reached down and touched her cheek.

"You've been a very naughty girl," he said, his voice a seductive purr. "Daddy's going to have to punish you."

Her skin crawled and her belly knotted and underneath it all, a sick and shameful heat.

"Playing dirty games behind Daddy's back." He slid his thumb over the curve of her lower lip. "Aren't you ashamed?"

"I'm sorry," she breathed.

"What did you say?" His eyes sparkled with blood and heat.

"I'm sorry," she said louder. "Daddy."

She was going to be sick. A heavy pulse thudded between her legs. He smiled.

"That's good," he said. "But you know as well as I do that bad girls have to be punished. It's for your own good."

He slid his hand down between her legs and she gasped. She was sure that he could feel how wet she was, even through her tights. Shame flared in her guts as he pressed his damp fingers to her lips, She could smell her own pussy, rich and undeniable.

"Daddy is very busy right now," he said, mouth inches from hers. "But he'll be back very soon to take care of his little girl. That's a promise."

He turned and pulled Jez with him. The girl glanced back at her, tears still fresh on her pale cheeks. Justine wrapped her arms around herself, nauseous and shaking. As soon as they were gone, she ran as fast as she could to the telephone.

———————

Back in his chambers, Absinthe pulled Jez close, holding the girl tight to his chest and resting his cheek against the smooth curve of her skull. He imagined he could hear the whispered workings of her unfathomable brain.

"No more sessions," he said, caressing the back of her neck. "No other Masters. You're mine. Mine alone."

Jez's only response was a tiny shudder and she burrowed deeper under Absinthe's chin, her thin arms curled between them.

"I don't care what that bitch says," he whispered. "You're mine. It's just you, me and Morrigan. We don't have to do anything that bitch says. From now on it's just the three of us." He giggled. "Mommy and Daddy and baby makes three. Just like a real family."

He kissed her tear-salty face, washed with emotion. Magnesium desire flared inside him and he was overwhelmed by a need to crush Jez's fragile bones, to eat her, to rip her open and bathe in her blood. A low noise escaped his lips and he shuddered, his cock pulsing angrily against the soft leather that confined it. He felt ravenous, uncontrollable, on the verge of rape, of murder, of true love. He had always considered himself jaded, a connoisseur of dark passions who had seen and done everything. But this strange child aroused such violent need, astonishing in it's depth and relentless heat.

He forced himself to let her go and stepped away, fingering the tiny key on a silver chain around his neck as he fought to clear his aching head. Deliberately slow, he poured himself a shot of brandy.

He tried to collect himself, to focus, but the brandy was cold and unsatisfying and the girl's frantic pulse beat so close to the surface. He threw the fragile snifter against the wall, fragments raining down around Jez's head, glittering like diamonds, like stars. They reminded him of the broken mirror, of Caitlin.

Using the key around his neck, Absinthe unlocked the chastity belt and flung it away. Gripping the largest of the glass fragments, he dug into the soft flesh of Jez's inner thighs, pressing his face to the welling blood. It burned like *jalepeño* on his tongue, like moonshine down his throat. He spread blood and saliva up into the cleft of Jez's ass. His body was screaming, his veins full of broken glass as he slicked his aching erection with a fistful of Jez's blood. Shuddering, urgent, he pressed his weight down on the boxkite body of his sobbing concubine, his cock nosing in the warm cleft, seeking entrance. Jez's back arched as it slid smoothly into her painfully tight asshole.

Locking his teeth on the back of Jez's neck like a rutting tomcat, Absinthe forgot himself, forgot everything. Jez's screams were like gasoline on the flames of his mad desire, the purpose of his entire life. There was never anything but this. If he lived a million years there would be nothing but this.

Orgasm was close, inescapable now, and he was screaming too, blood in his mouth and burning in his eyes. When he came, it was a razor-edged epiphany, a hallucinatory clutch of almost religious ecstasy. There were tears mingling with the blood on Absinthe's face as he withdrew and collapsed, wiping away the evidence of his weakness with clenched fists.

"Master?" Jez's voice was hesitant, cracking. Tiny hands snaked out and touched the curve of Absinthe's shoulder.

"Put on your chastity belt," Absinthe said without turning around.

Hurt and confusion played across Jez's face. Absinthe was still as death and Jez reached out again.

"Now." Absinthe snapped, the single syllable striking out like the crack of a whip, freezing Jez's fingers inches from his skin. There was an edge of panic in his voice.

Jez scurried to obey, buckling the chastity belt around her hips. The stiff leather dug viciously into her colorless flesh. The soft click of the lock was huge in the angry silence.

Absinthe stood and began searching through drawers, through tangled whips and clamps and fishnet stockings. He finally found what he was looking for, a heavy, iron belt with a lock and about three feet of chain.

"Everything is going to be fine," he told Jez as he locked the belt around her tiny waist and fastened the chain to a second lock on one of the four posts of the bed. "Be a good girl till I get back. I just have to take care of a little problem."

He smiled and then slapped Jez's face. The slave flinched, tears spilling over and Absinthe kissed the dark, tender flesh beneath her eyes, tasting salt.

"Be good," he said.

———————

All of the clean and groomed slaves had been rounded up and taken upstairs to be given tonight's assignments, but Justine stayed behind. She sat in a corner with her knees drawn up under her chin and her belly full of turmoil. Morrigan had agreed to meet her, but she had no idea what she was going to say.

She heard Absinthe's footfalls in the long hallway seconds before he pushed the door open.

"Justine," he said. His eyes were glowing spirals like the burners of an electric stove. "Come here."

Justine's heart clenched in her chest. She hung her head and crawled across the floor, kneeling before Absinthe's boots.

"Daddy's very proud of his little girl," Absinthe cooed, working his long fingers under her hair. "You waited like a good girl to take your punishment. You understand that it's for your own good, don't you?"

"Yes ... Daddy." Justine swallowed hard, blood pounding in her wrists and temples.

Absinthe tightened his grip on her hair.

"Say, 'It's for my own good, Daddy.'"

"It's ... it's for my own good, Daddy."

And between her legs, the hot spark of her body's betrayal.

Absinthe led her by her hair to a large, armless chair and sat, pulling her across his lap. She closed her eyes and struggled with the tide of emotions that threatened to rise up and drown her. As he yanked her panties down, she ground her teeth together.

"Naughty girl," Absinthe whispered, cool fingers slipping down into the cleft of her ass. He spanked her once, a sharp blow that took her off guard, and she gasped.

She held her breath, wishing he would just get on with it and spank her harder so she could lose herself in the familiar pain. But he kept stroking her ass, teasing her pussy with the tips of his fingers until she was ready to scream. Then, without warning, he pushed her away and she rolled down onto the floor, panties tangled around her knees.

"Whore," he spat. The contempt in his voice was rich and genuine. It made her skin crawl. "You think you have an easy life here, don't you?"

Justine shook her head, on the verge of tears.

"No, sir."

"Jez is my slave." Absinthe stood over her. "She belongs to me."

Then he did something no Master had ever done to her in the whole of her submissive career. Something that turned the whole world inside out and made a lie out of every rule she had ever been taught. He kicked her in the stomach. The pain of it was so huge and sudden that pale green light filled her vision and she doubled over, retching. Her mind was reeling at this incomprehensible breach of etiquette when the toe of his cowboy boot plowed into her face, erasing all further thoughts in a wash of red agony that stripped away all traces of civilization, reducing her to her tortured animal core.

He must have done more, but the sequence of events ceased to have meaning in the embrace of this vast pain. She came back to herself some time later, huddled against the wall with pain, her constant companion, curled around her like a lover. Her eyes were bloody and swollen nearly shut, but she could see Absinthe, sitting in the chair with a cigarette smoldering between two thin fingers.

"You have until tomorrow morning to be out of your apartment." He took a long drag off the cigarette. "Jonathan and Kyle will help you."

Two of the grey-suited security men were suddenly beside her, helping her up with strong and neutral hands. She sagged against them, dizzy and sick.

Absinthe dropped his cigarette on the floor and ground it out under his bootheel as he stood.

"Make sure I never see you again," he said without looking back.

Justine wanted to scream, wanted to fly at him and claw his arrogant face off his grinning skull, but as always, she did nothing. She let the men take her away without a word.

38.

Caitlin fought her way to an empty bar stool in a claustrophobic underground club on the Lower East Side. Around her, unwashed children competed in displays of almost catatonic apathy and indifference. There was a rich, dog blanket smell in the sodden air, the aroma of rained-on dreadlocks mingling with alcoholic exhalations and cigarette butts scavenged off the sticky floor and relit for the third time.

She had no idea why Justine had picked this roach motel as a place to meet, or even why she had wanted to meet anywhere when she would see her at the Club in less than an hour anyway. But her message had been urgent, insistent, and so Caitlin was here, waiting.

She had come straight from the dojo, where she had gone to submerge the pain of her confrontation with Mike in grueling exertion. She hadn't showered and she felt as though microscopic particles of this bar were sifting down and adhering to her sweaty flesh, nestling in her hair and on her lips. She shuddered and checked her watch. Justine was a half an hour late.

She watched the door with growing impatience. Her toybag felt so heavy, each whip and paddle replaced suddenly with lead and stone. Every redhead who walked in the door looked like Justine.

Sifting through a handful of warm change, she stood and made her way towards the elderly payphone. She didn't see Absinthe until he laid a chilly hand on her shoulder.

"Justine will not be able to keep her appointment," he said, dilated eyes full of mock solemnity. Jez was at his side, collared and pale with dark smudges of makeup around her rainwater eyes. Absinthe stroked the back of the girl's neck, wicked black nails tracing the blue lace of her fragile veins. There was crusted blood in the whorls of Absinthe's fingers and in the corners of his mouth. He took a step closer and touched an errant wisp of hair at Caitlin's temple.

"It doesn't matter," Caitlin said. "I'll see her later tonight."

Jez's gaze flickered up, quick as a reptile's tongue. She flushed and looked away.

"No," Absinthe said. "It doesn't matter."

He bent to kiss her, and at that moment, as a slick pulse of heat flared between her legs, she realized that something was very wrong. When she pulled away, she saw that Justine's wide leather belt hugged Jez's narrow waist. The silver buckle was tacky with dark blood.

"Where is she?" Caitlin wrapped her arms around herself, electric adrenaline unable to obliterate the tight quiver of sneaky lust in the back of her throat.

"Morrigan," he said, caressing the curve of her jaw. "It doesn't matter. The car is waiting."

He stepped back and offered his hand. His eyes burned with the patient viciousness of a cat poised before a mouse hole. All around them, conversation had evaporated. All around them, hungry faces, razor cheekbones and bottomless eyes. She watched her hand reach out to him, marveling at its familiar scars and calluses as if it belonged to someone else.

As they turned to go, Absinthe motioned to a pair of bedraggled squatter boys, their thin lips smeared black with shoplifted make-up. Their hair was filthy, one bleach yellow, one black with an improbable but apparently natural white streak down the center and their rangy bodies were clad in mismatched polyester rags stolen from church donation boxes. They blinked, unsure.

"Well, do you want to come or not?" Absinthe flashed his most seductive grin.

The boys glanced at each other and then scampered after them like puppies. Caitlin thought she saw a flash of jealousy in Jez's shadowed eyes but she looked away so fast there was no way to be sure.

———

In the back of the limousine, the boys peeled down Absinthe's leather pants and took turns sucking his lazy cock, giggling like children sharing a summer popsicle. Jez sat curled against Caitlin, her body tight as an uneasy animal. Caitlin found herself petting her smooth skull, speaking nonsensical soothing words. When she looked up at Caitlin, there were tears on her cheeks. Absinthe didn't seem to notice.

"Morrigan," Jez said, almost too softly to hear.

Caitlin pulled her close, fingers tracing the delicate points of her spine.

"What is it?" she whispered.

"I'm afraid that it's all falling apart." Her childish voice was jagged with emotion.

Caitlin glanced in Absinthe's direction. He had pulled one of the rats close and was lapping at a shallow cut on the boy's dirt-streaked face. The other boy was moaning softly around a mouthful of semi-erect cock, grinding his hips against Absinthe's boot.

Absinthe's eyes suddenly flew open and he held a hand out for Jez.

For the first time, Jez seemed almost reluctant.

Absinthe struck the girl in the face, anger burning like hot sulfur in his lemur eyes. He forced Jez down on her belly on the carpeted floor, pressing the toe of his boot into the back of the girl's neck.

"Don't embarrass me in front of our new friends, Jez," he said, voice low and nasty.

"I'm sorry, Master." Jez shivered, hands clenching and opening like dying insects.

"Good," Absinthe said, smiling as he removed his foot from the girl's neck. Caitlin could see the angry print of the boot's tread on Jez's pale flesh. He put his spit-slick cock away and buttoned his pants. "Now I want you to make it up to Skunk and Tommy."

Jez pressed her lips to the boys' grimy sneakers.

"I'm sorry, Master Skunk. Master Tommy."

The dirtier of the two smiled, displaying a tenacious handful of rotted teeth. He caressed the stiff crotch of his gritty trousers and unbuckled his heavy belt.

"Go on," Absinthe said, grinning. "Show Master Skunk how sorry you are."

There was a moment of thick tension where Caitlin was sure Jez was just going to refuse outright. The toothy smell of unwashed flesh was almost overwhelming in the claustrophobic interior of the sealed car.

Then, with dutiful resignation, Jez sat up on her haunches and pulled down the boy's rusted zipper. The thick, cheesy aroma released along with his massive, pierced erection was more that Caitlin could handle. She slammed her fist into the window control, the warm wash of city air a sweet tonic as the tinted glass slid open. She watched the progression of bland streets with dull obsession, determined not to listen to the slurping and grunting and low chanting.

"Oh yeah, that's right. Suck that cock. Come on, slut. That's right. Choke on it, you little slut. You know you want it. Oh fuck yeah, that's it. Yeah, that's it."

Caitlin flinched when Absinthe caressed the back of her neck. Without even realizing it, she had readied her body for a fight, turning and bringing her forearm up to block his questing fingers.

"Relax, my Lady." Absinthe uncurled her fist and kissed her palm, tongue dancing over her skin.

She felt seductive nausea fluttering in the back of her throat and adrenaline pulsing in her veins. Her body was coiled tight as a snake ready to strike, and she was sure that she would kill him, that she wouldn't be able to stop herself. She felt like she had woken up from an erotic dream to discover scorpions covering her body like a chitinous blanket. Watching the ticking pulse beneath his ear, she made herself breathe deeply, force her bunched muscles to relax. In her brain's manic search for calming images, she found herself thinking suddenly of Mike, of the simplicity of his touch, of the honest smell of his sweat. The memory felt a million years old, full of sad nostalgia, like a memory of lost innocence, a childhood hideaway that was too small to admit adult bodies.

Absinthe pressed his mouth to her temple and she let him unfasten the clip that restrained her sweat-damp locks. She felt that moment of bright awareness dimming fast, a insidious, sleepy sensuality creeping over her as Absinthe buried both hands up to the elbows in the spill of her hair. Over the curve of his shoulder, she watched Jez's head bobbing between the squatter's thighs, feeling detached, recording. The kid threw his head back and came, grunting, and Caitlin pressed her face into Absinthe's neck, her teeth working a small fold of skin, a deliberate distraction. He gasped and wrapped his arms around her, pulling her close. His body was tense and at the same time strangely pliant against hers. As she sank her teeth deeper, she watched Skunk tuck his enormous, half-hard dick back into his pants while Tommy fished his out. She caught a glimpse of Jez's damp face and hurt eyes before she bent to the new task.

Absinthe writhed against her, sobbing low in his throat and blood burst into her mouth like jism. The fragile crust of his dominance broke with his skin and the rich flavor of vulnerability was just as sweet as she remembered. He was painfully hard against the curve of her hip and she found herself fantasizing about breaking his neck, or chewing through his jugular vein and letting his corrupt blood spill out, untasted. She would take Jez and disappear, leave this adolescent dreamworld forever. The girl was crying freely now as the second kid filled her mouth with thick, unhealthy semen.

Galvanized by Jez's tears, Caitlin tightened her embrace, feeling Absinthe's body shuddering against hers, his soul opening to her penetration. She took a handful of his oily black hair and pulled his head back, gripping his face in her hand. She pressed her lips down on his, spilling the hot mouthful of his own blood down his throat. Catching both of his skinny wrists in one hand, she turned him around and pressed his face into the plush seat.

"Jez," she said, her voice strong and steady, like someone else. "Get my dildo."

The girl looked up, face smooth with shock.

"Quickly," she said.

Scrambling to obey, Jez dug through her toybag and extracted the black rubber dick with it's leather harness. Absinthe struggled half heartedly as she unfastened his leather pants and pushed them down to his knees. His cock was flush against his lean belly, hard as glass.

Caitlin let Jez buckle the straps around her waist and slick the latex-sheathed dildo with a handful of clear lubricant. She spoke low and close to Absinthe's ear.

"You know you want it, slut." she said, pressing the head of the dildo against his asshole. "Say you want it."

"Ah, no. Don't." He struggled, grinding his hips against the grey velour.

She slapped his ass and he cried out.

"Liar," she spat, pressing harder, spreading him wider.

"No." His head whipped back and forth. "Please."

She gripped his steely erection in one hand and squeezed hard. He sobbed, desire and submission pouring out of him like sweat.

"What's this then, slut?" She slapped his ass again. "You know you want me to fuck you."

"Please." His voice was barely audible.

"Please what?" Caitlin rubbed the slick dildo along the crack of his ass and he arched his back like a cat in heat.

"Please fuck me," he whispered.

Caitlin smiled.

"I don't think everybody heard that," she said. "Would you care to repeat it?"

"Please," he cried. "Please fuck me."

With one smooth thrust, Caitlin buried the length of the dildo in Absinthe's ass.

She fucked him hard, whispering hot obscenities in his ear. The grinding of the harness against her swollen clit was excruciating, infuriating, unbearable. Her hair spilled down over his arched back as she pushed up his leather shirt and gripped his hard little nipples, rolling them between thumb and forefinger. She wanted to tear him open, crush him, break his spine. Tears stung her eyes and she screamed, driving her cock in deeper. His hips bucked and he shuddered and came against the plush seat.

She withdrew slowly and unbuckled the harness, feeling cool and victorious, powerful. Absinthe turned and peered at her through his hair like a punished child. Jez watched with strange despair and the boys leaned against each other giggling.

Absinthe pushed his hair back and laughed, a soft, dangerous sound that chilled Caitlin to the bone. She passed a hand over her eyes and almost missed Absinthe launching himself across the car at the two boys. When she turned, Tommy was clutching at a fountain of blood from his throat and Skunk was wrestling with Absinthe, struggling to keep the razor away from his face. He was not successful.

Jez screamed and pressed herself into Caitlin's arms, hiding her face against her belly. Covered with blood and jism, Absinthe crouched over the twitching bodies, teeth bared. His pants were still around his ankles.

Caitlin sat perfectly still, ready to do whatever it took to get her and Jez out of this car. She was terrified and revolted and full of a thousand razor-edged emotions. She thought she might vomit, or smash a window with her fist. As she watched, Absinthe rubbed his hands over his belly and licked his fingers.

"My Lady," he said. He ran his tongue over his lips and then knelt before her and pressed his mouth to her shoe. "You are a rare and uncompromising woman."

He wiped blood from his face and arms with a clean white towel from under the bar while Caitlin sat across from him with fists and teeth clenched. He pulled the grey denim jacket off of Tommy's unresisting body and examined the arcane magic-marker symbols. Pressing it to his lips, he inhaled deeply and then slid it on. Rows of rusted safety pins jingled softly.

He punched a button on the intercom and told the driver to stop the car. Jez was staring at the oozing bodies with a blankness that was hideous in its purity. It was as if every ounce of Jez's personality had suddenly evaporated, leaving her as devoid of life as the dead boys.

"It's over," Caitlin thought she heard Jez whisper. "It's really over."

Caitlin shuddered.

"Come, Lady," Absinthe said, smiling as if nothing out of the ordinary had taken place. "Let's walk from here."

He opened the door and stepped out onto the sidewalk. Caitlin waited, unsure, for an endless minute, and then climbed out after him, wondering if Jez would be able to keep up if she ran. She knew now that she had to do something, that she had to get away from him, from the crazy desire that still drew her to him, even now. But she couldn't leave Jez behind. She turned to help her out of the car but Absinthe slammed the door and the car peeled out with Jez still inside.

Caitlin stood on the cracked pavement, arms crossed, wondering what he would do if she just turned and walked away, but knowing that she couldn't, not yet, not without Jez. He grinned shyly, hunched down inside the ratty coat like a high school girl wearing her boy-friend's letter jacket. She had to bite back a ferocious urge to slap him.

"Why did you do that?" she asked instead, surprised at her own words.

"Do what?" He looked away, up at the Cheshire-cat smile moon lurking between the buildings.

"Don't be coy with me," she spat. "What the fuck do you think?"

"Oh, that." He looked down. "Well, I can't let people walk around knowing that I'm still a submissive boy at heart."

He slipped his arms around her waist and nuzzled her like a calf.

"Please don't be angry," he said.

She closed her eyes and felt that strange melting sickness trickling through her. Liquid logic, rational madness. A sticky tar pit of untrustworthy emotion. She had to find Jez. There was no way she could leave without her. There was no choice but to play along. She returned his embrace and he made a sound like a happy cat.

He took her hand and dragged her across the street into a Korean deli. Brightly colored fruit and bunches of flowers swam and flowed together under the merciless fluorescent light. He piled bunches of white and pink roses into her arms and the smell was dizzying, nostalgic. He disappeared for a few seconds and returned with an enormous bottle of cheap malt liquor, grinning like a kid. Throwing handfuls of crumpled bills at the laughing woman behind the counter, he pulled Caitlin back out into the street.

As they walked, he took long drinks from the bottle and handed roses to homeless people who stared after them, flabbergasted. One woman turned to an imaginary companion and said, "Isn't love grand?"

The closer they came to the Club, the more intensely disconnected she felt. He was pressing her against the rough brick and kissing her, blood and jism, roses and malt liquor, a rainbow of flavors mingling on her tongue.

She turned her face away and planted both hands against his chest.

"Where's Jez?" she asked, twisting away from his questing mouth.

She was suddenly sure that if she did not see Jez right now, she would go crazy. The quiet sound of the girl's heart and cool vulnerability of her grey eyes seemed the only hope for sanity. Blood was rushing in her temples, in her wrists, behind her eyes. She felt disconnected, fragmented into a thousand contradictions.

"She'll meet us inside." Absinthe ducked into an alley, motioning for her to follow. "We'd be eaten alive if we tried to go in through the front."

A battered metal door lurked behind a rancid dumpster, its dented hide tattooed with scrawling graffiti. He flipped up a tiny, eye level door, revealing a glowing keypad. Instinct made her focus intensely on the dance of his long fingers against the numbered keys.

122448. She forced herself to repeat the number again and again as he ushered her inside. *122448 122448 122448*. Afraid to lose the number in the abstraction of repetition, she tried to dissect it, make it memorable. *Two twos is four. Two fours is eight. One at the beginning.* Then Wilson's voice spoke up in her mind and she almost laughed out loud.

Christmas Eve, 1948. Hellebore's birthday. It was just too simple.

Absinthe turned his head at the sound of her aborted laugh.

"What is it, Lady?"

"I was thinking of Jez." She was only half-lying.

He smiled, dreamy.

"Yes." He closed his eyes. "I have never had a slave as devoted and unique as Jez. She's everything I've ever wanted." Without warning, his face was inches from hers, crimson eyes wide, glistening. "Have you ever dreamed of running away, just you and me and Jez?"

That question again. As usual, Caitlin had no answer, but it didn't seem to matter because he continued without waiting for a response.

"Did you ever dream of an eternal night drenched in blood and passion and just the three of us together, away from all of this."

Caitlin blinked. He was hard again, a heavy pressure against her hip as he held her close. The thorns of roses pricked her skin.

"I love the things you do to me," he whispered, tongue warm and quick along the curve of her ear. "It's been so long. Not many women have that strength. I want you to stay with me and Jez from now on. Would you want that? I would love to live with you forever. I want to tell you secrets. I want to take you with me."

"You're a murderer," Caitlin said, fighting her traitorous body's desire to let him in again.

He looked up into her eyes, smile curling in the corner of his mouth.

"We all are," he said, long fingers teasing her nipples.

A sick shudder of electric pleasure crackled along her spine, but she refused to give in.

"No, that's not true," she said. "I'm not ... "

"Ah, but you are." He ran his hand up under her shirt, caressing her belly. "Just as you were a dominant before you ever picked up a whip."

Caitlin shook her head, pushing him away.

"Fuck you," she said. "You don't know me."

Absinthe's eyes went wide and mock-sorrowful. He sank to his knees before her.

"I'm sorry, Mistress," he said. He pressed a kiss to the toe of her boot and offered her one of the white roses in his arms. "What can I do to make it up to you?"

"Find Jez," Caitlin answered, refusing the offered blossom.

"Don't worry," he said. "She will join us in a minute. But until then ... "

He stood and pulled her close kissing her mouth. She knew he would not lay off until he had what he wanted, so she stopped fighting, let him touch her. But as his knowing hands roamed the surface of her skin, she knew in her darkest heart she still wanted this as much as he did.

He was pushing down her shorts, fingers sliding over her clit, down into the molten cleft of her pussy. She moved her hips against his hand, feeling any semblance of rational thought melting away. Roses fell around them like rain, releasing dying bursts of scent as they were crushed under Absinthe's boots. She could not concentrate. She wanted him to stop, but she thought she might not be able to stand it if he did. His mouth was sour with old blood and his cock was hot between her legs, sliding over the slippery contours of her intimate geography. He pushed her against the concrete wall and spread her legs wide, burying the length of his naked cock inside her.

Nagging thoughts of death and disease and murder and conception dissolved like wet tissue in the torrent of gluttonous sensation. She came almost at once, slamming her head against the concrete wall, stars glittering on the edges of her vision. Her fists were wrapped in thick locks of his hair and she screamed and came again and he came growling low and vicious like an animal and there was a starburst of pain in her shoulder as his teeth clenched and drew blood, more blood, trickling down her breasts, salty in her mouth.

Breathing deeply, Absinthe laid his head against her shoulder for a long minute. Her thighs were shaking. Her back was scraped raw from the concrete and her head was throbbing. He kissed her cheek.

"How sweet." A low voice in the dark. Hellebore, with Jez collared at her side. She bent and picked up a single pale blossom that had survived their passion, holding it to her lips.

Caitlin struggled to straighten her disheveled clothing, feeling sick and strange but stronger now, as if the shock of Hellebore's monster-mask face had pierced her scattered delirium. She watched Absinthe button up with false nonchalance.

"What did you tell her?" Hellebore asked, long hand caressing Jez's bird-boned shoulder.

"I love her," Absinthe said, his voice petulant, like a child.

He reached out for Jez and pulled the girl to him, taking her leash in his hand and snaking an arm around Caitlin as well. The three of them stood there facing Hellebore, a static tableau meant to represent Absinthe's dream of a *ménage à trois* that would last forever.

"Don't be ridiculous," Hellebore said, turning away.

39.

Caitlin stood carefully balanced on the curve of a man's well muscled chest, spike heels leaving tiny round indentations and triangles of bruise. She had a glass of sweetened absinthe in her gloved hand. It could have been any other night at the Club, except it wasn't.

She watched Absinthe making his rounds with Jez in tow and Hellebore close behind, watchful. Caitlin found herself following the ebb and flow of the crowd with her eyes and imagining escape is a thousand forms. Alone, it shouldn't be a problem to slink past the grunts. She came and went all the time, and was never questioned. But she could not leave Jez behind. Plans spooled out in her mind like plots for bad action films and she turned each one over and over searching for holes. She thought of murdered Eva, imagined her going through her own escape plans just like her, and at that point she felt as if no one in the world understood Eva as well as she did. She found herself thinking of her book again for the first time in weeks. It sprang up eagerly in her inner vision as clearly as if she had never put it down. Planning how she and Jez would escape together was not just survival, it was the climax of her story.

But her body would not let her forget the feel of Absinthe's long white fingers and the decadent flavor of his submission, and some part of her struggled vehemently against betrayal of this lunatic passion. The stronger side saw nothing but the anguish in Jez's eyes. She was sure that redemption lay in saving Jez and incidentally, herself, from Absinthe's sadistic vision.

Carefully stepping off the man's chest, Caitlin allowed him to kiss her feet and tuck a folded bill into the ankle strap of her shoe before dismissing him. She scanned the room for a chair to rest her tired body and a serving boy with a tray for her empty glass or maybe even a refill. Instead she saw Hellebore. The woman had appeared noiselessly at her elbow, her good eye shadowed and flat black, revealing nothing.

"Come," she said. "Sit here with me."

Caitlin allowed herself to be led to the same table by the cold fireplace where she had sat with Absinthe that first night. There was a long haired black and white cat curled on the plush cushion of one chair. Hellebore lifted the cat with surprising tenderness and held it like a baby as she sat, motioning for Caitlin to do the same.

"I don't know what Absinthe has been telling you," she said, stroking the cat's soft belly. "But you mustn't take him too seriously. We all have our delusions here."

Caitlin watched her, turning the empty glass in her hands.

"What are your delusions?"

Hellebore narrowed her eyes, her fingers suddenly still in the thick fur.

"You've been with us for almost two months now and we've hardly ever spoken." She set the cat down on the faded rug. "Yet you must know that you are only here because I have allowed it."

Caitlin was silent, unwilling to say anything.

"I suppose that my primary delusion has been my belief that Absinthe would be enough. You are here solely because I have been able to shake that delusion. Let me explain."

She removed Justine's silver cigarette case from an inside pocket of her man's suit-jacket and offered it, open, to Caitlin.

"Smoke?"

Caitlin frowned. She shook her head.

"Tell me what happened to Justine," she said.

"All in good time." She pulled out an antique lighter and dipped her cigarette into the pungent flame. "Soon you will know more than you ever wanted to about all the players in this game."

She took a deep drag and flicked ashes into a jade ashtray.

Caitlin did not allow her face to show any expression.

"Tell me," she said.

"I'm sure that Absinthe has tried to impress upon you his control of the situation and I am also sure that, being as observant as one of your profession must necessarily be, you must have noticed that he is not. I was counting on him and to my dismay, I have discovered that he is inherently flawed. He does not have even a fraction of the natural dominance required for this endeavor. However, I am never without a B plan, which is where you come in."

"My profession?" Caitlin blinked. It was hard to track the older woman's words. She felt distracted, as if every sound, every movement in the wide room demanded her total attention. "What do you mean?"

"Please," Hellebore said, shaking her head. "Playing dumb at this point is unnecessary as well as irritating. The fact that you are a writer is irrelevant except that it brought you here. No one can predict what twist of fate brings a true dominant to the realization of their nature. What matters is that you are here now."

Hellebore took a deep, final drag off Justine's cigarette and crushed it against the creamy green stone.

"I want you to take Absinthe's place," she said.

That quiet statement brought Caitlin's wandering mind into sudden, brutal focus.

"There is much you need to learn, but that doesn't matter. You are a rare creature. You have certain ... capacities. You are raw, unpolished, but the biological reality of your dominance is there. I can smell it." She paused, her eyes bright. "Jez can smell it."

Caitlin turned away, eyes picking Jez out of the crowd of revelers. She was strung up on a steel cross, wrists bound by metal shackles, pale ass crossed with angry red welts. A crown of razorwire circled her head like some industrial Jesus, a sacrificial lamb for the machine age. Absinthe, anachronistic in all his gothic splendor, slashed at the girl with a whalebone crop, face flushed with the high color of passion or madness.

"He is out of control," Hellebore said, noting the direction of her gaze. "His behavior tonight was absolutely unacceptable. It pains me terribly to be so close and have it all fall down because of a egomaniacal peacock whose dominance has proven itself to be nothing more that skin deep."

"Look," Caitlin said. "What does this mean in the real world? You want me to run the Club? If I agree, then what happens to Absinthe?"

"You know a lot more than you like to admit," Hellebore said. "Even to yourself. Absinthe is a liability. You know that as well as I do. What happens to him is not your concern."

Caitlin felt some uncontrollable reply rising in her throat when suddenly Absinthe was there beside her, his woman's nails brushing against her exposed shoulder.

"Speak of the devil," Hellebore said.

"Morrigan, we miss you terribly." He pressed his mouth to her neck. His speech was blurry around the edges.

"Think about it," Hellebore said to Caitlin, face hard and unnaturally smooth over her twisted bones.

She turned and walked away, but Absinthe filled Caitlin's attention utterly, pulling her close and kissing her face. There was a strange urgency in his grasp and the hungry sucking of his tainted mouth. She allowed herself to be pulled to where Jez was crucified.

Extracting herself from his arms, she bent close to Jez, running her fingers over the girl's welted back.

"Are you allright?" she whispered.

"I'm fine, Mistress." There were tears, but lately there were always tears. She stroked the girl's cheek.

"I'm going to get you out of here," she breathed, her lips brushing the curve of Jez's ear. "I promise."

Jez's face held a mix of resignation and sadness that broke Caitlin's heart and made her want to gather the girl up in her arms.

When Absinthe pressed his body against the curve of her back, she felt herself stiffen involuntarily.

"Lady," he purred. "It won't be long now."

When he turned away, she saw that he was holding a thin bamboo cane, fresh and greenish yellow.

"Just a little more," he whispered.

The cane whistled, slicing through the air as he brought it down sharply on Jez's ass. Jez hardly flinched.

Around them, heads turned, eyes focused and suddenly they were at the center of a hungry crowd. Caitlin felt a strange cold shiver, but kept her chin high, her gaze steely.

Absinthe struck Jez again and again with the viciously flexible little cane, leaving long purple welts that oozed blood through tiny pores. It was not long before the tortured skin began to split, more blood running free down the backs of Jez's legs and Absinthe's eyes burned with lunatic fire as the welts spread up her back and down her thighs. Before long, she was a raw, bleeding mess from the back of her neck to the back of her knees, but Absinthe showed no signs of stopping. Sweat glistened on his face and his teeth flashed as the cane snapped in half. Grunting angrily, he continued to lash the girl with the splintered fragment, ragged, needle-fine bamboo teeth tearing into her until she finally cried out, shattering her defiant silence.

That broken wail was more than Caitlin could take. Before she was even aware of moving, her hand flashed out and caught Absinthe's wrist. He turned wild eyes up to her as if he might strike out at her next and she said, "Enough."

Again, like the first night, Caitlin found herself at center of a ring of eyes. The crowd was funeral silent around them and standing amid the gawkers with a little smile on her hideously sexy lips, was Hellebore. She tipped her head in the barest hint of an approving nod.

The broken cane slipped from Absinthe's fingers and he leaned heavily against Caitlin as if his own weight were suddenly to much to bear. Wrapping a supporting arm around him, she set about freeing Jez.

She forced her fingers to move slowly over the metal cuffs, unlocking them and massaging Jez's icy hands. The girl limped heavily as Caitlin led her charges protectively through the crowd, away from the hungry scrutiny and Hellebore's poisonous approval.

40.

Back in his private chambers, Absinthe lay in a sodden lump on the bed with tangled sheets clutched tight around him, face hidden by a sweaty spill of hair. In the bathroom, Caitlin cleansed and disinfected Jez's welts. The tile was spattered with a foaming pink blend of blood and peroxide.

"Just hang on," Caitlin whispered, soothing away the sting with soft words. "He'll pass out soon, and then we'll go."

She didn't know how, but they would make it. They had to. Absinthe was a lost cause, lost in his own private hell, and in her heart she found a kind of pity for him. He was like a genetically engineered organism, perfectly adapted in the environment he was created for, but useless in the outside world. When he lost his ability to function even in his own specialized environment, there was nothing left for him at all. Hellebore would undoubtedly have him killed or institutionalized but Caitlin could not allow pity to keep her and Jez from freedom.

When Caitlin cautiously returned to the bedroom, she saw that Absinthe had gotten a bottle of brandy off the bedside table and poured a massive dose into a glass as fragile as a soap bubble.

"We'll be legendary," he was saying, hands cutting the air in wide sweeping gestures, sheets crumpled in his lap. The golden liquor sloshed over the glass' edge, staining the coverlet. His voice was slurred, his eyes rimmed with scarlet. Then, suddenly intimate, he pulled Caitlin and Jez close. "You are my family."

Caitlin gritted her teeth.

He'll pass out soon if we fuck him hard enough. Slip out while he's sleeping. There's a window in the hallway. Does it open on the crowded street, or the alley? If it doesn't open, break it. But what about Jez? Can she make the jump?

A thousand plans were born and murdered in her head. She was so absorbed in her thoughts that she didn't immediately notice why Jez had gone still and tense against her.

"It's over," Jez was saying. Her face had gone blank and empty, in startling contrast to the hectic color in Absinthe's cheeks. When Caitlin looked down, she saw the nose of a gun pressed against Jez's belly.

Her heart clenched like a fist in her chest and all the rich saliva in her mouth vanished. She looked into Absinthe's amber eyes and saw nothing but gleeful madness.

"We'll all be together," he whispered, caressing Jez's ribcage with the gun barrel protruding from beneath a fold in the satin bedcovers. "Forever. Don't be afraid. It's the only way."

He pulled the key from around his neck and pressed it into Jez's hand.

"But first," he said, gesturing with the gun. "Show her."

Jez swallowed, eyes shock glazed and empty. She stepped away, fingers toying with the tiny key.

"Hurry," Absinthe stage whispered, as if grownups might overhear. "There isn't much time left."

Jez struggled to fit the key into the little silver lock at the center of her chastity belt, but as curious as she was, Caitlin was hardly watching as she let her hand inch imperceivably closer to the swaddled weapon. Absinthe was so fixated on the desperate movements of Jez's fingers on the lock's delicate mechanism that he did not even notice as Caitlin carefully closed the distance between his hand and hers.

Out of the corner of her eye, she watched Jez pull the lock open, waiting, waiting, her hands flexing and teeth working the inside of her lips. The straps were complicated and she took her time unbuckling each one. Absinthe watched this striptease with obsessive fascination. Caitlin's fingers were millimeters from his when Jez undid the last buckle and let the leather belt fall.

The soft jingle of the buckles against the rug punched through her like a starter's pistol and she grabbed the wrist of Absinthe's right hand and threw all her weight against him, toppling them both to the floor.

The brandy snifter shattered. Flinching from the spray of glass, she slammed the hand that held the gun against the bed frame.

Absinthe screamed with rage and brought his thick nails raking across her face, gun hand struggling like a caught snake in her grasp. A shot, deafening in her ears and a trail of liquid fire seared a path across her shoulder. A candelabra crashed down on them from above, hot wax splattering her face and a galaxy of orange flames licking the brandy soaked carpet.

The stink of burning was thick in Caitlin's throat and she dug her thumb into the soft inside of his wrist as hard as she could. His fingers opened convulsively, the gun thudding on the burning rug beside them. Jamming her other fingers into his throat, she reached into the flames and grabbed the searing hot metal.

Rolling away from him and the heat of the fire, she leapt to her feet and held the gun in both hands, training it on his heaving chest. The hot rubber grip stuck to her fingers.

The fire was tasting the gauzy curtains around the bed, reaching bright arms across the rug. Smoke was everywhere. Caitlin could hardly see.

She thought she could make out the dusky shape of Jez, who stood alone and unflinching in the madness.

Absinthe stood silhouetted in flame, fingers jittering wildly through the air. His expression seemed more hurt than surprised. He tried to take a step towards her and she screamed and pulled the trigger. His lanky bicep bloomed with a spray of sudden blood and he staggered to his knees. Fire was surrounding him, kissing his outstretched hands. The heat was unbearable, tightening Caitlin's skin across her cheeks. Smoke filled her mouth, choking her and she backed away, dropping the gun to the burning carpet and groping for Jez in the haze. She thought she saw her by the open door beckoning and when she came close she saw smooth nakedness and at the delta of those coltish legs, *what secret?*

But Caitlin was coughing, pain wracking her chest and there was the sound of running feet and shouting and she couldn't see, just thick, endless smoke. Jez was gone, lost somewhere and Caitlin was down on her knees crawling.

There.

Hot smooth glass and she slammed her fist two, three times until it shattered. A wave of heat rolled over her, flames reaching for her as she pressed through, spears of broken glass clawing her body and she fell.

———————

In the alley, stinking garbage slick under her palms and she pulled herself to her feet. There was no part of her that didn't hurt. Her lungs felt packed with metal shavings. Her eyes stung. Her shoulder throbbed. Somewhere close, people were screaming and there were sirens. She leaned against the wall, sliding along until she reached the mouth of the alley.

The street was chaos. People were crushed together, eyes frantic and rimmed with white like cattle being herded up the ramp to the slaughterhouse. More people poured from the main entrance, some still buckling their pants as they ran. She saw Bettina and Jeremiah huddled together under a grey police blanket. Eager reporters filmed naked slave boys vomiting into the gutter and disheveled celebrities ducking into waiting cars. She saw Hemlock carrying the limp form of his sister, screaming for an ambulance. Red and blue lights played across anxious faces. Smoke and anguish filled the hot night sky. Caitlin turned and walked away.

Part Four

AFTERMATH

41.

On the dim streets of Fieldston, putting down one foot after the other, numb and frozen, empty. If this were a movie, it would all be over. The credits would have rolled over the raging flames and then the lights would have come up and every one would go home to their ordinary lives. Caitlin felt like a character that had outlived it's usefulness. *Was she supposed to go to sleep tonight? Finish that seventh Vic Steele novel? Get on with her life?* She could still feel the heat of Absinthe's kisses and the kick of the gun in her aching bones.

The sanctuary of the Bergin Manse loomed ahead and she made her way towards it like a plant growing towards the sun. It was the only place that made sense, her childhood safe-house, an unchanging refuge when the rest of the world was too crazy. All the windows were dark, unwelcoming. If no one was home, Caitlin would just sit here on the cold stone steps and wait. She rang the bell.

Nothing. She leaned on it, tasteful, musical tones echoing through the hallways over and over.

No answer. She let go and slid down, sitting dazed and unthinking on the flagstones.

The door opened on its chain, a pale slice of face in the crack. Then the door closed and opened again.

"Wilson?" She couldn't stand the sound of her own voice. She pushed the door open all the way.

But it was not Wilson. It was his mother.

Caitlin barely recognized her. Her eyes were swollen and sticky, mascara smudges giving her a raccoon mask that reminded Caitlin of her dead sister. Her hair was skewed from its normal perfection, hanging in her face like seaweed.

"Mrs. B," Caitlin whispered. There was a terrible fear gnawing at her guts. "What is it?"

Without answering, she turned and walked away, leaving the door hanging open. Caitlin followed, silent, closing the heavy door behind her.

The tiny woman moved like a ghost through the dark hallways and Caitlin followed like a mortal led to buried treasure or the spirit's desiccated remains. She made the last turn and led Caitlin into a nearly empty room that she didn't recognize. Narrow bed, scarred desk, these things seemed naggingly familiar, but she could not think. There was a small curl of copper wire on the scruffy blue carpet next to her foot and she stared at it like it was an alien hieroglyph that held the secrets of the universe. When it clicked, the sensation of brutal understanding was physically painful. This was Wilson's room, and all the hardware was gone.

She looked up. Mrs. Bergin had sunk down onto the bed, hands covering her face.

"They took him," she said.

"Who?" Caitlin took a step closer to her and she turned away, eyes squeezed shut.

"They took all his things and then they took him."

"Who took him?" She reached out and lay a hand on Mrs. Bergin's shoulder. The older woman flinched and pulled away.

"Fucking pigs," she said, tears flowing freely.

Caitlin stood, dumbfounded. She had never heard Mrs. Bergin say a bad word before. To see her so unraveled, so helpless, was almost sacrelegious. She had always been so cool, so competent. It just added to Caitlin's conviction that the world had ended.

"My lawyer will have him home soon," Mrs. Bergin said, speaking through her laced fingers. "All I can do now is wait."

Caitlin looked away, watching the hypnotic sign-language of the swaying tree branches outside the window, feeling nothing. She found she was able to conjure some emotion for her friend, some small sadness, but it felt as hopeless as the dying embers of a lonely bone-chip fire in the vast night of a nuclear winter.

"Here," Mrs. Bergin said suddenly, thrusting a crumpled piece of paper into Caitlin's chilly hand.

Caitlin unfolded the little scrap and squinted at it in the dim blue light.

Written in Wilson's meticulous hand were two words that refused to make sense. They slid over her brain like slick nonsense-words and the more she struggled to understand them, the more they defied her.

Kaiichi Kobiyashi.

"He told me to give this to you," Mrs. Bergin said, looking up finally. The cool light sparkled in her tears. "He didn't have the time to post it, before ... " Her mouth tightened. "He said it was very important, that you would know who it was."

"Who ... ?" Caitlin frowned. Then she knew, and the guilt hit home like a hypodermic needle to her frozen heart.

She heard Wilson's sardonic, nasal voice: *I think someone is investing in her silence.*

Hellebore's absentee father. So Wilson finally found the source of Hellebore's hush money and now he was in jail because of it.

Caitlin shook her head. Wilson was into a thousand extralegal endeavors and any one of them could have lead to his arrest. But in her guilty heart, she was sure it was her fault.

"I better go," she said, clenching the damning note in her closed fist.

Mrs. Bergin said nothing, just hung her head and covered her face with her hands.

42.

On the sidewalk in front of her apartment building, Caitlin stood, unmoving, her keys on the cracked cement at her feet. She did not remember dropping them, did not remember how she got here. For the two hundredth time, she read the neatly printed sign that read, "No Menus." The sun was up already, but she didn't remember dawn.

The super of her building, a lanky Hispanic man with an anemic mustache that looked as if it could be scrubbed off, was standing next to her, saying something that required a response, but she couldn't understand it.

"Hey, honey, you OK?"

She blinked.

"Sure yeah, I'm fine," she made herself answer.

"You dropped your keys," he told her, pressing the ring into her hands.

She took them and held them so tightly the jagged brass teeth dug into her palm.

"Come inside," the super was saying, opening the door and ushering her in. She allowed him to lead her up to the elevator and put her inside, pushing the button of her floor. "Get some rest, OK?"

The elevator door closed on his worried face and she leaned against the gouged wooden paneling, watching the changing numerals with bland concentration. When the doors opened on her floor, she almost took too long to get out. The doors bounced indignantly off her hip as she jumped through at the last minute.

She was afraid to open the door to her apartment. It was ages before she was able to turn the last key. Inside, the familiar scent of her old life and her old things was overwhelming, gutwrenching and the tears finally came.

Lying on the floor with her cheek pressed to the smooth, dusty wood, she cried, each tear dragging up a long root of razor wire, tearing at her, ripping her apart. She could still feel Absinthe's mouth on hers, still feel the smooth curve of Jez skull against her breasts. Crawling to the bathroom, chilly tile against her hands and the unyielding porcelain of the toilet. Angry fists clenched in her guts and thick streams of vomit spilled down her chin, splashing in the sparkling blue water. The taste of blood and absinthe. She wretched again and again. She could feel Absinthe's cock inside her and hear the insidious cadence of his voice. Black and red abstractions fluttered at the edge of her vision and needle teeth bit deeply into her legs and arms. Dark unconsciousness swallowed everything and she slid into its gullet with tired gratitude.

The phone.

The phone was ringing and her body was cramping and the tile was cold against her skin. She scrambled to her feet and staggered toward the source of the noise, head spinning, muscles screaming. She groped blindly for the receiver.

"Yeah, hello."

"Caitlin?" It was Eric. "Jesus Christ, didn't you get any of my messages? I been trying to reach you all night."

"Eric," she said. Her mouth was dry and awful. "What is it?"

"It's Mike," he said. A long pause, and then, "Caitlin, he's been shot."

"Shot," she said, uncomprehending. She felt the recoil of the gun in her hand and Absinthe's hot blood on her face.

"I been trying to reach you." Eric's voice was rough, broken. "He's in the trauma unit here at Saint Vincent's. He wants to see you."

Silence. Caitlin could not speak.

"Caitlin, are you there?"

"I'm here."

"It's bad, Caitlin," he said. "It's so fucking bad. You gotta come and see him as soon as you can. The doctors say he might not make it through another night."

"Fine," she heard herself say. "I'll be there as soon as I can."

When she hung up the phone, she started laughing. If anyone had been listening, they might have thought she were being murdered. She slumped down to the floor, laughing and crying and wondering just how many hits the human psyche was capable of taking before it checked out completely. How much more could she take before her mind just went spinning off into the void? She took a deep breath and struck herself in the face as hard as she could. Glitter danced in her vision like artificial snow and the pain warmed her, focused her. She did it again and a third time. Then she stood and went into the bathroom to wash up.

The hospital was just like every other one, dismal and antiseptic, its aroma bringing up memories of her fragile and dying mother. The lounge down the hall from the trauma ward was stale and full of people who hadn't slept in days thumbing listlessly through irrelevant magazines. Eric was there, staring at a greenish television. He looked awful.

Caitlin stood in the doorway for a long moment, wondering what would happen if she just turned around and left.

Then Eric looked up and saw her. He stood, face weary and ravaged. He smelled like cigarettes and bad, sick sweat.

"Jesus Christ, Caitlin, I thought you weren't coming."

"Tell me," she said.

They sat in a pair of molded plastic seats with a white plastic table between them.

"We were talking to this chick whose boyfriend threw her baby out a window. Typical shit, no surprises. He used to beat her, y'know, like that. So we're in this shitty little apartment all full of booze bottles and stuffed animals and she's telling us how he used to beat her, how he used to tell her he was gonna kill her and the baby, that kinda thing, and she's crying and shit. She's got snot all on her face and she starts digging in her purse like she's looking for a tissue. Mike, he leaned down to give this chick a tissue and she pulls out a fucking gun."

He paused, swallowing. Caitlin felt nothing.

"He just stared at her. I mean, shit, Mike did 28 months with Hostage Negotiation back in '84-'85. He's always been great with these kinda situations. Cool, y'know, even when everyone else was flipping out. But it's like he wasn't even trying, like he didn't even care." His voice became monotone. The story took on the reheated flavor of something repeated a thousand times for various officials. "She fired two shots. The first one hit him in the face. The second one hit him in the throat. I returned fire, hitting her once in the shoulder and twice in the chest. She's down the hallway."

He wiped his mouth on the back of his hand.

"I feel like it's my fault, like if I hadn't made him come ... "

Caitlin nodded silently.

"It's so fucking bad, Caitlin. He's all sewn up now, so you can't really see, but I know how bad it is. I could see his fucking jawbone. All these little pieces of teeth." He closed his eyes. "I tried to hold him, tried to tell him that it was OK, that the ambulance was coming, that he should just hang on, but he was all over the place, knocking shit over, making this fucking sound like a cat throwing up. I kept telling him to just lay still, to just hold on. I don't even know if he heard me."

Caitlin tried to feel something, anything. She tried to picture the scene Eric was describing, but all she could see was Absinthe, baptized by flame. She tried to remember making love with Mike, walking with him in Washington Square Park, drinking Cafe Bustello with him on the fire escape, but the memories seemed to belong to someone else.

"The doctors say even if he survives, there's a good chance that he'll have brain damage." Eric shook his head. "Brain damage. Christ."

"Can I see him?" Caitlin asked. If she could see him, then maybe she would believe in the memories again.

Eric nodded.

"The nurse'll show you to his room. It's the first on the left." He reached out and put a hand on her shoulder. "It's really bad, Caitlin. Try to prepare yourself before you go in. I know you're a tough chick, but I'm pretty tough too, and I just about lost it when I saw all them tubes and stuff. It's real good of you to come. He really cares about you a lot, you know that, don't you?"

"Yeah," she said. "Yeah, I know that."

43.

The nurse was Philippino, with shiny red lips and a pale green smock. She was silent and respectful as she led Caitlin to Mike's room.

The thing that shocked her the most was that there were hardly any bandages. There was a folded square of gauze over one eye and sucking pouches of yellow and red fluid that seemed to be draining hidden wounds. Rows of metal staples ran the length of his distorted jaw and his skin was a rainbow of bruises, horribly swollen, glittering with wire and angled struts. Piss flowed sluggishly down a tube taped to one leg and a complex tree of IV bags fed into his distended veins. A curled length of tubing hung from one nostril and an open, hissing pipe protruding from his throat dribbled and sucked, dribbled and sucked. There was blood crusted in his hair.

"Mike?" She stepped up to the bed. She forced herself to take his hand. It felt hot and bloated, like a latex glove filled with warm water. "Mike, it's Caitlin."

His uncovered eye was barely more than a sticky purple slit. She could not tell if it was open. His fingers twitched slightly and she jumped, biting back a scream.

His left hand was curled around a red plastic pen with no ink and poised under his fist was a magic slate, the kind little kids use to write secret messages. His fingers jerked across the slate and pulled back the grey film that erased the old messages, but not before she saw her own name scrawled over and over.

He lay still for a long moment, then drew a lopsided heart and tapped it hard enough to leave scratches on the plastic.

A huge wave of dizziness surged through her body and she bit down hard on her lower lip. Cold sweat prickled on her stomach and the back of her neck. She felt hollow, scooped out on the inside.

"I love you, too," she said, too late of course. She was shaking, knees soft and weak and she saw tiny splashes of water on her forearm, glistening on the delicate blonde hairs. She did not know if they were tears or sweat.

"CAIT," he spelled in drunken, childish letters. He tapped the heart again.

"It's me," she said. "It's me, I'm right here."

"SORY," he wrote. She struggled to follow each painful letter.

"What?" She frowned at the scrawl.

A sharp hiss of air from the mucus-crusted tube in his neck as he pulled up the film, erasing the words. He began again, writing slow.

"S O R R Y," he spelled.

"Oh, baby, no." Caitlin held his limp fingers to her lips. "No, don't be sorry. I was stupid. I'm the one who should be sorry. It doesn't matter now."

She knew that it was the right thing to say, but inside, she still felt nothing. A cold, sneaky voice in her head told her to just keep making the right shapes with her mouth, since he would be dead soon anyway. Dead like Eva. Like Absinthe. Like Caitlin.

She stood for three hours, holding his hand, watching the clock turn and listening the liquid suction of his breath, the blip and hum of unobtrusive monitors. Nurses came and went noiselessly on soft white shoes, checking and injecting and replacing. Caitlin was not sure if he was conscious, but every time she tried to take her hand away, his fingers would clutch tightly and his single eye would roll towards her. That cold voice kept asking, *how much longer?*

Once again, if this had been a movie, he would have died right after he told her that he loved her. But the writer of this script seemed to have no sense of timing and the moment just went on and on with no purpose and no hidden meaning. When Caitlin was finally asked to leave by the nightshift nurse, she was obscurely grateful.

Back in the lounge, Eric was still waiting with a blue paper cup of coffee and a new layer of rings under his eyes. Beside him sat an older woman who Caitlin had only ever seen in photographs. She was delicately pretty with wide brown eyes, and she hugged herself like a frightened child. Her dark hair was twisted up off her neck and her make-up looked hastily applied in an airport restroom.

"Caitlin," Eric said, standing as if to deflect her away from the red faced woman.

"Maura," Caitlin said, her voice cold and measured. "I'm surprised you had the nerve to show up. How's the new sucker?"

"Caitlin," Eric repeated. "I don't think ... "

She stepped past Eric and stood inches from Maura's chair, wielding her height like a weapon.

"I just wanted to make sure he was OK," Maura said, her voice high and shaky, intimidated.

"Oh, now you care whether he's OK. I think you've caused him enough pain for one lifetime. The last thing he needs is your pathetic attempt to make yourself feel better about it by sucking up to him when he's fucking dying."

Caitlin was crying, tears like slow lava, burning, because she wasn't really talking to Maura at all. She was talking to herself. Eric tried to take her arm and she shook him off.

"Don't fucking TOUCH me!"

She felt out of control, ready to smash everything. She wanted to kill everyone. Maura was crying, too, and Caitlin wanted to break her neck and crush her face. She covered her eyes with both hands and sank into a plastic chair, turning a mental stream of liquid nitrogen like a firehose on the raging emotions. When she uncovered her face, she was calm.

"Sorry," she said.

In her mind she saw his big scrawling letters and the crooked heart with the long scratches inside.

44.

Cold morning. The city grey and reluctant outside Caitlin's window. The phone was ringing and she stared at it, waiting for the machine to pick up.

"Hello, Caitlin?" A perky voice emanated from the plastic box. "My name is Judy, I'm Mike's cousin. I just wanted to see how he was doing. I think it's so wonderful, what you're doing for him. We are all praying for him and for you, too. If you ever need anything, or if you just want to talk ... "

A sharp tone cut across the woman's voice and the tape rewound. Caitlin stared at the machine for a long time, her mind idling in empty neutral. She brought her thumb up to her lips and set to work ripping a chunk of dead skin from the corner of her nail. Blood flowed. It tasted like memories, like the other side of the wall. She could not make herself care. She watched the red numerals on the answering machine, waiting for them to tell her it was time to go to the hospital.

In Mike's room, nothing ever changed. Caitlin sat in the uncomfortable chair next to his bed, watching the ticking clock and marking time in wet exhalations and the satisfied rhythm of busy machines. He could no longer be roused to anything resembling consciousness. He had not written any messages in over two weeks, but she kept the magic slate on his bedside table, just in case. It was impossible to tell if he understood anything she said, but she always recited the list of people who called, always read his letters and cards to him, always told him that she loved him.

Doctors came and recited complicated pronouncements that slid smoothly over Caitlin's brain with out making the slightest impression. She learned to memorize these periodic updates in order to regurgitate them for the caring relatives to lick up.

Intracranial pressure is still high ... still a slight fever ... no he hasn't regained consciousness yet ... it's really too soon to tell.

But they never told Caitlin what she wanted to know. In all the condescending attitudes and false optimism, no one told her how much longer.

Because inside, Caitlin was convinced that it would never end, that he would never get any better, but he would never die either. She was in hell, doing eternal penance for loving the way Justine had bucked and writhed under the lash, the way Absinthe's fine skin had torn and bled beneath her teeth..

Eric, in the doorway, his suit loose over newly assertive bones. His cop-belly had melted away and his round, comedian's face had acquired a new severity. It reminded Caitlin of the softness that had rounded out the rippled definition of her abdomen, smoothed the cuts in her arms and swelled her tiny breasts. What he had lost, she had found but she couldn't make herself care. He kissed her cheek and pulled a chair up to Mike's bed.

"How ya doing, buddy?" His voice was painfully cheerful. "You know Leary's still got me flying a fucking desk. Talking to that idiot Priesinger three times a week, too, just to make sure I don't go psycho. I don't know why I didn't get what's-her-name, remember, that hot blonde shrink. Figures, right? You know my luck."

He paused, face flushed red. Caitlin knew what he was thinking. *Luck is not getting a sexy psychiatrist. Luck is a bullet taking off your partner's face and passing you by.* She wanted to tell him that she understood, but she could not speak. All her emotions felt like dark cruising shapes under heavy ice. Dangerous, but inaccessible.

"Anyway," Eric was saying. "If everything goes the way I hope, I'll be back in the real world by the end of the month. Sara sends her love, and all the guys are pulling for you. You know that."

Silence and sucking breath and Eric's uncomfortable guilt as tangible as the wet-bread stink of unchanged bandage and slowly dying flesh.

"So, I uh ... " He rubbed his big hands together. "I guess I better be going. I'll be back to see you again tomorrow, OK buddy?"

More silence, long and excruciating.

"See you tomorrow, Eric," Caitlin said, turning her face to be kissed.

"Yeah, right." He pressed dry lips to her cheek. "See you tomorrow."

She watched him leave, his shoulders sharp and hopeless under his wrinkled jacket.

45.

A chilly, autumn morning decorated with black and orange construc-
tion paper in honor of the coming holiday. Caitlin was underdressed on
her way to the hospital. She had forgotten it was not still July. The three
months that had passed could have been a single day. She was shivering
in her unwashed t-shirt by the time she pushed open the heavy glass
doors and swallowed the day's first breath of tainted hospital air. She
followed the familiar corridors with blind resignation, a sorry handful
of well meaning but irrelevant letters from friends and family under her
arm. When she came to his room, his bed was empty.

She stood in the doorway, staring at the neat white expanse of clean
sheets. Her mind was as empty as his room.

A Jamaican nurse was touching her shoulder, speaking in soft
lilting tones that made no sense to Caitlin at all. She turned her head,
struggling to focus on the movements of her dark lips. Something
about emergency surgery, about swelling of the brain.

"He had a bad night," the nurse was saying.

"A bad night," Caitlin repeated, the phrase meaningless on her
tongue.

The nurse was directing her to a lounge where she should wait.

"Three hours," she was saying. "He'll be down in surgical ICU. You
can see him there."

It was not three hours. It was less than fifteen minutes.

"You are Caitlin McCullough?" An Indian doctor with long white
hair and a round, child-like face. "You are here for Michael Kiernan?"

"Yes," Caitlin standing, mouth full of ice.

"Can you please step into the office."

She followed the doctor, unable to do anything else.

The office was sea green and pale rose, soothing colors selected by a psychologist. When she saw those colors, she knew without a doubt that he was dead.

The doctor was explaining things that made no difference at all to Caitlin. She watched the doctor's mouth.

"I'm very sorry," she was saying. "We did everything we could for him."

Tears on Caitlin's face, but she could not feel them. She wanted to grab the doctor's white lapels and scream into her face: *Now what am I supposed to do?* The only thing that had kept her from eating three bottles of Sominex and never waking up was the dry routine of obligation. How could she go home and watch the numbers on the answering machine, knowing that it would never again be time to go to the hospital? Instead of screaming, she nodded, competent, responsible, listing names of people to be notified. It was an excellent act.

When she stood, razor-petaled flowers bloomed inside her abdomen and she cried out, blood soaking through her jeans. The gentle, soothing colors were eclipsed by angry, pulsing red. The doctor's brown hands were on her as her legs buckled and swirling blackness obscured everything.

A long blur of impressions. Endless hallways and probing hands. Hot blood between her legs and sour vomit in her mouth and underscoring it all, pain like a neverending drumroll in her belly. Disassociated images floated in her head. She could smell Absinthe's breath, his hair. Jez's soft, apologetic voice whispered to her. Megan's shrieking guitar, full of unquenchable pain. Caitlin saw herself at 17 gathering up dirty laundry and yelping with surprise as long pins sank into her fingers. Thirteen pins threaded carefully into the stiff crotch of her sister's panties. She knew that her sister cut herself for pleasure, that she devised endless tests of endurance that lasted days, but holding those panties with their subtle teeth made it that much more real. Megan was dead the next morning.

The parade of memories seemed to have no end.

She saw her father hunched shape over Megan's bed, dragging her sister up out of sleep, lifting her in her rumpled nightgown and carrying her, fighting silently out into the bathroom. He would press his finger to his thin mouth and wink at Caitlin where she huddled sleepless in her clammy bed, confident of the safety of their shared secret. He knew she wouldn't tell, because in the darkest part of her heart she enjoyed her sister's pain.

Megan took her secrets with her when she died. Caitlin never told anyone what she had seen.

A woman was leaning over Caitlin, demanding her attention.

"Am I dying?" Caitlin asked.

"Don't be silly," she said. "You're having a miscarriage, that's all. We've scheduled you for an emergency D&C. I'll need you to fill out some forms."

"What?" Everything snapped suddenly into sharp focus. "That's not possible."

"I know this must be hard for you, dear. But you're young and healthy, you have plenty of time to try again."

"What are you talking about." The bright pattern of the woman's smock hurt Caitlin's head, a nauseating swirl of yellow and red, like bloody egg yolk. "I'm not pregnant."

The woman frowned.

"Well, I understand how hard this is ... "

"I am not pregnant." Caitlin repeated. "It must be some mistake."

She tried to sit up and knives slashed at her belly.

"Please," the woman eased her back down. "Try to relax."

Miscarriage, she thought. *She means a baby. A dead man's dead baby is inside me, has been inside me for months and I didn't even know it.* A wave of nausea swept over her and she was reminded of a time when she found a nest of albino cockroaches behind her refrigerator. Who knew how long they had been there inches away from her food while she went about her life. She thought of Absinthe, of the delicious friction of his bare cock inside her, of the liquid heat of his semen bursting in the fertile darkness of her pussy. She thought of the pain and betrayal in his eyes as he lay burning, dying.

The woman narrowed her eyes at Caitlin. Mascara clogged her lashes.

"You mean to tell me that you had a pregnancy this advanced and didn't know it?"

Caitlin couldn't speak. She shook her head.

"When was your last period?"

Caitlin struggled to remember.

"I don't know."

"What do you mean you don't know?"

Anger swelled in Caitlin's guts, a hot slippery sensation that was curiously compatible with the dull pain there.

"I mean, I don't fucking know. My mind has been on other things."

"Well you obviously have not been practicing safe sex." The woman's pink lips clenched like a reluctant sphincter. "That's not very responsible."

There was a feeling of stepping back, a physical tearing of her soul disconnecting from her flesh. She watched her hands fly at the nurse's face like the hooked talons of a bird of prey, heard her voice like the wailing of some insane hardcore vocalist on PCP, but she felt nothing. A needle's alcohol sting and insidious chemical blackness speeding through her veins, then more nothing.

46.

Caitlin woke with a horrible empty feeling and a creeping sickness in the back of her throat. Her head felt packed with sodden cotton and whirling vertigo swirled around her when she tried to sit up. She was dressed in a blue and white hospital gown that was rucked up around her hips. A slow drizzle of sluggish blood flowed between her legs. A young black man with a kind face was standing over her with a paper cup.

"See if you can suck some of this ice," he said.

"Is it out yet?" she asked.

"What?" He blinked.

"The dead baby," she said. "Is it out?"

The corner of his mouth turned up in a sad smile.

"Yes," he said, pressing the cup into her hands. "It's over."

She stared into the refracting surfaces of the cubes. It seemed to take forever for her to bring the cup to her lips. The ice was cold bliss on her parched tongue.

"Where are my clothes?" She was suddenly sure that they were going to try to keep her if she didn't escape immediately. She sat up, clenching her fists around the dizziness.

"Here," a woman who she hadn't noticed handed her a white plastic bag. Her soiled jeans were neatly folded. She thought of the neat pile of folded clothes on Absinthe's chair that first morning.

"I need to get out of here," she told the man.

"Do you have anyone who can come and get you?" the man asked, politely turning his head as she dressed.

The jeans were stiff and horrid with old blood. She peeled the printed backing off the maxi pad the woman gave her and pressed it to the stained crotch.

"No." She shook her head. "I'll be fine."

"Take a cab home, OK?" He was giving her forms to sign and an orange bottle of pills to take three times a day with meals. She nodded like a good girl and forced herself not to run.

She was in a part of the hospital that she didn't recognize. The dim hallways smelled like boiled cabbage and bleach, like soiled sheets and pureed meat. She followed the twisting maze, taking turns at random, seeing fewer and fewer people. She was passing a soda machine that glowed like an alien monolith when she became aware of a skulking shadow tailing her.

She took two more turns and the shadow followed. As she passed under a bank of fluorescent lights, she saw the shadow was a shabby figure with a dirty overcoat and a wool hat pulled low over a face like a grey and pink puzzle. A thin spurt of adrenaline spurred her trembling legs faster. The next turn revealed a bank of elevators. A dead end.

Caitlin dug frantically in her pockets for coins as she spun to face the homeless man turning the corner behind her. She could smell him. A hot, sick smell that dug hooks deep in her gullet. He pulled the shapeless hat off his head and Caitlin's change slipped through her numb fingers to scatter uselessly on the green linoleum, because it was Absinthe.

Screaming wasn't even an option. She was sure that her voice had vanished for good, that there was just nothing left to say in the face of this walking dead man. Inescapable blankness crept across her mind and she was still as death was supposed to be as she stared into the familiar crimson madness of her lover's eyes.

His beautiful hair had been burnt to patchy fuzz on his blistered scalp. One arm hung useless in a dirty sling, the hand a twisted claw. But the face ...

That angelic, demonic face. The beauty that had inspired lust and loyalty and desperate obsession was gone, buried under slick burnflesh that glistened like the melted plastic face of a doll Megan held against the radiator as an experiment. But the eyes were unchanged, bright, nearly crimson rings around pools of blackest lunacy.

A narcotic peace stole over Caitlin as he took another step closer. She was not afraid at all. It seemed perfectly logical that he should kill her.

I kill you, you kill me.

It saved her the trouble of having to do it herself. Death was all the rage lately, it seemed, and who was she to argue with fashion? Idly, she wondered if it would hurt much. Not that she minded, it was just that the uterine rotorooter had hurt so much. She was struck with an urge to tell Absinthe about the baby.

I was pregnant with your baby, but now it's dead, just like Daddy.

A sick giggle rose in her throat like a bubble of vomit. He cocked his head at her like a curious dog.

Caitlin bit down hard on her tongue and a bright burst of dizzy pain shot though her. Warm blood ran down her chin like drool.

Absinthe's eyes followed that scarlet trickle with starving intensity. He took the last step between them, reaching out with his filthy, black nailed hand.

Caitlin felt sure that she must be screaming now, but there was no sound but the low buzz of the fluorescent lights and the drone of the distant elevators.

He touched a delicate finger to her lower lip. His amber eyes were wet and glistening and, as she watched, fat tears spilled down his ravaged cheeks. He knelt down and, for an exquisitely surreal moment, she was sure that he was going to kiss her feet. Instead he laid a crumpled sheet of smudged yellow paper on the linoleum inches from her boots.

Then, with no word or explanation, he turned and ran, disappearing around the corner.

Caitlin struggled to convince herself that the entire episode was a hallucination brought on by extreme stress and pharmaceutical pain suppressants, except for the folded paper at her feet.

You don't have to pick it up, you can just walk away.

She bent her knees, her fingers reaching.

Just walk away!

The paper was cold and slightly clammy. Instead of walking away, she picked it up and held it tightly, as if she was afraid she might drop it. She unfolded it with numb fingers. In scrawling letters, three lines.

Don't be afraid of me
I have to tell you
I will find you again

Caitlin shuddered, crumpled the note and threw it, wiping her hand on her stained jeans. She thought maybe she ought to be scared, but the idea was just too abstract. When she turned the corner, she knew exactly where she was.

47.

Caitlin could not bear the dark silence of her apartment. All her things seemed like traps to catch her mind and hold it forever in empty contemplation. She pulled off her filthy jeans and studied the stiff bloodstain as if it were a psychiatrist's test. It was an angel. It was a grinning mouth. It was an open book. It was a bloodstain, the rich blood meant to cradle a vampire's baby, now dead and flushed away. Pain pirouetted in her belly and vomit caressed the back of her throat. She stuffed the jeans into the trash.

It took her almost an hour to find a pair of sweatpants that were only slightly cleaner. Her head was woozy and spinning, chilly sweat slicking her back and armpits. Just as she was fumbling with the locks on her door, she remembered that it was cold outside. She groped blindly in the closet and came out with her leather motorcycle jacket. It felt heavy, but reassuring. Slipping into its warm weight, she stuffed her hands into the pockets and her fingers brushed the herbal charm given to her by a kid with the bluest eyes. She could not remember any of Crow's words, just the sound of his voice. She shook her head and threw open the door to her apartment.

Standing across the hall, nearly lost in a shabby cloth coat many sizes too big, was Jez.

Her mouth was dirty, her eyes wide and haunted. She wore a green knit hat with the name of some team stitched in yellow, and her bare and grimy feet were stuffed into cracked rubber beach sandals.

"Morrigan," Jez said, so softly that Caitlin might have imagined it.

Raising her hands against this new apparition from her other life, Caitlin took a step back. Her thoughts were a chaos of razors and broken mirror fragments. Her belly ached, violated uterus clenching like teeth chewing on nothing. Washes of sweat and vertigo made her stagger against the door frame.

"Morrigan," Jez said again, louder this time, undeniable.

Then cool hands took hers and led her back inside, so helpful and unobtrusive as they steadied her, guiding her to the couch and laying her down. Her head swam, her heart pounding.

"Jez?" Caitlin heard herself say. "Is it really you?"

Her vision cleared suddenly and she saw Jez kneeling beside her, just like the old days.

"I'm here, Mistress," Jez said. "I'll take care of you."

The next few days, Caitlin spent in a kind of fugue state, punctuated by pain and cool cloths across her forehead and ice water and bitter pills. Jez's soothing voice underscoring it all, reassuring her.

She woke with a start in the middle of the afternoon, drenched with sweat, but cool and aware for the first time in what seemed like forever.

Jez was there beside her, clean now and dressed in one of Caitlin's white t-shirts that slid down off one bony shoulder when the girl leaned in and laid a hand on Caitlin's sweaty forehead. One of her faded blue bandannas covered the girl's head, intricately knotted at the nape of her neck. She looked like the world's meekest gang-member.

"Your fever broke," Jez told her, brushing wet strands of hair away from Caitlin's face.

"How long was I out of it?" Caitlin asked, struggling to sit up.

"Three days, Mistress," Jez said, handing her a glass of water.

Caitlin drank deeply, lost for a moment in the pure pleasure of parched tissues gratefully absorbing the cool liquid.

"Listen," Caitlin said, setting the empty glass down on the coffee table. "You don't have to call me Mistress anymore."

Jez bowed her head.

"But I want to," she said.

Caitlin felt a strange, hot emotion uncurl inside her, something almost maternal in it's primal strength. She reached out and pulled the girl close to her, fingers wandering up the back of her neck to the knot in the bandanna. The girl shuddered and hugged back fiercely. She smelled like Caitlin's soap.

"I thought you were dead," Caitlin whispered.

Jez didn't answer, just hugged tighter.

Caitlin pulled away slightly, taking Jez's narrow face in both her hands.

"What happened to you?"

Jez blinked and tried to look down, but Caitlin held her chin.

"I was ... " she said, eyes darting back and forth, looking anywhere but at Caitlin. "I was lost in the smoke." She paused. "I ... I didn't have any clothes. It was so hot and I couldn't breathe and then somebody saved me."

"Who?" Caitlin asked. "Who saved you?"

Jez's forehead wrinkled and Caitlin realized that her eyebrows had not grown back.

"A boy. A slave, maybe." Jez struggled to look away and Caitlin let go of her chin, her hand resting on Jez's razor-thin shoulder. "I just remember him looking at me in the alley. Staring at me." She shook her head. "Then everything got all mixed up in my head and the next thing I remember I was hiding. Always hiding."

Caitlin pulled the girl close again, soothing her. She could feel the girl's desperate heartbeat against her belly.

"Who were you hiding from?" she asked, thinking of Absinthe, of his wild eyes and cooked skin.

Jez shuddered.

"Hellebore," she whispered. "She wants me back."

Caitlin felt cold creeping fingers down her spine as she hugged Jez tighter, suddenly protective. The girl's scrawny body felt so fragile, as delicate as the transparent husk of a cicada Caitlin had once found clinging to a blade of grass in the park. The t-shirt was old and thin and as Caitlin ran her hand down Jez's scarred back, over her sharp bones and angles, her fingers automatically sought the rigid edges of the leather chastity belt. When her hand slid smoothly over the small of Jez's back and down over the knot of her tailbone to the smooth cheeks of her narrow ass, Caitlin realized that the girl was naked beneath the white cloth.

This realization brought a rush of blood to Caitlin's face and a slow pulse of heat between her legs. For the past few months, her body had been cold and dead and after the grinding pain of her miscarriage, this cautious awakening felt strange and wonderful.

"I'll protect you," Caitlin said, her voice unsteady with perilous emotion. "I won't let anyone hurt you."

Jez made a soft noise in the back of her throat and pressed her cheek to Caitlin's. Her skin was cool and smooth as marble. Diving down into warm and familiar waters, Caitlin tipped her face up and kissed her.

Her tongue was hot and slick against Caitlin's lips. Feeling as if she were falling, spiraling backwards into the long untended garden of her forgotten desires, Caitlin pulled Jez up into her lap, hands strong and purposeful as they slid over Jez's skinny hips and up her rippled ribcage, thumbs teasing her childish nipples. She pinched hard and Jez groaned, tossing her head and grinding her hips.

A fierce new energy was coursing through Caitlin's veins, burning off the dull grey mindlessness that had held her brain hostage for so long. She felt strong again. Alive. It seemed that the dominant soul that had been awakened and nurtured by the Club had not died with its destruction. That place might have been her training wheels once but now she could ride alone, defiant, unbound by the endless rules and restrictions of that obsessively ritualistic atmosphere. For the first time in what felt like ages, Caitlin could imagine a future. Laughing, she gripped the back of Jez's neck and forced the girl's face down between her legs.

The rich waves of pleasure that washed over Caitlin as Jez worked teasing circles with the tip of her tongue felt so cleansing, so right and she gave in to the sensation completely, forgetting everything.

When the heat of orgasm gripped her, it felt like coming home.

They lay still together for a long moment, Jez's head resting against Caitlin's bare belly. Then, Caitlin pulled the girl up and kissed her pungent mouth, tasting blood and her own pussy.

She pressed kisses to the curve of Jez's throat, biting gently at first, then harder. Her fingers slid over Jez's pale thighs and up under the t-shirt, again surprised to feel flesh instead of leather but not nearly as surprised as she was when her questing fingers reached the delta between Jez's boyish legs.

It felt like thrusting her hand into a dish of live worms, but hot, nearly burning. She yanked her hand away, horrified, sucking air through her teeth.

Jez pushed away and crouched down on the floor, pulling the thin fabric down to cover herself. Her eyes were huge, her nostrils flaring.

"Jez?"

Caitlin reached out to touch her and the girl swatted her hand away with shocking strength.

"Don't touch me!" Jez turned her face away, tears in her bright eyes.

Caitlin frowned. She swallowed her momentary revulsion and crouched down on the floor beside the shivering girl.

"Hey Jez," she said, speaking softly, non-threatening. "It's OK honey, don't cry."

"Get away from me!" Jez stood and backed away, pressing against the wall with her arms wrapped around herself.

Caitlin stayed down on the floor, showing her palms.

"I'm not going to touch you unless you want me to. See?" She sat and crossed her legs. "I'm just gonna sit right here."

They stayed that way for a good half hour, Jez flat against the wall, crying silently and Caitlin sitting on the floor, waiting.

"Do you hate me?" Jez asked suddenly, wiping her nose on the back of her hand.

"Of course not," Caitlin said. "Why would you think that?"

Jez frowned.

"If I show you, you have to promise not to hate me."

Caitlin smiled.

"You probably saved my life, taking care of me the way you did," she said. "How could I ever hate you?"

Jez watched her like a suspicious wild animal, unsure. Then, suddenly, she yanked the t-shirt over her head and threw it down on the floor where it lay, crumpled, between them.

Naked, Jez looked just as she always looked, breastless, hipless, her childish body nothing but thin white skin over her delicate bones. She could have been a boy except what was between her legs was certainly

234

not a penis. It was not really a vagina either. What had been done to Eva had also been done to Jez.

But Eva's butchered labia was a cruder version, the cuts more ragged, more hasty. The artwork between Jez's legs was smooth and fluid, curling tendrils of red flesh clustered like the stinging arms of a sea anemone and soft, fleshy wings, impossibly delicate, so thin as to be almost translucent in the pale afternoon sun. There was nothing that resembled a vaginal opening, just a tiny dark slit like a closed eye in the center of all this chaos.

Caitlin struggled to keep her face neutral, non- judgmental. Her stomach churned.

"Who did this to you?" she whispered.

Jez blinked, as if she hadn't understood.

"It's OK," Caitlin said, her voice low and soothing while her heart pounded in her chest. "You can tell me."

"It ... " Fresh tears spilled down Jez's cheeks. "It was Absinthe."

She crossed the space between them and threw herself, sobbing, into Caitlin's arms.

Caitlin held Jez's trembling body, hyper-aware of the hot, wormy press of the girl's mutilated genitals against her bare thigh.

"Eva was going to take me away," Jez said, speaking fast and breathless against Caitlin's shoulder. "When Absinthe found us, he killed her and he ... he cut her up." Jez shuddered. "The whole time he was doing it, he was telling me that I was next, but that he wouldn't kill me first. He would let me live like this for the rest of my life as a punishment for running away. I tried to tell Eva that this would happen, but she wouldn't listen."

Jez's words were swallowed up by choking tears and Caitlin held her, stroking her bare back, and whispering soft reassurance.

"You poor girl," she said, fingers wandering across the thick bands of scar that cris-crossed her back and ass.

Absinthe, that bastard. How could he do something so inhuman to an innocent girl? Suddenly, she thought again of Absinthe's note, of his burned, twisted face. Jez felt her go stiff and looked up, curious.

"He followed me to the hospital," Caitlin said.

Jez's eyes went huge.

"He's alive?"

Caitlin nodded.

"He wanted to talk to me," she said. She saw him kneeling down before her in the bright hospital hallway, the dull fluorescent lights glistening in his mad eyes.

Jez hugged Caitlin tighter.

"Don't do it!" she pleaded. "He'll kill us both."

"Don't worry, Jez," Caitlin said, arms tight around her skinny ribs. "I won't let anyone hurt you, I promise."

Caitlin lifted Jez in her arms and carried her to the sofa.

"Everything will be fine," Caitlin said, wrapping her blanket around Jez's shoulders.

"I love you, Mistress," Jez said. Her eyes were shiny, rainwater puddles reflecting a stormy sky.

Caitlin smiled and pulled her close.

They lay like that as the sun went red and bled away into New Jersey and the streetlights started to come on in the pale, lavender twilight.

Caitlin wondered if Jez were sleeping. Her arm was full of pins and needles, but she felt too good to move. This quiet peace was hard won and well deserved. She had fought a terrible battle and come out the other side. Like ancient Inanna, she had descended into the Underworld, and emerged triumphant. The hell of the past few months had not broken her. She felt as if she had gone crazy and come back again and now maybe she could begin to live again.

She felt the girl shift slightly and she shifted with her. As she moved, Caitlin's stomach rumbled loudly and she suddenly realized that she hadn't eaten in days. Jez looked up and giggled.

"Hey, you know what?" Caitlin said. "I'm starving!"

"Me too," Jez said, as if she were ashamed to admit it.

"There ain't shit in the house," Caitlin said. She had been mostly eating in the hospital cafeteria and there was maybe half a bottle of flat seltzer water in the fridge.

"I found some crackers," Jez told her in that same, apologetic voice.

"You mean all you've eaten in the last few days is some crackers?"

Jez nodded.

"Well shit!" Caitlin sat up and stretched. "We better go get some Chinese food or something."

Jez smiled, and Caitlin realized that she had never seen the girl smile before.

———————

In the fragrant, steamy cave of a tiny Chinese restaurant, Caitlin ate spicy ginger shrimp and hot rice and vegetable soup with little brown mushrooms that she fed to Jez with chopsticks.

"They're like little dicks," Jez said, poking one of them with her pinkie.

Caitlin laughed out loud.

"All the more reason to eat them, slut!" she said, forcing one between Jez's lips.

"Yes, Mistress!" The girl laughed and licked it's tiny cap with the tip of her tongue before sucking it into her mouth.

"Good girl," Caitlin said, brushing Jez's cheek with her scarred knuckles. "Now clean your plate, or you'll get a spanking!"

Jez smiled and again Caitlin marveled at the way it changed her face. Her grey eyes seemed almost violet, her strange, high cheekbones plump as apples. She left a single shrimp on her plate, eyes glittering with mischief.

"Did I say you were a good girl?" Caitlin paid the bill and took Jez's hand. "God, what was I thinking?"

Jez giggled, a flashing silver sound.

On the street, people gave them strange looks, ranging from disapproval to disgust to blank confusion. Their inability to get it made Caitlin feel special, a member of a secret society. Jez looked so sweet in that big white t-shirt and a pair of Caitlin's black bicycle shorts. They were skin tight on Caitlin, but Jez needed a belt with a new hole poked into it to hold them up and they still hung down over her knees. Caitlin's fleece-lined denim jacket with the sleeves rolled up kept Jez warm in the chilly night. It made Caitlin feel good to keep her warm. Waiting for the light on 24TH Street, she put her arm around the girl's skinny shoulders.

In the elevator of her building, Caitlin pressed Jez against the cheap paneling and smacked her ass six times in quick succession.

"Teach you to be a smart-ass," Caitlin whispered in her ear, hand sliding up under her shirt. "Nasty girl."

"I'm sorry, Mistress," Jez breathed.

Caitlin turned her around and kissed her mouth, tasting ginger and chilies.

When the door opened on her floor, Caitlin lifted Jez off the floor and threw the girl over her shoulder like a sack of potatoes. Jez giggled and squirmed.

"I'm going to teach you to behave like a proper young lady," she told Jez as she carried her down the hallway and dug out her keys. "I'll make you into a good girl if it kills me."

She swung open the door and inside, sitting on her sofa with a cigarette burning between long fingers, was Hellebore.

48.

"Morrigan," Hellebore said, nodding her head slightly. She brought the cigarette to her lips, pale eye jittering in its deep socket. "Good to see you again."

Caitlin let Jez down gently and the girl clung to her, burying her face under Caitlin's hair. There were two men in the room, standing together before the window, watching. They were both Asian, both dressed in expensive suits, but one was thin and arrogantly handsome with heavy eyebrows and fine, pale skin and the other was bulky and moon-faced like a sumo wrestler. Caitlin noticed that the big one was wearing a bolo tie shaped like a silver cow-skull and a leather shoulder holster like Mike's beneath his open jacket.

"What the fuck are you doing in my apartment?" Caitlin clenched her fist around her keys and wrapped a protective arm around Jez. Adrenaline hammered in her veins.

"No need to be rude," Hellebore said. She cupped a hand under the long ash of her cigarette. "Have you got an ashtray?"

"I quit smoking," Caitlin said, teeth clenching.

Hellebore shrugged and tapped her ash in an empty glass on the coffee table.

Caitlin drew herself up straight and took a step forward, keeping Jez behind her in the entryway.

"Will you please tell me why you've seen fit to break into my apartment?" She kept her voice even, but her heart was pounding.

"I want you to come back with me, Morrigan," Hellebore said, taking one last drag and dropping her cigarette into the sludge at the bottom of the glass where it died with a tiny hiss.

"Back to where?" Caitlin asked, frowning. "Your precious Club is nothing but ashes."

Hellebore smiled, just the thinnest smile.

"With you and Jez, I can rebuild. Start over in a new city." She took out Justine's silver case and extracted another cigarette. She held it out to Caitlin. "Oh, that's right," she said, closing it and slipping in into an inner pocket of her dark suit jacket. "You quit."

Caitlin could feel Jez pressing into her from behind, covering her face.

"Really, Morrigan," Hellebore continued. "You can't tell me you want to go back to your old life. Writing bad novels for next to nothing and dating men who just don't get it. Be realistic. Once you've tasted the kind of power I can give you, you can never go back."

"I don't need you to feel powerful," Caitlin said, taking another step forward. "I own who I am and Jez owns who she is and we don't need you. You need us. Without us, your money and your Club doesn't mean shit."

Hellebore bowed her head, cigarette burning unsmoked between her fingers.

"What can I say?" She turned her deformity away, good eye looking out at the night city. "You're right, I know."

She motioned to the men and the handsome one came forward with an aluminum briefcase. A Halliburton case. Caitlin only knew that because it was the kind of briefcase evil drug dealers in Vic Steele novels used to carry cocaine. Or money.

Sure enough, he laid the case on the coffee table and when he popped the lock, she saw that it was packed with stacks of bills.

"That is ten thousand dollars," Hellebore told her. "For starters. Taki will drive you and Jez to the Hotel Nikko where you will stay tonight. In the morning, he will take you to the airport. Your flight leaves for San Francisco at 3:00 PM."

Caitlin shook her head.

"Well," she said, eyes bouncing from the cash to Hellebore's twisted face and back again. "You sure have it all figured out."

"Your rent on this apartment has been paid for the next year, so your things will be safe until you decide to send for them." Hellebore dropped the cigarette into the sludge beside its dead sister. "If you have any other concerns, Taki will take care of them for you."

"What about Jez?" Caitlin asked, pulling Jez in front of her and wrapping an arm around her ribs. The girl was trembling like a frightened bird. "Doesn't she get any money?"

Hellebore laughed, a low breathy sound.

"Jez is a slave. What would she do with money?" Hellebore stood and closed the briefcase. "Besides, she's going regardless of your decision."

The two men stepped up to flank their Mistress.

"After all," Hellebore said. "She is my property."

Jez turned and pressed her face into Caitlin's armpit, shaking her head blindly. The desperate vulnerability in that small body made her decision for her.

"Fuck you and your money," Caitlin spat. "I want you and your goons out of my house, right now."

Hellebore sighed, almost regretful, sad, even.

"I'd really rather it didn't have to go this way," she said. "It will take me years to find another dominant as perfect as you."

"Well," Caitlin said. "It'll take even longer since you'll have to find a new submissive, too."

Jez looked up at her, joy and tears filling her violet-grey eyes.

Hellebore shook her head and made a subtle gesture with both hands.

"Let the girl go," she said.

When Caitlin looked up, the handsome goon had a big, butch Automag trained on her forehead.

Her heart clenched and her bowels went loose and hot. There was no doubt that this beautiful, cold-eyed man would put a bullet in her head without a second thought. Her mind worked furiously, an animal in a trap, all panicked teeth and claws. She was hideously sure that once Jez was out of the way, that man was going to shoot her anyway. It would be easier, cleaner than having her walking around after. She thought of what Vic Steele would do. That wily redhead could talk, shoot, or fuck her way out of any sticky situation, but Caitlin's mind was blank, empty of answers.

"Let her go, Morrigan," Hellebore said, more firmly this time.

Caitlin clenched her fist around her keys and the hot flare of an idea burst across her vision.

The hand that held the keys was behind Jez's narrow back. Eyes darting from the gun to Hellebore, Caitlin thumbed open the miniature Swiss army knife on her keychain until the pinkie-length blade clicked into place. She took a deep breath, blood screaming in her temples.

She lifted Jez off her feet with one arm and pressed the little knife against the soft flesh under her eye.

"Drop it, motherfucker."

The man's black coffee eyes went wide, flicking to Hellebore for guidance.

"Do it, pretty boy, unless you want to be responsible for your boss' precious slave doing the rest of her sessions with a fucking eyepatch."

Caitlin could barely believe her mouth. Cheesy, hardboiled dialogue always was her strong point. Those brave and stupid words hung in the air between them as if waiting for a laughtrack, or a bullet. There was something so exquisitely unreal about this exchange, something comical and horrible and utterly impossible. She swallowed hard, dry throat muscles clicking too loud in her ears.

"Morrigan, don't be stupid," Hellebore said. "You don't want to hurt Jez. She innocent."

"Call off your dog, Hellebore, or I swear to God ... "

Caitlin dug the point of the knife into the delicate skin and blood flowed with the tears. Jez cried out, instinctually sensing her role in this drama.

Hellebore made a hasty downward gesture and the man lowered his gun.

"On the floor," Caitlin said.

The man looked to Hellebore and she nodded, anger flashing in her good eye. He laid the gun on the scarred wood floor, palms out. The heavy clunk was sharp and hyper-real in the tense silence.

"That's it, just back away." Caitlin turned to the other man. "You too, Bubba-san. Just lay it down nice and easy."

The big man took a pistol out of his shoulder holster and laid it carefully beside the first. In a burst of pointless realization, Caitlin saw that it was a lightweight Glock 9mm with a long, 19 round magazine. By some utterly irrelevant coincidence, it was the same gun that Vic Steele had swiped from a dying hit-man in her latest epic. She had only ever seen a picture of it in an old copy of *The Shooter's Bible*. They used to be porcelain, but the new ones were some kind of high-tech polymer. Undetectable. Caitlin had to bite down hard on her lips to keep from laughing.

"What are you going to do now, Caitlin?" Hellebore asked, stepping back. "You can't kill us all."

Hellebore had never said her real name before and the sound of it brought her mind into sudden sharp focus. She remembered the slip of paper pressed into her hand by Wilson's distraught mother.

"You want to talk about names, Lily?" Caitlin said, triumphant heat pulsing in her throat. "Let's talk about Kaiichi Kobiyashi."

Silence. The goons glanced nervously at each other.

Caitlin grinned and pushed her advantage.

"If anything happens to me, in exactly twenty-four hours the dish on Kobiyashi's illegitimate daughter is gonna be spooling out of every fax machine in the offices of every tabloid from here to Tokyo and I'm the only one who knows how to stop it. Now, you wouldn't want Daddy to lose face in front of the whole world, would you? Not because of your deep abiding love for the old bastard, or even love for his hush money, but because after that, shame and family obligation would no longer stop him from having you killed."

For a long stretch of seconds, Hellebore said nothing, her crooked face utterly blank and Caitlin felt elated, like an action hero, destined to win if for no other reason than the fact that she was the good guy. Just as long as Hellebore didn't call her bluff.

The handsome gunman leaned in slow and began to speak in soft Japanese to Hellebore.

"Shut up," Caitlin said, setting Jez back down on the ground but not taking the blade from her eye, just in case. "Get in the bathroom."

Hellebore's crooked eyebrows knitted.

"What?"

"Do it," Caitlin said, stepping forward to stand between the men and their guns.

The men looked at each other and then at Hellebore. Hellebore made a soft spitting sound and began to back into the bathroom with her grunts behind her.

"Why do you have to make it so hard on yourself?"

Caitlin kicked the door closed in her face.

———————◆———————

With a shaky laugh, Caitlin let go of Jez and wiped blood from beneath her eye.

"Pretty tough, huh?" She covered her mouth with her hand. "Quick ... "

She wrestled her heavy armoire across the floor and leaned it against the bathroom door.

"Go open the front door." She pointed with her chin. "Hurry!"

Obedient, Jez ran and pulled the door open, glancing nervously out into the hallway.

Caitlin brushed her palms on her jeans.

"Now," she said. "Get the money."

Jez nodded and Caitlin set to work opening the bolted window by the fire escape. She felt full of the same blazing energy and subsurface hilarity as she had felt during that first scene with Justine. When she got the paint-sticky window open, Jez handed her the case. The goons were starting to pound on the bathroom door, so Caitlin laid the case on the iron fire escape and climbed out after it. She reached in to help Jez and the girl ducked away. Caitlin's guts knotted.

"Jez," she called in a loud, harsh whisper. "Jez, come back."

The girl reappeared with a pistol in each hand like a miniature gunslinger. Caitlin was amazed that the girl could hold the enormous Automag in one hand.

"Here," she said, handing Caitlin the Glock. She tucked the Automag into the belt holding up her too big shorts. It looked obscene beneath the thin black cloth, bigger than an average strap-on dildo. "Just in case."

Caitlin laughed, weak relief rushing through her belly. Tucking the Glock under her own waistband, she helped Jez out onto the fire escape and shut the window. Back in the apartment, the armoire was beginning to jump and splinter under relentless blows.

"If we're lucky," Caitlin said, climbing up fast and hustling Jez ahead of her. "They'll see the open door and think we went that way."

Up on the roof, Caitlin ran with the case in one hand and Jez's hand in the other.

"Even if they take the fire escape, they'll assume we went down."

Caitlin paused by a slit in the chainlink separating her building from its neighbor.

"We all used to get on the super's case about fixing this." She grinned, flying on the cold speed of victory. "Lazy shit might just have saved our asses."

She squeezed though, wire scratching at her face. Jez pushed the case through and then wiggled through after it.

On the other side, Jez paused briefly, eyes deep and wet in the faint city glow.

"Thank you," she said, bowing her head. "Mistress."

Caitlin pulled her close, holding her for a precious moment.

"C'mon," Caitlin said, pulling Jez to the new fire escape.

"Where are we going?" Jez asked, climbing.

Caitlin looked out over the glittery night street.

"I don't know," she answered. The metal case banged against her hip as she descended.

Jez paused, balanced on the wrought iron ladder.

"I know a place," she said. "A safe place where we can hide for a little while, until Hellebore gives up."

Caitlin looked into Jez's shiny eyes. She smiled.

"Alright then," she said.

49.

Little West Twelfth Street, just like Caitlin remembered it, but utterly different, like a slightly inaccurate movie set of itself. The Club was bricked up, black with smeary soot and sprayed with scrawling street mythology. Some guerrilla artist had painted Absinthe's portrait with diffuse spray-can colors, sensuous red lips peeled back from silver fang teeth, black hair wild, highlighted with glossy blue. Underneath, the words "LORD ABSINTHE WILL RETURN!"

Caitlin felt icy cold inside the heatless shell of her leather jacket. She held Jez's tiny hand tighter.

"This way," Jez whispered, urgent as she led Caitlin down into the narrow alley.

She wasn't sure why they were here, or what memories might be hidden in the soft ashes. Her adrenaline high had ebbed away, leaving behind a profound fatigue. Lazy fear danced slow spirals in her belly but she pressed on, following Jez in silence. The shrieking love of alleycats was the only soundtrack.

Jez froze in front of her and then squatted down on the cobblestone.

"Shit," she said, running her fingers over fresh, pale boards held across a low window by shiny new nails.

"What is it?" Caitlin asked, squatting down beside her, touching a smooth nail-head with the tip of her finger.

"They sealed it up." Jez looked up, eyes shadowed. "I used to hide here, but they sealed it up."

"Hellebore?"

Jez shook her head.

"City people, must have been," she said. "Hellebore wouldn't come here. She's superstitious."

"Yeah?" Caitlin looked up and down the long alley. The battered metal door that she and Absinthe had slipped through that night was still there. She took Jez's hand again.

"C'mon," she said.

She reached up and ran her palm over the little panel covering the electronic lock. It opened easily, its keypad glowing helpfully.

"Looks like there's still power."

Her fingers moved quickly over the keys.

1-2-2-4-4-8

A soft tone sounded and the door clicked open.

The narrow crack was dark and seductive, a thick charred smell wafting out into the chilly night air. She squeezed Jez's hand and pushed the door open. The feeble yellow streetlight barely penetrated the aromatic darkness. Fumbling in her pockets, she extracted a cheap lighter and sparked it, holding the tiny flame ahead of her as they stepped into the doorway.

On the cement floor ahead, a sad litter of crushed roses, their dry, skewed stalks like broken bones. Irrational heat flared between her legs and she pulled Jez close, letting the lighter's flame go out. The greedy darkness rushed in to fill her senses and she reeled. She was sure she heard passionate whispers. She thought suddenly of Absinthe, of the warm friction of his lithe body against hers, of the corrupt flavor of his kisses. Memories flapped like bats around her blind face. She forced her shaking fingers to spark the hot plastic lighter. The dull light burned her eyes.

"Are you sure this is a good idea?" Caitlin asked. The flickering light played over the curious angles of Jez's face.

"Don't worry, Mistress," Jez said softly. She fumbled around amid the dead flowers and came up with a candle stub.

"Here." Jez thrust the dusty wick into the lighter's flame until it caught. "I'll show you."

Caitlin allowed herself to be led down cement steps and through long, soot-washed corridors. The stink of burning was huge in her sinuses. Stinging plastics. Warm, organic wood. And underlying it all the rich ghost of cooking flesh and burning hair, of burning leather mingling with the living skin beneath. How many people died here? She felt so tired, her belly aching dully as she put one foot in front of the other, one hand numb on the handle of the druglord briefcase and the other thrust deep in her pocket.

Her fingers closed again around the lumpy shape of the herbal charm. She wanted to throw it away, but it seemed too important, an artifact from a time where the weirdest thing in her life was an articulate four year old. Imagining the small pouch sitting forgotten on the stained cement floor of a burnt building made her feel hopeless and sad. Uncontrollable tears transformed the candle's flame into a glittering rainbow wash.

As they moved, echoes threw back their own breath and the sliding shuffle of their shoes on the gritty floor, creating flocks of chuckling ghosts. Jez led her through a low doorway and into a long room with padded walls, torn and stained. There was a little nest of blankets at the far end and a milk-crate up on end full of dog-eared magazines. All around, candles of different colors and sizes. Some were set in glass tubes that pictured gory saints or bleeding, impassioned Jesus with his wicked crown of thorns. Others were stuck into the mouths of scavenged bottles. Jez kissed each with the tiny flame of her lit candle until the cramped space was lit with a warm romantic glow that seemed so out of place inside this lonely monument to their dead lives.

And with this new light, Caitlin suddenly knew where they were.

They were in the slave quarters, the padded stables where Absinthe's slaves slept when their services were not required. Moving away from Jez, her fingers trailed over the gouges in the wall, and it was too easy to imagine the panicked slaves desperately scrabbling at the unyielding door, screaming while smoke filled their lungs, choking them. She could imagine fire fighters breaking in and finding the sad, forgotten bodies with their bloody broken fingers, like dead children in a Nazi gas chamber. She was horrified that she couldn't remember a single slave's name. She shivered.

"Jez," she said. "How could you stay here in this haunted place?"

Jez looked up, frowning.

"Haunted places are always safe," she said, as if it were the most obvious thing in the world. "Ghosts don't hurt me, but they keep everyone else out." Jez held out her hand. "Mistress, please. Come lie down."

Caitlin smiled and took those last few steps, the last of her manic energy burned away in that simple act, and when she felt Jez's hands on her, drawing her down into the musty nest of blankets, she let go, asleep almost instantly.

With wide open eyes, Jez watched over her in the candlelight.

Ejected suddenly from violent dreams of fire and Absinthe, Caitlin sat up wide eyed in perfect darkness. She groped around her, lost in a maelstrom of disorientation until warm arms closed around her, soothing and whispering and she remembered everything.

A match scratched in the dark and orange light filled her skull. She blinked, eyes tearing against the sudden intrusion. When she could see, she made out the curve of Jez's back and the gloss of her bare head.

"Thirsty?" Jez asked, turning and offering a scratched plastic bottle of water. Caitlin could see black grit floating in the murky depths. She shook her head.

Jez shrugged and drank before capping the bottle and stashing it behind the milk crate.

Caitlin stretched and groaned, her bones a clinking xylophone of aches and grinding joints. Her hair was horrificly tangled, a hopeless mess. She gathered the thick, knotted locks up on the top of her head and fastened them with two long splinters of wood.

"Listen, Jez," Caitlin said, pulling the girl close and stroking her smooth head. "I'm gonna make a supply run. Get some juice and something we can eat. More candles, some bottled water."

Jez tightened her grip on Caitlin's waist.

"It isn't safe."

Caitlin gently peeled the girl loose and opened the briefcase. The bills were all different denominations, tens and hundreds and fives and fifties. She slipped a pair of twenties from their paper band and stuck them into the pocket of her jacket.

"If were gonna hole up here," Caitlin said. "We've gotta eat. Don't worry." She checked the Glock's extended clip. Full. She checked the safety twice before she stuck it back in the waistband of her jeans, feeling absurd, like Vic Steele's less competent little sister. She smiled. "I'll be back soon. And while I'm gone ... "

She bent and kissed Jez's smooth forehead.

"Can we move up into the main room upstairs? There might still be some furniture and even windows. It's like a fucking tomb down here."

"But this place is the safest." Jez crossed her arms. "There's only one door."

"Yeah," Caitlin stood. "And no escape routes." She shook her head. "I want the stuff upstairs when I get back, understand?"

Jez closed her eyes.

"Yes, Mistress," she said.

Caitlin smiled and pressed a finger to Jez's lips.

"Good girl," she said.

Jez looked up and smiled back.

Out on the street, Caitlin's skin crawled with paranoia. The Glock felt enormous and obvious against her belly and she changed direction every time she saw a young Asian man, convinced he would shoot her in the back of the head as soon as she turned. Every sense was screaming, wide open, scanning the early morning street for signs of Hellebore or her goons.

She took a random, nonsensical route through the empty neighborhood until she found a small bodega with heavy bars over all its glass. Inside was dark brown and fragrant with the aroma of coffee and she had to buy a paper cup full before she could do anything else. She drank it down scalding and bitingly black and felt instantly better, warmer and more focused. The task of picking out non-perishable food and bottled water soothed her, a simple sensible task, nonthreatening. She even bought two little bottles of gourmet juice and a packet with three miniature croissants inside, thinking they would have a special breakfast, with roses even, since there was a bucket of sad blossoms out front.

With her purchases on her hip, Caitlin made her way back to the Club, still careful to take a round-about path.

But as she walked, she began to feel the slow creeping return of that deep paranoia, fed on caffeine and stronger now. And with it was born a kind of anger, anger at being forced to hide, to be afraid. It might be fine for Jez to hide out like a hunted animal, but not for her. She looked up and down the empty street and gritted her teeth.

There was a payphone on the corner of Jane and Water, in front of an old abandoned hotel. Caitlin laid her groceries on the sidewalk between her legs and began to dig for change, itching with shaky resolve.

"Fuck this," she said out loud, dialing from memory.

"Tenth, Antonucci," said the voice on the other end, picking up on the third ring.

"Eric," she said, her voice rougher than she wanted, unsteady.

"Caitlin, that you?"

"It's me," she answered. Her heart was beating too fast, her hand coiled too tightly around the receiver.

"We missed you at the funeral," Eric said.

"I know," she said. "Listen, Eric. I need your help."

"Sure, anything."

"Eric." Her mouth was dry as dust. "I know who killed Eva Eiseman. I have a witness."

A long pause over the line. She could hear a typewriter and other phones in the background.

"Caitlin, are you sure?"

Caitlin closed her eyes and told Eric everything.

When she was done, her joints felt loose and her stomach felt tight, full of boiling insects.

"Can you help us?" she asked.

"Caitlin, honey," he said. "You get your ass back to that club. Don't go anywhere. Stay with the girl and I'll meet you there as soon as I can."

She hung up the phone, plagued with uncertainty. When she turned to pick up her groceries, Absinthe was standing behind her, his filthy boots inches from her bag, crimson eyes wide and wet.

"Caitlin," he said, his voice horribly unchanged, still as sweet as ever. "We have to talk."

She pressed back against the telephone.

"Get away from me," she hissed, eyes darting one way and the other. Cars passed oblivious. The sidewalk was empty.

"Listen to me," he said, leaning closer. She could smell poisonous sweat and dying breath.

Her fingers clenched around the Glock's textured grip, hand pushing up the t-shirt to make her threat clear.

"Get the fuck away from me!" She shoved him away with her free hand. "I know what you did. Jez showed me."

"What?" Then, out of the chaos of his ruined features, a flash of the old Absinthe and he laughed, tossing his head as if to throw back hair that was no longer there. "She told you that I ... ?"

"Yeah," she said. "Real fucking kneeslapper, murdering one innocent child and mutilating another."

Absinthe shook his head, smile revealing rotted teeth.

"Caitlin, I thought you were much smarter than that."

She frowned.

"What are you talking about?" Her grip faltered.

"That is no innocent you are so valiantly protecting." Absinthe shook his head. "And no child either. Do you even know how old she is?"

"What does that matter?" Caitlin's head was spinning.

"She's older than I am." Absinthe looked away down the street. "Won't you come inside. It's not safe out here."

He held his hand out to her, just the way he had that first night.

"Think about it, Caitlin," he said. "I have all the answers you wanted when you first came to me all fresh and full of questions. If you want to know what really happened, you have no choice."

Caitlin felt as if the world had turned inside out. Her hand released the gun's sweaty grip, went slack and fell to her side. She stood there for a long ticking minute. Then, veins pulsing with a cold inevitability, she gathered up her bag of groceries and followed a madman into an abandoned building.

50.

Inside the old hotel, it was dusty and cool. Thin slices of morning sun found their way through the boarded-up windows, providing the only illumination. While the Club had been murdered in its prime, this place had expired quietly from old age and neglect. Caitlin felt as if all the buildings in the city were like this, abandoned, desolate, symbolic somehow of the destruction of her safe, simple life. To counter this irrational feeling, she imagined the decayed lobby new and immaculate in ultramodern, thirties splendor full of glamorous but shady dames smoking cigarettes and men in dark suits with weathered, film noir faces.

"I used to live here," Absinthe told Caitlin as he led her through the debris. "Before Hellebore found me."

Caitlin frowned, following.

"You say Jez is older than you are." She paused. "Tell me how old you are, then."

He turned back, eyes glistening in the pale light.

"I'm thirty. Too old to be trusted." He looked away. "I'll be thirty-one next month, on December first. If I live that long."

She wasn't sure what sort of answer she was ready for, but that was not it. She followed, silent.

There was a single, wobbly table left upright and undamaged in the long space that must have once been a bar.

"I used to rent a room upstairs on flush nights, when I was a teenager. Turning tricks for beer money. That was just before they closed it down." He sat down on a milk crate just like the one that held Jez's magazines, gesturing for her to do the same. "I got in trouble with the law. Got too rough with a rich trick. The trick wound up dead, and I wound up in baby-jail. Hellebore rescued me."

He laughed, a short cynical sound.

"Just like picking out a puppy at the pound." His hands knotted together in his lap. "Oh, she had big plans for me. Come with me, little boy, and I'll make you a star. Shit." He spat. "Do you have a cigarette?"

Caitlin shook her head. Absinthe sighed heavily, pulling a blowzy white rose from her grocery bag and touching it to his thick, twisted lips. Caitlin struggled not to stare.

"For a while it worked." There was damp nostalgia in his slitted eyes. "Like a dream. I don't have to tell you what it's like to have everything that's missing in your life handed to you on a silver platter. It was perfect."

He laid the rose on the table between them.

"I know that you're a writer, and that you first came to us to find out what happened to Eva Eiseman. Well ... " he leaned forward. "Consider this to be your final interview."

Caitlin thought of all her careful notes and wondered if they would ever add up to anything. She took a deep breath, wishing that she had her little tape-recorder or at least a pen.

"Go ahead, then," she said.

———————————

"I really loved Jez," he said. "I still do. It's not her fault what happened. I know what it's like to strike out at someone you love in the heat of passion."

He paused, lost in reflection. Caitlin wanted to slice him open and rip the truth out with her bare hands. She waited.

"I knew what was going on between Jez and Eva, but I didn't care. I was too lost in my own love and lust and confusion. Jez inspires that kind of reaction in everyone she meets. That's her gift."

He looked at Caitlin, amber eyes unflinching and the feel of Jez's fragile body against hers rose clear inside her, followed swiftly by the familiar cool caress of guilt.

"That's why Hellebore wanted her. The perfect submissive. She thought if she could control Jez, she could control the emotions of the world's rich and famous. I thought she had set me up to be that submissive's counterpart. A totem image for the ones who long for pain and submission. But I was really nothing more than bait." His voice was low and bitter. "A tasty morsel to attract her perfect submissive. Then when her precious monster bites, she already has her new Domina set up to take my place."

Caitlin refused to look away from the pain clenching Absinthe's stiff, tortured features.

"But I digress." He took a deep, rattling breath. "I was going to tell you about Eva.

"Poor Eva. She had no idea what she had stolen. Jez's unique abilities do not come without a hefty price tag. She's as unstable as nitroglycerin, a dangerous pleasure. When Eva saw the true nature of her new toy, she was horrified."

"What do you mean," Caitlin asked, knowing the answer, but hating it.

"Jez's ... singular anatomy is no fault of mine." He held out his hands as if volunteering evidence. "I may be a brilliant dominant, but I'm no surgeon."

"But, she told me ... " Caitlin said, softly, with no conviction.

"Come on, Morrigan. You don't really believe I pulled out her goddamn eyelashes too?"

Caitlin shook her head, words frozen in the back of her throat. She thought of Jez's strange grey eyes, how they always seemed so wet and vulnerable and she could never put her finger on the reason why.

"She's a freak. A little genetic typo. And it was Hellebore's opinion that same gene or lack of a gene that left her underdeveloped and sexually ambiguous made her the ultimate submissive, capable of bringing out the dominant tendencies in virtually anyone. She's been fishing for years but Jez is the closest she's ever come to her mythical perfect slave from all those mad, ancient writings and lunatic ravings her crazy mother collected. And she intends to get her pretty fish back." He shook his head. "You can't stop her."

"So, if you didn't ... ?" Caitlin bit her lip, still several minutes behind in her comprehension. "Who killed Eva then? Was it Hellebore?"

Absinthe looked up at her, puffy burnflesh rendering his features unreadable.

"I knew about Eva's plan to run away. The Twins told me. If Eva had gone alone, I would have let her go, but I couldn't lose Jez. Hellebore would never have allowed it. So I had the Twins play along with Eva's scheme, thinking a little sport might be fun. When the Twins let them out, I followed.

"I watched them go down into the Crypt and then back out again, down 14TH and into an alley. By the time I had caught up with them, Eva was already dead."

He paused again, fingers spidering over the curve of his patchy scalp

"Jez was lying next to the body with blood and tears on her cheeks and a cheap knife clenched in one hand. She was stroking that ... that mess between Eva's legs and whispering 'It's OK now' over and over. 'We're sisters now, see?' she said."

"No," Caitlin shook her head, horrified. "No that isn't right."

But in her mind she saw the pain and rage in Jez's eyes as she pulled her t-shirt down to cover the source of her shame. She felt the disproportionate strength in the girl's angry hands as she threw off Caitlin's attempt at reconciliation. She knew in her guts that it was true.

"I can't lie to you anymore, Morrigan," he said, almost whispering. "Even if I wanted to." He toyed with the rose, plucking at the satiny, brown edged petals. "After that I kissed her bloody little fingers and took her home. She came, because I was the only one who knew everything and loved her anyway."

Absinthe stared off into the air between them for a long minute and then reached across the table and took her hand. She wanted to flinch, but her body refused to obey.

"Morrigan," he said. "I've given you everything. Now it's my turn to ask something from you."

He stood and pulled her with him.

"One last scene," he purred. "With your indulgence."

He pushed her shirt up over her breasts and for a cold moment, she thought he would kiss her. Instead, he backed away and stood still and straight, pulling the tattered remains of his lost dignity tight around his wasted frame.

"Kill me, Mistress," he said.

Caitlin blinked, sure that she had misheard. She pushed her shirt back down, covering her breasts and the handle of the gun.

"Please, Mistress." His strange eyes were clear and sane, glittering with unshed tears. "I have nothing left to give but my life. There is no reason for me to live now, without you, without Jez." His fingers wandered up, over the ravaged contours of his face. "Without myself, even."

He let the shabby coat slide down over his shoulders, began to slowly peel the encrusted layers from his dirty skin. His scrawny chest was coated with gaudy-pink burnflesh, his arms striped shiny with scar. His dark pubic hair was gone, his pale thighs mottled with desperate new tissue. Even his penis had burned and healed strangely, seeming stiff and almost corrugated, like cardboard. He looked as much as monster as Jez. More so even. Caitlin was transfixed as he knelt, naked before her.

"Please," he whispered.

Her fingers caressed the Glock's warm grip. There was a slick heat in her belly and she realized that a part of her wanted to do it. Wanted to press the barrel against his bowed and compliant forehead and pull the trigger, to finish what she started the night the Club burned. It would be the most intimate penetration, the ultimate domination. Her heart was pounding in her ears as she pulled the gun from her waistband.

It felt so heavy in her shaking hand. Absinthe smiled as she pressed its muzzle against his lips. A thick pulse of blood surged between her legs as he opened his mouth and slid his lips down over the length of the barrel. He closed his eyes and she remembered his words, the night of the fire.

Just as you were a dominant before you ever picked up a whip.

She denied it then, but could he have been right? Was she a murderer, too?

The moment spun out, endless as they stood in the dusty sunlight, frozen in this excruciating tableau. It was such a tiny movement, to pull the trigger. Just the smallest tightening of the smallest muscles, but seemed like moving a vast weight, like traveling though the millions of lightyears that separated the woman she thought she was from the woman she would be, a killer, like him. She had blown through every other sin with such instinctual ease, but this was the last and biggest, on which the last shreds of her own shattered sense of morality hung by a thread. It hadn't mattered when she thought Absinthe had died by her hand, but now that he stood before her as living proof of her second chance, could she really take that final step? She thumbed off the safety and Absinthe's scarred penis twitched, swelling to a lopsided erection.

She closed her eyes, full scale war raging in her mind and heart. Sweat bathed her, beading on her hairline and making the Glock's grip treacherously slippery. It was such a tiny movement, pulling that trigger. She bit down harder on her lip and shook her head.

"I can't," she said.

As she pulled the gun from Absinthe's mouth and turned away, a huge noise split the world in half as something too fast to see screamed past inches from her face. An explosion of splinters sprayed her, clinging to her hair and stinging her skin. She found herself staring stupidly at a sudden pale spot on the wall beside her, a sunburst of clean, white wood. Did she fire the Glock without realizing it? She was looking down at the gun in her hand when Absinthe screamed her name and slammed into her with his full weight, knocking her sideways through the doorway into the lobby. A puff of plaster sifted down on her face.

When she opened her eyes, she saw Absinthe lying a few feet away with a gaping hole in his belly that opened and closed like a hungry mouth with each breath. Blood was everywhere, more blood that she ever imagined a single body could contain, but his eyes were wide open and he was looking right at her. Her first thought was that she had shot him after all.

"I'm ... " She crawled towards him. "I'm sorry."

She wanted to throw the gun away, but it felt welded to her hand.

"Mistress," Absinthe wheezed, good hand pressing into his belly, trying to keep his insides in. With his broken hand he gestured at the dark doorway. "Mistress, look out."

Caitlin spun and saw one of Hellebore's goons, the handsome one, standing in the doorway. She wondered, irrelevantly if he was the one named Taki. He had a new, identical Automag to replace the one stolen by Jez. Caitlin imagined that the new gun had grown in to replace the old, like a shark's tooth. All these thoughts tumbled through her brain in the fraction of a second before she brought the Glock up level to the crotch of the man's expensive suit and fired.

Really, it was so simple. Squeeze, nice and easy, just like that time with Mike at the firing range and then it was too late to take it back because the man (Taki, her brain reminded her pointlessly) was clutching his crotch and shrieking like a woman while blood soaked though the fine wool of his well-cut trousers. Since she couldn't think of a reason not to, she fired again and a third time.

The next bullet hit her grocery bag. It fell over and died in a spray of pineapple-guava-raspberry juice. The last hit the flailing man in the face, churning his beautiful, classic features into a chaos of blood and bone and he went down amid the scatter of roses and broken glass.

Caitlin staggered forward, back into the bar. Kneeling beside the man, beside Taki, she watched him fight to breathe through the shattered hole that had been his mouth and nose. She couldn't just leave him like this. In the neat, fictional world of Vic Steele, the bad guys died like flies, but this man was real, flesh and blood, like her and she felt she owed him somehow. He had been awfully handsome and under different circumstances, she might have flirted with him, instead of killing him. In a world where right and wrong were no longer as clear as she once thought, it seemed like the right thing to do. But that didn't stop her hands from shaking as she pressed the Glock against what was left of his forehead and pulled the trigger yet again. The recoil felt almost good, like stretching an aching muscle. The man's body jumped, arms and legs thumping hard against the floor and then he was still.

She sat back on her haunches, staring mindlessly at the unmoving corpse. She wondered if she ought to take the new Automag, start a collection. She laughed, a dry cackle that sounded like something from a children's Halloween special.

She crawled back through the doorway, hands and knees sticky with blood or maybe just expensive juice, leaving the Automag and its late owner together behind her. Absinthe was splayed out on the floor beside her and she gathered him into her arms, uncaring of the blood and other more unsavory fluids that gushed out when she lifted him.

"I'm sorry," she said again, running her fingers over the ruin of his face.

His eyes rolled up to hers.

"Get out of here," he said. He coughed and blood sprayed from his lips. Swallowing hard, he nodded towards the door. "Go on, hurry. There'll be more soon."

Tears blurred her vision as she bent to kiss his mouth, tasting blood and memories. She was becoming a regular angel of death, wasn't she, but this felt different, more intimate, an act of love, rather than obligation. She pressed her cheek to his for nearly a full minute before letting him down gently and touching the barrel of the Glock to the soft, unburned flesh beneath his chin. He smiled. This time, there was no hesitation.

51.

"Mistress," Jez said, her face lighting up as she turned towards Caitlin with the water jug in both hands like a kid, so innocent.

The huge space that had housed the main room of the Club was a charred wasteland with Jez standing at the lip of a huge hole in the floor. Caitlin wanted to tell Jez to get away from there before she got hurt, but all she could think of was that curious puzzle between those coltish legs. She knew instinctively that Absinthe had told her the truth. A thing of such hideous delicacy, such complexity had to be organic, a wild and accidental occurrence that no scalpel could ever reproduce. On the heels of that thought came a vision of Eva's mutilation, seemingly intricate, but so crude and brutal next to the living organ it strove to imitate. There was danger and rage hidden like a nest of hornets inside that smooth, hairless skull, twisted paths of unfathomable logic that Caitlin could never hope to understand, but in spite of it all, she still felt an overwhelming need to take Jez into her arms. Like a junkie craving chemical oblivion, she still felt a hunger for that sweet submission that oozed from Jez's skin, dripping from her sad, crazy eyes and her vulnerable mouth.

"Come here, Jez," she said.

Jez could see the smears of blood on Caitlin's shirt, even in the dimness and she hesitated, pale face unreadable.

"Jez," Caitlin repeated, firmer this time.

"What's wrong?" Jez asked, skirting the hole and inching carefully closer.

Caitlin reached out to the girl and took both her tiny hands. Murdering hands, but then again, so were Caitlin's.

"Tell me what really happened to Eva," she said.

Jez's eyes went huge and she tried to pull away, but Caitlin held her wrists.

"I have to know the truth, Jez. I won't hurt you or judge you, but I can't stand anymore lies."

Jez wrenched away.

"You talked to Absinthe, didn't you." The girl's lips skinned back from her tiny round teeth. "You said you wouldn't and now you're all bloody!"

"Absinthe is dead," Caitlin said. "I need you to tell the truth if I'm going to help you."

"I already told you. Absinthe is the liar!"

Jez looked desperate now, wild-eyed, and Caitlin was suddenly very aware of the Automag's phallic bulge beneath Jez's shorts. She thought of the woman who shot Mike and her heart clenched, imagining the feel of angry metal punching through her fragile skin and hidden organs.

"Don't be afraid, Jez," Caitlin said, palms out as she took a step towards the girl.

Jez's face was twisted with a thousand emotions. Her eyes swirled with pain and bright insanity and Caitlin felt for her, for her suffering and self-hatred. She wanted to gather the girl up in her arms and kiss away the hurt, and seeming to sense this, Jez closed the distance between them, pressing up against her like a cat, mask of innocence sliding so deftly over her child-like features that Caitlin could have imagined the madness.

"I'm not afraid, Mistress," she whispered, her body so fragile in Caitlin's arms. "I trust you."

She slid down to the floor, pressing kisses to Caitlin's boots.

Sucking in a deep breath, Caitlin reached down and hauled the girl to her feet. She needed to be firm.

"If you trust me," she said, holding Jez's strange feline face between her thumb and forefinger. "Then you have to tell me the truth."

A part of her wanted to punish Jez for her reluctance, to make her suffer, but that desire was Jez's weapon and if she gave in, she would lose her advantage. She held Jez's gaze for nearly a full minute before the girl looked away and began to speak.

"She was disgusted," she said, her voice almost inaudible.

"Who was?" Caitlin kept her voice soft, non-threatening.

"Eva." Shadows of remembered shame chased each other across Jez's face. "She thought she loved me, but when she saw ... " Such pain in those lashless eyes. Alien eyes filled with human suffering. "When I was little, my grandfather used to tell me it was because of my momma's sin. He never told me what the sin was and I couldn't ask her cause she was dead. He tried to love me, my grandfather. He used to do things to me, to make me pure, save me from my momma's sin, but I knew that he wanted to keep me for himself, just like everyone else."

Caitlin couldn't think of anything to say. Her pity for this lost girl deepened.

"Eva wanted to keep me, too, but I never meant to hurt her. I tried to make it up to her, after. You know, make her like ... like a sister. Like me. But I realize now that it was a stupid idea. There is no one like me. There never was and there never will be. I could lie, or tell the truth and it would never matter, because no one will ever really understand."

Jez pulled her shirt up over the handle of the gun and at that moment a loud gunshot filled Caitlin's head and made her stagger as something seemed to snatch at her clothes, wrenching her shoulder. When she looked down, she saw a smooth hole in her leather jacket just above the buckle. She could suddenly smell burnt sage, a curious clean smell and she was filled with exquisite terror. She felt no pain but she knew from research that a person could be shot and not even realize it because of fear and adrenaline. She also knew that there was no time for reflection. She dove towards Jez, pulling the girl down to the ground.

"Enough fucking around, Caitlin!"

Hellebore again, with all pretense of politeness evaporated from her jagged voice. The huge gunman was with her, and as soon as Caitlin noticed him, the floor next to her head exploded. She grabbed Jez and rolled away, behind a charred metal skeleton that might have been a sofa.

She could still see them through the twisted springs, standing together at the other end of the room. Bullets pinged off the sofa's metal frame and Caitlin screamed.

"Dammit, Hellebore, did you forget what happens if you kill me?"

"Don't be afraid," Hellebore said, her voice smooth again, suddenly reasonable. "If Eiji shoots you, you won't die. I won't allow it. We only want to encourage you to reconsider your little computer stunt. Be realistic, Caitlin." Her voice dropped and Caitlin could make out something Japanese.

There was a long silence and when Caitlin peered through the springs again, she saw that Hellebore was alone. At that same moment, a huge weight slammed down on her, knocking her head against the floor and crushing the breath from her lungs. She was amazed that someone so large could move so swiftly without making a sound.

As she struggled with the gunman, she fought for air, sucking in shallow breaths scented with the clean, babypowder aroma of the man's heavy flesh. He dragged her to her feet, massive arms clamped tightly around her ribs, pinning her arms to her sides. She couldn't see Jez anywhere and was filled with fierce panic. She refused to give in. Instead, she brought her heel down along the gunman's instep, stomping on his foot as hard as she could. He reacted only by grunting between his teeth and tightening his grip on her chest. Struggling felt like fighting a brick wall. She was beginning to weaken from lack of oxygen, bright glitter floating around the edges of her vision. Fast running out of options, she slammed the back of her head into the gunman's face. Pain shot through her skull, bringing her consciousness down to a thin dark tunnel, but she felt a burst of wetness against the back of her neck and the gunman's grip loosened enough for her to break free.

When she turned, she saw the man clutching his face, blood pouring from between his fingers. Without stopping to think, she kicked him as hard as she could in the center of the chest, driving him back. She strode forward and delivered a second kick to the bloody sponge of his face, bones crunching horribly beneath the sole of her boot. He staggered and fell and as his massive weight hit the floor, the charred boards gave way beneath him, cracking with a ear splitting sound. She watched, astonished as he vanished in a rush of debris crashing through to the lower floor.

"Caitlin," a new voice called. "Are you OK?"

Eric. In the chaos, Caitlin had completely forgotten that he had promised to meet her here.

"Stay out of this, little man," Hellebore said. "This does not concern you."

When Caitlin turned, she saw that Hellebore held a gun, trained on the shadows behind Caitlin.

"What are you, nuts?" Eric stepped into the dim light. His own gun was drawn and leveled at Hellebore. "Drop that shit before somebody gets hurt."

"I'm afraid that somebody will be you," Hellebore said and then the crack of a shot and Caitlin screamed Eric's name, pulling the Glock from her jeans and trying to make her shaking hands aim at the fluid shadow of Hellebore.

"Motherfucker!" She heard Eric's voice from behind a supporting pillar.

Sweat stung Caitlin's eyes, blurring her vision. She felt sick and weak. She wanted to shoot Hellebore for all the pain she'd caused, for Jez and even for Absinthe, but a part of her rebelled against the growing body count. Could she just keep on shooting forever, and if she did, could she ever stop? She was a killer now, no question about it, and what difference did all her bullshit rationalizations really make? She might have squeezed the trigger then when Jez's voice pierced the gloom with a cry of anguish.

"Enough!" she wailed.

Standing alone in the center of the room, the slender figure of Jez, poised like a marble saint with both hands together beneath her chin. Her pewter eyes were dull and hopeless.

"It has to end," she said.

She pulled the Automag from her belt.

"Jesus, kid," Eric said from his place behind the pillar. "Put that goddam cannon down before somebody gets hurt."

"I can't stand this anymore," Jez said. "You all keep fighting over me like I was some kind of toy." She trained the gun on Hellebore's forehead, then on Caitlin's. "None of you really love me. It's time to stop all this."

As Caitlin watched, belly full of slow dread, Jez turned the huge gun on herself. Time seemed to elongate, seconds like hours as those tortured eyes settled on Caitlin. Tombstone-colored eyes like deep holes filled with all the pain in the world and Caitlin thought of Imogene's warning. All this time, she thought it was Absinthe who was the monster, but now she knew, it was Jez's pain and isolation that had made Imogene feel so cold. As cold as Caitlin felt now, in the endless years before ...

The sound of the Automag spewing death into Jez's always-receptive mouth was one that Caitlin would never forget. And as Jez's nearly headless body crumpled awkwardly to the floor, her tormented brains raining down around her, Caitlin felt she finally understood. For the first time in her life, Jez had taken an independent action and, in her own way, freed herself.

The room was suddenly swarming with yelling and people, and Eric was beside her, clutching his side like an old man. She was barely aware of him, lost as she was in a endless replay of the obscenely large gun barrel sliding into Jez's mouth and that terrible, terrible sound. In her mind, the image got strangely mingled with Absinthe's twisted face and his honeyed voice saying, *Kill me, Mistress.*

She felt as if she was tottering on the edge, ready to plunge headfirst into the insanity she had so recently escaped when Eric laid a hand on her shoulder.

"Are you OK?" he asked.

His familiar voice was like a beacon in the dark and endless ocean threatening to swallow her. She made herself reach out to him, allowing him to take the Glock from her unfeeling fingers.

"Eric," she said. "I shot somebody."

He looked up at her, his eyes warm and concerned.

"Did he deserve it?" he asked.

Caitlin smiled, shaky.

"I think so," she said.

"Then you did the right thing," he told her.

She noticed then that blood had stained his white shirt just above the belt.

"Are you hurt?" Caitlin asked.

"The bitch shot me," Eric said, wincing. "Just clipped me, but still ..."

Turning away from Eric, she suddenly remembered the hole in her jacket. Her fingers flew to her belly, racing over the length of her abdomen, but she felt no blood, no pain. She discovered entry and exit holes in her left pocket and inside, her fingers closed around the lumpy cloth charm. When she pulled it out and held it up in the dim light, she saw it had a clean and perfect hole through its center, herbs and colored powder leaking like dry blood into Caitlin's palm.

She watched as kevlar armored men surrounded Hellebore. The strange, twisted face was frozen, expressionless for a moment and then she threw herself forward, knees skidding in the slick fluid that had once been Jez's head. A high wail unfurled as she beat Jez's body with desperate fists.

"No," she sobbed, struggling as they cuffed her and pulled her to her feet.

She lunged toward Caitlin, mismatched eyes wild and ringed with blood. She screeched like a banshee, black strands of hair that had escaped her braid whipping across her contorted face, but the men who held her dragged her away.

"Crazy bitch!" Eric yelled after her.

Caitlin smiled again, wider this time. Her body hurt all over and she couldn't take her eyes off the sorry heap of Jez, but she still felt a little saner and she was filled with a jittery sense of relief. She wondered what would happen to Hellebore, if Daddy Kobiyashi would set her up in a posh nuthouse, if maybe, just to be safe, he might send in a night orderly with a syringe full of air.

Shivering a little, she let Eric put his arm around her and leaned against him. She wondered what would happen to her.

52.

At Loesman's delicatessen on Sixth Ave, Caitlin sat across from Eric, a cup of coffee warming her cold hands.

"So how's the book going?" Eric asked, dragging a french fry through a puddle of ketchup.

"It's almost finished now," she said, looking out the rain-streaked window. "The writing helps me a lot, y'know? Helps me sort shit out."

She had been plagued with dreams at the beginning, dreams of Jez and Absinthe and the kick of the gun in her bones.

She looked back at Eric, his round, familiar face crinkled with the simple pleasure of a good greasy meal. He had grown a moustache and Caitlin liked to tease him about it, since his picture had been in the paper and all over TV once the details of the Eiseman case went down.

"What'll you do next?" he asked.

Caitlin shrugged, crossing her legs and letting one high-heeled shoe dangle off her big toe. She had discovered it was impossible to fit her new self into the old jeans and t-shirts. Instead she wore leather, short skirts and seamed stockings and high heels, enjoying the furtive reaction from the men around her. It was the one thing that she brought with her out the chaos of the past year, like a precious heirloom saved from a burning building, the one thing that was hers alone.

"Thought I might go impose on Wilson for a little while out in sunny Southern California." She chuckled. "It's hard to believe he finally moved out of his mother's house. Guess his little brush with the Feds put the fear of God into him, turned him into a lawful citizen."

"Yeah, well, as lawful a citizen as a kid with his kinda talent will ever be," Eric said, grinning over the rim of his coffee cup.

A comfortable silence spun out between them and Caitlin leaned back in the booth, staring out the rain-streaked window at the flashy blur of passing cars.

"Think you'll go back to writing them detective novels?" Eric asked.

"I don't know," she said, shaking her head. "I guess I kinda lost the stomach for that sort of shit."

Eric nodded sympathetically.

"Yeah, I know what you mean. I never really went for that kinda thing myself."

"Eric" she said, suddenly. "How do you live with it?"

He looked up at her quizzically.

"Live with what?"

"Death. Y'know, killing someone."

Eric chewed his lower lip.

"Well," he said, thoughtfully. "It's like a lot of the shit that wears you down on the job. Fucked up things that eat away at your soul, y'know. The only way to fight it is to keep your sense of humor and accept that the innocent person you were before, well that person is dead too. It's OK to miss 'em, just like it's OK to miss Mike or anyone else that's gone, but then you gotta move on."

Caitlin nodded, sipped her coffee, but she wasn't sure it was that simple. She sometimes missed her old life, but most times it seemed to her that the person she used to be was nothing but an ill-defined blur, an uninteresting movie she once saw. The new Caitlin was still growing, still stretching her wings.

At that moment, the waiter showed up with a piece of cake. He was young and dark with wide eyes and a baby's mouth. His shoulders were hunched, apologetic as he slid the plate in front of her. She couldn't help noting the direction of his hungry gaze, not at her tits or even her legs, but at the dangling shoe.

She looked down at the plate and then up at him.

"This is chocolate cake," she said, stern, eyes burning into the squirming boy. "I asked for carrot cake."

"Um ... sorry," he whispered, snatching the plate and scuttling away as if it was difficult to walk.

Eric laughed.

"You sure are something, girl," he said.

"Something?" she said as the waiter hustled back with her carrot cake, an extra large slice. "Yeah, I guess I am."

This book was designed by Lydia Marano for Babbage Press using a Macintosh G3 and Adobe FrameMaker. It was printed by LSI on sixty pound, offset cream-white acid-free stock. The text font is Minion, a Garalde Oldstyle typeface designed by Robert Slimbach in 1990 for Adobe Systems. Minion was inspired by the elegant and highly readable type designs of master printers Claude Garamond and Aldus Manutius in the late Renaissance. Created primarily for type-setting, Minion lends an aesthetic quality to the modern versatility of digital technology.

BABBAGE PRESS

... books you can count on

JAMES P. BLAYLOCK
    The Digging Leviathan   1-930235-16-X   18.95
    Homonculus   1-930235-13-5   17.95

RAMSEY CAMPBELL
    The Height of the Scream   1-930235-15-1   18.95

ARTHUR BYRON COVER
    Autumn Angels   1-930235-12-7   17.95

DENNIS ETCHISON
    The Dark Country   1-930235-04-6   17.95

CHRISTA FAUST
    Control Freak   1-930235-14-3   18.95

JOHN FARRIS
    Elvisland   1-930235-21-6   19.95

GEORGE R.R. MARTIN
    A Song for Lya   1-930235-11-9   17.95

WILLIAM F. NOLAN
    Things Beyond Midnight   1-930235-09-7   17.95

MICHAEL REAVES
    The Night People   1-930235-25-9   19.95

DAVID J. SCHOW
    Crypt Orchids   1-930235-26-7   18.95
    Lost Angels   1-930235-06-2   17.95
    Seeing Red   1-930235-05-4   18.95
    Wild Hairs   1-930235-08-9   19.95

JOHN SHIRLEY
    Eclipse   1-930235-00-3   17.95
    Eclipse Penumbra   1-930235-01-1   17.95
    Eclipse Corona   1-930235-02-X   17.95
    A Splendid Chaos   1-930235-23-2   18.95

JOHN SKIPP & MARC LEVINTHAL
    The Emerald Burrito of Oz   1-930235-17-8   19.95

S.P. SOMTOW
    Dragon's Fin Soup   1-930235-03-8   17.95

The Fallen Country   1-930235-07-0   17.95

Chelsea Quinn Yarbro
False Dawn   1-930235-10-0   17.95

Available from your favorite bookstore or order direct. Discounted to the trade.

Babbage Press • 8740 Penfield Avenue • Northridge, CA 91324
www.babbagepress.com • books@babbagepress.com

Distributed by Ingram Book Co. and Baker & Taylor.

Printed in the United States
1307500002BA/37